there are more things

Yara Rodrigues Fowler

abacus
books

ABACUS

First published in Great Britain in 2022 by Fleet
This paperback edition published in 2023 by Abacus

1 3 5 7 9 10 8 6 4 2

A CIP catalogue record for this book is available from the British Library.

ISBN 978-0-349-72672-4

Typeset in Garamond by M Rules
Printed and bound in Great Britain by Clays Ltd, Elcograf S.p.A

Papers used by Abacus are from well-managed forests and other responsible sources.

Abacus
An imprint of
Little, Brown Book Group
Carmelite House
50 Victoria Embankment
London EC4Y 0DZ

An Hachette UK Company
www.hachette.co.uk

www.littlebrown.co.uk

For Laura, Cleide and Thália, three revolutionary mothers

When a song plays on the page, listen to it out loud.

When the characters speak in chorus, when they read from the iphone at meetings, speak out loud with them.

'Comigo' by Elza Soares, from her album
A Mulher do fim do Mundo,
2015

I take my mother with me
although she has already gone
I take my mother with me
perhaps because we are so similar

I take my mother with me
in a way I don't know how to tell of
I take my mother with me
because she gave me her own being

ως ἄραμαι
τούτο τω
Βόλλαμαι

Sappho
c 630 – c 570 BCE

because I prayed
this word:
I want

Sappho translated by Anne Carson
2000

Prologue

I

This a love story the length of a life
   as big as the city
   the size of the sea

Once upon a time the city whispered – stay
   die here

imagine a country
   the size of a continent
imagine, a country
   the size of an island

This is a story of –

   how much sugar
   how much coffee
   how much gold

   how much wood
   how much iron
   how much oil

   how many hands

        the city shouts

What is five hundred years in the life of the land
   of the sea of the forest of the sky of the stars

(What are seven or eighteen or twenty-nine years in the length of a life)

No one has seen LAURA since she died but you can hear her shout –

THERE ARE MORE THINGS IN HEAVEN AND EARTH

II

This is a story of –

Did you ever have a sister?
  Yes her name was Catarina

Did you ever have a sister?
  Yes her name was Melissa

Did you ever have a sister?
  Yes her name was Glória

Did you ever have a sister?
  Yes her name was Sônia

Did you ever have a sister?
  Yes her name was Lamis

Did you ever have a sister?
  Yes her name was Laura

(on Amen Corner we have had many sisters)

Did you ever have a sister?
  Yes I have had three
  Janine, Jasmine, Jean

Did you ever have a sister?
  Yes, her name was Ruthie

(na Rua do Bomfim I have had many sisters)

This is a story of

  (this is a story of sisters)

What was your mother's name?

(tell us her name)
  Her name was –

Tell me

(tell us)

  what happened?

III

This was a beginning –

We saw from the window
We saw from the door
       where the net curtain was blowing

      in the purple sky

The lights were on
He was in the bath

There was a purple towel
lying on the floor
   They say

He was in the bath
We heard a door slamming

His wife
what is her name sounds like
       She was carrying shopping bags

      all the water sparkle spilling
over and
out of the bath with the bath

There were sounds
Yes and we heard screams
On other days

Nobody saw it
And then he was gone

(There were no witnesses)
(Except us)

Except us

But my eyes are old
Yes and so are mine
And the net curtain was blowing
through the window

      into the purple sky

MILE END I
(2016)

It was the year that Prince died and the guy who played Professor Snape died. It was the year that George Michael died at Christmas, and bright flowers and handwritten notes and laminated photos of him piled up outside his Highgate mansion in the frost. Ever since that winter, everywhere you go in London you can hear the buskers playing 'Careless Whisper' on their saxophones. They play it at the fullest volume. They play it after dark into the dark. They play it to tourists in Covent Garden; at the bottom of the mosaic escalators at Tottenham Court Road tube; on the crowded pavement outside Brixton station. They play it on summers' nights into the night, into the smell of bin bags. *Bah* nah nah na *Bah* na nah na. The older-looking man outside Mile End station plays despite the rain, his body bent into the worn out instrument.

Melissa's new housemate arrived in January 2016, in the rain.

Melissa waited in the flat to give her new housemate the key. She lay on her back on the L-shaped sofa, white socked feet against the armrest. She read the news on her phone and then she put her phone down and began to roll a cigarette. As she stood up, she licked the rizla paper and slipped her feet into her trainers, squashing the backs of the shoes with her heels. On the balcony, she leant against the wall, the storey above sheltering her body from the rain. Across the road, a child ran along the first-floor walkway of the opposite building, hitting a bookbag against the railings.

The doorbell rang.

Melissa stubbed out the roll up and went back inside. She checked the time on her phone before opening the front door. The woman in the doorway was shorter than her. She looked about the same age as Melissa. Her elbow-length hair was wet through. She had a backpack and two suitcases with her, one big and one small, both with purple ribbons tied around the handles. She looked Melissa up and down, and then she smiled.

Hello

Catarina?

Yes

Hi

Melissa stepped backwards into the small hallway. Catarina followed her. She looked around. Melissa cleared her throat –

The kitchen / living room, as the estate agent calls it, is through there. This room right here is my bedroom. It's smaller than the others and I pay £490 per month, a bit less than everybody else. There's the downstairs bathroom. The other bedrooms are upstairs. Your room is the one next to the bathroom. There's a bath.

Catarina raised her wet eyebrows, her gaze moving up the stairs. A bath?

And a shower.

Melissa walked ahead of Catarina into the kitchen / living room.

Catarina followed her. Melissa picked up a key from the dining table and held it out.

Here's your key.

Thank you.

They stood together in the space between the dining table and the L-shaped sofa. Outside was grey. Catarina noticed the balcony door and, walking up to it, peered out, first at the concrete square immediately in front of her with its bucket collecting rainwater and cigarette butts, and then out at the street below. Melissa sniffed. The wet suitcases and Catarina's wet hair and wet coat made the room smell damp.

Um, do you want a cup of tea?

Yes. Thank you.

Where did you come from?

Kennington

Melissa nodded.

Catarina gestured at her bags – I will take these upstairs –

Melissa boiled the kettle and put two teabags in two mugs on the counter. Catarina was a PhD student from somewhere. Melissa had found her online in a hurry. Her accent made Melissa's chest tense and twist. The kettle clicked. She poured the water onto the teabags and took the milk out of the fridge, pouring a little into one mug and removing the teabag. She sat on the sofa with the tea and took her phone out of her pocket.

Catarina re-entered the room, barefoot. She picked up the mug on the counter.

This is for me?

Yes

Thank you

There's milk –

I am vegan

Sorry there isn't any soy milk or

That's okay

You'll just have it black?

Yes

Catarina leant against the counter. The kitchen / living room smelled like rice cooked with onions.

So your name is – Melissa?
There was a pause.
Call me Mel

Like honey

Melissa did not reply. She touched her glasses and looked at her phone screen. But Catarina was looking at her. Catarina shifted the position of her body against the counter.

Mel I have a question. I saw your last name on the advert. I was wondering, are you Brazilian?

Um

You grew up here?

I grew up in *South* London.

Catarina nodded. She tried to make eye contact with Melissa.

That is so cool. An English person who is a Brazilian person.

I've never been to Brazil.

Never?

No.

Catarina did not speak straight away. She took a sip of her tea, which still contained the teabag.

That is interesting. Do you intend to go? I had come to England twice before I came to live here. I had read many books set in England.

Melissa nodded.

Catarina put both hands around her mug. She looked up.

Fala português?

No.

Catarina sat down at the dining table. There was a silence. Melissa put her phone down and looked up at her –

People say I look Brazilian

Catarina moved her head to the side – Anyone can look Brazilian

Melissa made a sound.

Your mum and dad are from where?

Um

Melissa stood up. Actually – Melissa put her phone and her tobacco papers in her jeans pocket – Actually, I have to go now. She emptied her mug into the sink then washed it.

Sure

I've got to go out.

While you are gone I will unpack.

Okay

Then I think I will skype my boyfriend, Pedro – he is in Brazil.

Cool.

Is it a problem if I do that in here?

No. Anyway Olivia works late and Julieta is always at her boyfriend's, don't know why she even keeps the room. So

OK.

Catarina stood in her bare feet in the grey light.

Melissa held her jacket in her hand. Bye.

Tchau, Melissa.

The spoken sounds of her name held at the back of Melissa's throat. When Catarina reached out to hug her, Melissa let herself stand in her embrace.

Melissa ran down the steps out of the building two at a time, almost slipping on their rain wet surface and bumping into a grandma-looking woman in a hijab who was climbing up them.

Sorry –

In the street she walked quickly, checking her phone, reading the news until the screen became blurry with rain and she couldn't see through her glasses. Her thighs were getting wet through her jeans. Outside Mile End tube the man who played the saxophone stood with his knees bent in the mouth of the station. He was playing a song she knew and riffing, adding notes. His sax was worn and dappled as if it had been bent by the sound. She dropped a pound coin into his open saxophone case. She ran down the steps into the station against the crowd. The station floor was black with black city water.

Melissa stood in front of the Central line signs

EASTBOUND

WESTBOUND

For a whole second, people strode past her and her feet did not know which way to go.

Catarina, who was sat at the dining table, opened her laptop. She had not understood what had just happened. English people were weird. But this woman was not English. Or, not only English. She had looked younger than Catarina and had almost purple hair. Her accent was not what Catarina was used to from books and films set in England. It was a new accent that she had first heard in shops and on the bus in London.

Catarina dug her toes into the carpet. She would finish her tea and then unpack. And then perhaps even take a bath. She would not forget to call Pedro. She looked around the kitchen / living room of the apartment that she should call a *flat* even though it had two floors. The ceilings were low. This room had the kitchen on one side – fridge, stove, oven, sink – lined by a metre or so of yellow fake wood flooring, and then a carpeted space. The dining table was cheap and made from glass. They had pushed it against the wall. The walls were cream and totally plain. This must be because of the no nails and bluetack clause, Catarina thought. Out of the window she could see the street below and across the road another apartment block. Both blocks had only four floors, enough for two apartments of two storeys. The inefficient use of space bemused Catarina; it was so characteristic of this small, densely populated island. But the flat was a good quality, good value with two bathrooms, a private balcony and double glazing. Her room was big, with a desk and space for a bookshelf. Her toes in the carpet were warm.

As the result of online research, Catarina had come to know some facts about the area. Her mother had quizzed her on it the last time they had spoken.

Is it safe? her mother had said. Querida, querida is it safe?

And she had cleared her throat, Ahem-ing Ahem-ing before paraphrasing Wikipedia.

Mãe, the East End was heavily bombed in World War Two. And then it became a place where many government houses were built. This was part of the grand socialist reforms in the UK to recover from the war by your favourite European Prime Minister, Clement Attlee. She had looked up at the screen, addressing this last sentence to her father whose forehead filled the left side of her laptop.

I wish Pedro was staying with you

Harold Pinter was born here. You know who he is? She had clicked on the name.

Her father had sighed.

Catarina had squinted at the screen.

Yes he is a very famous English playwright. Her mother had sighed. It is a shame Pedro will not stay.

Catarina had squinted at the screen, speaking then in English. *Harold Pinter was awarded the Nobel Prize in Literature in 2005. Pinter was also an outspoken opponent of the War in Iraq—'*

Larissa wants to know if you will come back for Carnaval? And Tia Lygia is asking does the apartment building have a porter?

Não. Catarina had exhaled. I'm not coming back for Carnaval. And tell Tia Lygia that I am not living in Recife, I am not living in São Paulo!

No. She was living in the East End, the London of Monica Ali.

Outside was dark. Catarina crossed her feet under her chair. She looked up at the screen.

The name 'Sônia' came up on her phone and then on Skype.

For thirty seconds she listened to the ringing sound and then pressed mute.

The next morning Melissa was in the kitchen / living room when Catarina came down at half past eight. Catarina looked at her black jeans, black boots and hoodie. Melissa was taller than Pedro and Catarina's father, at least 180cm. She was strong looking in her legs and shoulders. She wore eyeliner and no other makeup.

Melissa put her mug in the sink. I'm just leaving.

Are you going to work?

Melissa nodded. Are you going into uni today?

Yes. Catarina looked down at her robe – I don't have to go until later. I will get dressed –

Melissa smiled. She put on her jacket.

Where is your office Mel?

Tottenham Court Road.

It is near my university!

Yeah?

Can we 'Go For A Pint' this evening? Catarina made air quotes with her index fingers.

Melissa smiled at her. Yeah we can 'Go For A Pint'. Melissa made air quotes with her index fingers also.

OK.

Turning to leave the room, Melissa pointed at the stove. There's coffee – it's still warm.

Brigada Melí.

Melissa nodded. This new version of her name softened something in her throat.

When Catarina reached out to hug her, Melissa let herself stand in her embrace.

Catarina rang the bell of the ground floor office in a backstreet near Tottenham Court Road station where Melissa worked at 6pm. The front of the office was glass and she could see Melissa sitting at her desk, boots crossed, screen reflected in her black frame glasses. There was a young man sitting next to her and an older man on the phone at the back of the space. The rest of the desks in the office were empty. Lightbulbs hung from the ceiling over tables made from curving white plastic. The young man answered the door. His face was friendly. She asked him for Melissa.

We haven't finished working yet. Can you wait ten minutes?

Sure.

He looked back.

Maybe half an hour.

Sure.

But come in, come in.

Warm air rushed her face.

My name is Femi – he said, holding out a hand. She shook it.

Catarina sat down at one of the empty desks and opened her book. She took off her coat and her scarf and put them on the table. Melissa waved at her.

Femi sat back down in the seat next to Melissa.

New flatmate?

Yes.

He pressed his lips together and said nothing.

Even if she hits on you, you can't get with her.

I won't.

Don't hit on her

I won't!

Melissa frowned at him.

I can't vouch for Marc though.

Melissa turned to look at the wiry middle-aged man making a phone call in the corner of the room. She made a vomit sound with her mouth.

Femi laughed. He put his hand on her shoulder.

Melissa looked at Catarina and then at Femi. She turned to her screen.

What does she do?

She's doing a PhD.

In what?

Um. History? I don't know

Femi turned back to his screen.

Probably a Marxist

Melissa spoke without looking at him. She's from Brazil.

Oh

Yeah.

How's that?

Melissa paused.

Fine

Melissa breathed in.

The way she pronounces my name reminds me of my mum

Two hands with large fingers landed on the table in front of them.

Drink? Marc said. I'm buying. He turned his head to the corner of the room where Catarina sat, her legs crossed in front of her. He leant into Melissa. And *who* is your friend?

The pub was tiny and Femi and Melissa had to crouch to enter through an arched entrance. They squeezed into a corner table and the cyclist-looking man who Catarina presumed was Melissa's boss pushed his legs against Catarina's legs to fit. He spread his fingers across his thighs under the tabletop.

Right I know what you two want —

Estrella

Guinness

But what about you?

The same as Melissa, I will have a pint of Guinness

Marc nodded and stood up. Good Good.

Femi looked across the table at Catarina. She looked around the pub.

Melissa tells me you're a historian?

Yes

And you're doing a PhD —

Yes, in Latin American history of the late nineteenth and twentieth centuries

Oh really, what aspects

The rise of the popular novel at the time and its relationship to gender and race and the nation state

What do you mean

Catarina was nodding. She moved her hands. You know like nationhood, romance, the marriage plot, Pocahontas and John Smith, you have similar texts here, the new middle class or the virtuous chambermaid and the landowner, uniting for the consolidation of private property and —

Marc lifted a glass in each hand and called from the bar –

Femi! Come

Femi stood. I'll be back in a second.

Melissa looked at Catarina. She stood quickly and moved to sit next to her.

Femi came back, holding two glasses. Please continue —

I am using a Marxist framework, historical materialism —

Marc bounced into the seat next to Femi, beer slipping over the edge of his glass onto the table.

Oh Marxism, my dear did you say you are using a Marxist framework, I hope you don't mind me saying but as someone who has been in the real world, you know the world of politics, of government, of getting things done for real people, I just find it extraordinary the continuing purchase of Marxist ideology among academics. Remarkable. I mean —

Catarina opened her mouth but Marc continued

I mean let me tell you that in my time I have come across ideologues, you know I am older than you and I've seen it all. Northern Ireland. East Germany. And the truth is that it all died, died in 1990 when the wall came down. And we cracked it. The Good Friday Agreement. Even in China everyone's got an ipad. Now. Policy – that is something else.

Let's be like Finland by all means, and when we were in government we loved policy, Tony, Gordon, loved it, bring on the data, the meat, the evidence —

Tony?

Oh yes Tony Blair

Melissa looked up. Catarina's mouth was hanging open.

Femi was nodding. He raised his eyebrows. Marc used to work for Tony Blair

Catarina's hands were on the table.

She turned to Melissa, who was looking down, rolling a cigarette.

Marc was standing, pointing, Who'd like another? Another Guinness? Estrella?

On the Central line home Catarina told Melissa that she felt sorry for her.

It must be very hard to work with Femi and Marc.

Melissa frowned.

They are so rightwing.

Rightwing?

Yes.

You think Femi's rightwing?

Oh yes.

Melissa moved her head to the side.

Femi's my best friend.

Really?

Yeah. I've known him since school.

Ah old friendships

Mm

They shifted in their seats as people filled the carriage around them.

And Marc—

He is terrible! I cannot believe he worked for Tony Blair. That is truly unforgivable.

Melissa nodded.

He is your boss?

Yep.

I suppose there is nothing you can do.

Melissa studied one of the adverts on the tube carriage wall.

He always pays for the drinks, at least. Melissa laughed.

Catarina did not reply. For a couple of stops the train was loud and they were quiet. At Liverpool Street Catarina turned her head to face Melissa.

Melissa I have some questions for you.

Yeah?

I want to ask you if our flat is a previously government owned flat sold off in Margaret Thatcher's infamous privatisation scheme?

Melissa considered this. Her thick shaped eyebrows moved.

Probably. I dunno when the landlord bought it. He owns a lot of houses. But yeah I would think it used to be council housing. For a family of four. My bedroom was probably the kitchen. Some of the flats in the block still are owned by the council I think.

Catarina considered this.

Mel

Yeah

I have another question

Yeah

Melissa inhaled. She listened to the sound of the train in the tunnel.

Mel, and will you tell me about your parents?

Melissa coughed. She spoke over the sound of the train.

I never had a dad. He left before I was born

Oh

I'm sorry

No – it's not a thing.

Got a feeling he was a dick anyway

Really?

Melissa shrugged.

Is that stupid?

No.

And he was Brazilian?

Yep.

Melissa looked around the carriage

And your mother?

My mum?

The tube carriage rattle slowed.

Melissa stood up.

This is our stop, Melissa said.

The next day, on her way back from buying soy milk, Catarina came across a bookcase surrounded by scattered wooden chairs on the pavement outside the second hand furniture shop by Mile End Park. It was plain dark wood and tall. She placed the milk carton on a middle shelf and then pressed her palms into the back and side of the bookcase. Satisfied, she went into the shop and paid an older-looking man £25 in cash. Outside, she reached around her bookcase and lifted, her wingspan just about the width of the shelves. She could not see where she was going and she could not see the ground. Her right leg juddered forwards and then her left, stepping sole, toes and ankle, into a puddle. Water and grit soaked her socks and the leather of her shoes.

A young man in a tracksuit helped her carry the bookcase to the front door of the flat. They didn't speak while carrying it, their faces blocked from each other by the wooden back of the bookcase. At the door to the flat, she said thank you and he shrugged.

That day she unpacked. (She met – briefly – Olivia who emerged bleary eyed and wordless from her bedroom to use the bathroom and helped Catarina carry the bookcase up the stairs before returning to sleep.) Catarina hung her clothes in the wardrobe and arranged her photographs on the desk (mum, dad, Pedro, the sea hitting the side of the city). She called her bank and told them her new address. She found the local GP surgery online and spent four hours trying to tell the Home Office where she was living. She would have to report to the local police station to tell them where she was living. She had a bath. She lay in her new bed. She messaged Pedro but he was at work. She listened for the sounds of her housemates and heard Julieta shifting in her room. At 8pm Catarina heard the front door slam.

The next morning, Catarina walked down around the estates by the park up the road to Mile End station. From there she got the Hammersmith and City line all the way to Euston Square, instead of Central line to Holborn. The Hammersmith and City line was slow but well ventilated. The Central line was fast but grimy.

Catarina sat at a desk by the window on the 10th floor of Senate House. She read alternately from a book from the Social History of Western Africa section and a book from the Critical Theory section. Until 1pm they swallowed her whole and she sat in the dark and cavernous silent belly of them. The wind wuthered outside the windows of Senate House. Under the desk, she kicked off her shoes and touched her socked toes onto each other.

Catarina left the library to eat lunch. She sat on a bench in Torrington Square eating a hummus and falafel wrap from the falafel van with the student discount. The rush chatter of undergraduates was all around her – spotty teens from the English countryside, queer kids from SOAS, their hair dyed pink and blue, East Asian fashion students in A-line coats. She finished the wrap and licked the hummus off her fingers. She would give herself another ten minutes before returning to the library. She watched two women with grey hair embrace. She joined the queue for a proper espresso made by a man with a ponytail. Oh, coffee on her tongue. Feet against the pavement. The rush of all these people, convivial and full of purpose. These streets and squares were frothing, hallowed, she felt sure. She thought of everyone who had stood there, drunk coffee there, before her. Virginia Woolf, writing *Orlando*. Vladimir Lenin, plotting the 1917 revolution. Maybe Sylvia Plath, who had killed herself on the other side of Regent's Park.

She got off the tube at Mile End in the dark. She went to the supermarket for toiletries and then she went to the chicken shop. As she stood in the queue she let her supermarket bags lean against the black and white floor. The men in the chicken shop stared at her.

Chips, please.

Catarina walked home through the estates by the park, balancing the chip box on her fingers between the plastic bag straps. The night was cold. The chips were too hot, burning her tongue and fingers and mouth. She ate them while she walked past the neat front gardens of residential blocks built in the craters left by World War Two. Lights on. Net curtains pulled. She had never been free like this. What would her mother say if she could see her only daughter walk home at night through a strange city, unaccompanied by Pedro or anybody else?

Catarina pushed her clothes into the washing machine under the stairs. It was not clear if Julieta was in her room. The door to Olivia's room was open and Catarina looked through it and saw bowls piled up on the desk. She would not be back from her night shift at the radio station until 2am. Last night Melissa had come home late wearing gym clothes and heated up food from the tupperwares she kept in the fridge. Catarina had noticed Melissa wiping and scooping Olivia's crumbs from the counter and sweeping the small kitchen floor although her name was not marked on the cleaning rota. That night Catarina waited but she did not hear Melissa come home. Catarina wondered if she had a boyfriend and had listened for the sounds of two sets of footsteps in the corridor, two sets of voices, but none came. Only the hmm hmm humm of the washing machine.

In the morning, Catarina woke to the sound of the front door slamming and the smell of coffee. When she went downstairs she found a clean mug and a half full pot of coffee on the counter, still warm.

Catarina, who was in her room, could hear one of her housemates taking a shower. Catarina opened her laptop.

She looked at the pixels of his face. She could see him clearly, clean shaven and squinting, his hands in his hair, his body wiggling in a swivel chair, the image catching up with the body 5000 kilometres away.

Pedro was dressed for work. White shirt and blue tie and glasses. Pixelated white yellow sunlight filled half the image.

His face looked at her on the screen.

They think they can impeach her

No—

Yes. Here, you go out onto the street in São Paulo, stand on your balcony, every evening you hear the paneladas – Fora Fora Fora

Catarina looked at him.

It would be a coup. To remove the democratically elected president – for political motivations, without an election –

Pedro said nothing. His hands were on his cheeks.

They are trying to say Oh she has committed financial irregularities –

These are technicalities, nothing that they have not done –

Pedro looked at her.

He nodded and then he spoke.

Yes. Yes it would be a coup.

Catarina didn't look at him. She closed her eyes. She opened her mouth to tell him about the protest outside the embassy. But Pedro spoke first –

How's your family?

The same.

Always calling?

Uh huh

Pedro nodded.

Have you been answering?

I answered the eighth time she called yesterday.

Pedro nodded. She must be very anxious.
Catarina bowed her head.

How is your family?
Not so good. My sister's company are making redundancies
Oh shit
She has not heard yet about her job
Catarina nodded.
They were quiet.

It is only another 18 months until you are finished in England
That is when the funding will finish.
Pedro moved his head. She heard the sound of his fingers against the table. She watched him move his hand to his neck. She watched the sunlight move on the wall behind him as she spoke.

Pai says I made the right choice to leave Brazil, he says now is the time to leave Brazil –
Pedro made a sound. His face on the screen broke into unrelated pixels. The sound of his voice broke up also.

Now – is the time – to stay

He seemed to be laughing. Catarina made a laughing sound also. For ten seconds he was frozen on her screen. There was a quiet

I cannot hear you Pedro
Pedro?

His face refreshed, moving, smiling.
I have to go to work, he said.
Okay.

Tchau
Tchau amor
She closed her laptop.

That day Catarina did not go into the university. She read an article her supervisor had written for an academic journal called *Historical Materialist Perspectives on the Twentieth Century* on her laptop and then she watched a YouTube video showing aerial footage of a protest in Salvador. Red balloons. She composed a long email to her supervisor and made herself a toastie. She had a shower. Before it got dark she left the flat and walked to the park. It was a strange shape – only 200 metres wide but over a kilometre long. A canal ran up one side and a big road that went south all the way almost to Canary Wharf ran down the other. Catarina walked across the grass to the canal. Two small children in school uniform skipped past her, trailed by a woman in a long skirt talking on the phone. The canal water was black.

Catarina stood there. She rubbed her hands together. She took a picture of the canal on her phone and sent it to her cousin Larissa on WhatsApp. She walked home.

Melissa came into the flat at 9pm. She was wearing soft tracksuit bottoms and her hair was wet. When she appeared Catarina was sitting at the dining table eating supermarket soup.

Hey

Hello

Melissa turned to take a container from the fridge.

How was your day?

Good. How was yours

Also good. I was reading some academic articles.

Uh huh

I skyped Pedro.

Melissa put the container in the microwave.

Your boyfriend?

Yes. He is very worried about the political situation

In Brazil?

Yes

Melissa nodded.

What did you do Melissa?

Marc was in meetings all day so I watched *Lost* on my computer.

He did not notice that?

Melissa shook her head. He doesn't understand what I do or how long it takes.

Catarina nodded. She smelled a familiar smell.

Did you make – did you make feijão?

Melissa took the tupperware from the microwave and sat on the sofa with her legs apart. She ate with a spoon straight from the container.

Uh huh

Catarina peered at the brown dish. The bean liquid was a thick and rich orange brown.

You use a pressure cooker?

Melissa looked up. Yep.

Catarina watched Melissa mix farofa into the beans in the tupperware.

Where did you buy that?

A shop near work.

Catarina nodded.

I would give you some but it's got bacon –

I can show you a vegetarian recipe, if you want.

Melissa wrinkled her nose.

It's my boyfriend's recipe, he is also a vegetarian. He's adapted loads of Brazilian recipes. Do you know moqueca?

Melissa shook her head

Oh, it's very nice. Perhaps we can make it together one time. I know a recipe with – I don't know what you call it – we call it banana da terra –

Plantain

Yes.

So you do speak Portuguese.

Melissa ate from the tupperware. Her mouth was full. No

Before Catarina could reply, Melissa said – My friend Ivy is coming over tomorrow evening. And Olivia's got the night off. If you don't have plans, you should eat with us.

Catarina did not have other plans. She had made friends in England – there was Matt from her PhD programme, who was more Pedro's friend than hers, and her supervisor Professor Henrietta, who occasionally invited her for Sunday lunch at her house in Stoke Newington – but she did not have Friday night, weekend friends. She had not had Friday night friends or weekend friends in Brazil. It had been her and her mother and father, sometimes her and Larissa, and then her and Pedro.

A woman arrived – late. Melissa opened the door. And Olivia emerged, hair wet and washed, her eyes alive, from the bedroom next to Catarina's. Catarina watched as the three women greeted each other in the doorway with big bodyful hugs, shouting compliments at each other like Have You Been Working Out and Dinner Smells Really Amazing. They touched Melissa's cheeks and shoulders with their hands, and Catarina watched as Melissa's face and her arms and shoulders turned warm. Catarina heard Melissa laugh.

Ivy, a management consultant, wore suit trousers and trainers, her hair in two thick plaits. She had fuchsia-coloured lipstick on and sat with her legs apart. She looked East Asian and Catarina heard her speak in the same accent as Melissa. Olivia, blond and pale-skinned, wore jeans and a wool jumper. She had a long ponytail and a pointy face and arms. Melissa was herself – eyelinered and scowling and that evening wearing contacts. All three of them wore hoops.

They sat around the cheap glass kitchen table in Mile End. Melissa had made a coconut spinach curry and rice cooked the Brazilian way with onions, and Ivy and Olivia had brought gin and Melissa had sent Catarina out for tonic half an hour before. Melissa cut lemons into their drinks. Melissa lit candles. Frank Ocean was playing. Melissa had forgotten to make ice so all their drinks were room temperature.

They ate in the yellow brown light of the candles and the streetlights outside the flat. Catarina ate and drank and listened. She tried, in real time, to piece together who they were talking about and what the slang words they used connoted. At the appropriate-seeming moments, Catarina made sympathetic sounds. I am in *Sex and the City*, she thought. What would Pedro or Larissa say if they could see me, she thought.

After half an hour, Olivia asked Catarina to explain what was happening in Brazil – If you don't mind, that is, someone mentioned it at work. You must be sick of being asked –

Catarina shook her head. It is fine. I don't mind

The candlelight moved over her face. Let me – I will – begin at the beginning?

Ivy and Olivia nodded.

Okay. Catarina inhaled. She spoke for thirty-five minutes without pause.

She was breathless.

My boyfriend – we were skyping yesterday – he thinks that they will try to impeach Dilma. My parents are also scared of this. I don't know if it is what will happen. Our democracy is only two years older than I am, you must understand this

Catarina felt embarrassed, like she had said or given or shown too much. She cleared her throat, touched the table.

Olivia replied too quickly – Of course you hear there is corruption on both sides. People say that Rousseff herself was implicated—

Catarina interrupted, feeling the alcohol rush to her cheeks and mouth – That is not the point – Dilma is not – their motivations are political – a technicality is not a reason to remove a democratically elected president. You would not countenance such a thing here, in your own parliament

Melissa looked at Olivia.

Olivia made a sound of agreement.

No no obviously.

They ate.

It was Ivy who rebegan the conversation.

Your boyfriend is in Brazil then?

Yes. His name is Pedro.

Right Pey-*droo* not Ped-*row*

Yes.

Ivy and Olivia looked at Catarina. Melissa raised her eyebrows.

Show us a picture then!

Catarina was embarrassed but she got her phone out. She flicked through until she got the photograph of Pedro at the university in Recife, books in thick arms, under the shade of a tree. The photo was over a year old. She held her phone out.

He's cute!

Is he mixed race?

Um he doesn't call himself mixed race –

What does he say

Black or of African descent

Uh huh

The three women turned to her again.

How's long distance

Do you think it's going to work out

For two more years? I couldn't do it

Catarina breathed in, she was drunk, the room was dark

Two years is not so long. We've been together since I was seventeen. Eight years

Wow

And he wants to stay there?

He was here for a year to study English and study for the public exams to be a government lawyer but he passed the exams and he has just started his job. It is a hard job to get, a permanent appointment in São Paulo, which is not where we are from, we are from the Northeast –

And you?

My PhD funding is for three years, I am halfway through.

And then?

I don't know.

Was he your first boyfriend?

Yes.

Mmmn

So he's the first person you ever –

And are you ever curious about

Catarina felt blood rush to her face. Curious? Catarina felt the blood rush to her hands and throat. He's an amazing person. He's the only male vegetarian I know in Brazil. He's an amazing lawyer – very political – I have learnt so much from him

Ivy nodded and Melissa nodded.

Would you want to stay?

Catarina felt the alcohol speak a secret thing into the room – Yes.

There was a quiet.

But it is not so easy to stay, the visa specifies that I must leave after my studies are completed

Catarina looked up at them.

Frank Ocean spoke to the low light room, he whispered, *in the hearth of your hotel.* Melissa poured out more gin and more tonic.

The conversation continued. Ivy was in a Long-Term Relationship with Will who she'd met at uni. Will was Very Nice and Gentle and everyone approved of him. He was also a management consultant. They lived together in Camberwell. Olivia was having a *thing* – she waved her hand in the air – with this guy she had met on Tinder who owned a kombucha company.

My last night off we went on a second date to a soft drinks convention in Holborn. I drank a lot of lemonade samples

Uh huh

Catarina stared at Olivia as she spoke. Catarina asked a question

And Melissa?

Ivy and Olivia looked at each other.

Melissa shook her head at them. She rolled her eyes.

They turned their heads back to Catarina and said, at the same time –

Melissa doesn't do relationships

No?

No.

Never?

Never.

Catarina frowned. Why?

Melissa drank from her glass.

I just – I don't want anything deep – she put her glass on the table – I mean the world is ending, we're all going to be underwater, people are already underwater, so – she held her arms out – Fuck everyone, snog everyone – everyone who wants to obviously – I mean the world is so big and life is so short –

Ivy looked at her

Melissa put her hands on the table. I'm just living my best life

Catarina tilted her head.

Olivia leant forwards – Melissa is not a commitment person

Not in a bad way like we admire it

Mel has game –

Melissa nodded.

Catarina finished the food on her plate. And you never find someone who – Catarina shook her shoulders and closed her eyes – who you want to be with?

Melissa frowned.

What are you searching for?

It's about sex – Olivia said.

No. Melissa closed her eyes then opened them. I mean yeah it's about sex, in the way that everything is about sex. But the sex isn't all great. It's something else –

The light and dark moved around them and Ivy put her hand on Melissa's back.

Melissa spoke –

I hate the idea of someone else in my things and hanging around and sending me messages all the time, but it's not that – she screwed up her face and pressed her lips together – It's like, when I have a one night stand everything is new. It's newness from the kissing to the trying to get to sleep and waking up in the morning in their bed. And then I can leave. I know the edges of myself. I feel free.

They kept talking. At some point Julieta moved from the front door to her bedroom without saying hi. Ivy was having a problem with a woman at work who wasn't even her manager assigning her tasks at 6.25pm. Olivia's boss wouldn't give her a contract and nowhere was hiring reporters anymore. So she would keep freelancing, picking up nightshifts. Melissa made fun of Marc, putting on his accent and holding a salt shaker up to her ear, saying – Excuse me. Excuse me, Melissa darling I'm getting a *very* important call.

Melissa and Ivy smoked cigarettes on the balcony, leaving the door open so the night air and smoke spread into the living room. Olivia joined them, taking Melissa's cigarette out of her fingers for a puff and putting it back. Catarina moved onto the sofa. The air was cold; she put her arms around her knees.

At 11.45pm Ivy started looking up her route home on her phone. Catarina listened as the other three said fizzing incoherent things about transport infrastructure like –

The night tube will be the eighth wonder of the world
and
The Victoria line is the FERRARI of tube lines

Catarina frowned and slurred at them.

You know New York City has had the 24-hour subway for like ten years? Melissa waved her hand.

You gotta understand Catarina. When we were growing up we used to get night buses everywhere. They were crazy let me tell you

Cray-zee. One time I smoked crack by accident on the top deck of the N333

For the record I never did that—

So the night tube is like – Melissa moved her hands around her temples to show her brain exploding.

The three of you talk like you're old ladies

No we don't

Also we're not old

You know Catarina I had three grandmothers growing up

She held out three fingers
Three?
Yes. Jean, Janine and Jasmine.
One was your step-grandmother?
No all of them were my main grandmothers
Catarina looked at Melissa. She looked at Ivy, who was busy putting on her coat and did not react.

As she turned to leave, Ivy pointed at Catarina's phone, which was on the table.

Someone called Sônia is calling you.

By January 2015 it was still deep winter, and they had been living in the city for four months. Pedro had turned to Catarina and said –

Quero voltar pra casa.

They were in their double room in Kennington for which they paid £850 a month, £425 each. Pedro had wanted an en suite but that was not how apartments were built in London. Most of them were houses that had been split up, their living rooms turned into bedrooms – and the ones that were in purpose-built blocks did not have en suites either. At the start of their search – when their move to England had been a shared Google sheet into which they pasted meticulously categorised hyperlinks – Pedro had hopefully suggested new builds to rent in Wembley. Wembley? She had said to him over the phone – Where is that? Google maps said that there was a big Ikea and a very big stadium in Wembley.

In the end they had moved into a four bed in Kennington. It had no communal spaces, except a kitchen so narrow that Pedro could stretch left and right and flatten both his palms on the walls at the same time. The estate agent asked them if they had registered at the police station when they arrived. He asked for their passports and visas. Their housemates were always in their rooms and no one ever cleaned the kitchen or the corridor. Their room was painted grey and the floors were brown. The sink was in a different room from the toilet. They had to report to the police within seven days of arriving in the country. Neither of them liked to cook in that kitchen. They took to wearing outdoor clothes in their double bed.

Pedro had looked at her when he said it.

Catarina had frowned.

I don't like this country

Catarina looked at him.

I never liked this country. The people are cold and the weather is cold. I do not see the sun. The whole city is the same colour apart from in the nighttime. My feet are always wet.

There are some nice days

I do not like the politics here. They hate foreigners like us, they hate brown people like me. I do not like the new government that was just elected.

40

Catarina opened her mouth.

There is nowhere to go dancing after 2am. The people are all alcoholics.

Catarina made a face.

I miss home. I miss not feeling pain in my fingers when I am outdoors. I miss making jokes. I miss being funny. I miss my family. I miss my sister. I miss my friends. I miss *having friends*. I miss the open university campus in Recife where no one asks for photo ID. I miss my baby nephew. I miss music with drums in it. I miss not being mistaken for Middle Eastern—

But you're harassed in Brazil too—

That is not the point Catarina. My heart is not here.

He looked at her.

And I do not have a Portuguese grandmother like you do, there is not a European passport I can apply for

Catarina swallowed. I don't know if that will—

Pedro continued – I want to sit these exams and go. I want to get a job and send money to my family. The people – here – they do not want me in to stay in this country. I don't want to try to get another visa. I want to go home.

Catarina felt the outside dark close in on her body.

Matt is your friend –

Pedro shrugged.

Catarina looked at him.

I miss my family

You miss your family –

Yes.

Don't you miss yours Catarina

I have to stay.

Pedro looked at her. I know

She moved her body into his, her hand into his hand.

I want you to stay with me.

Pedro did not reply to this. He sat back from her on the bed.

41

It is already spring. The weather will get better –

And then it will get worse. He spoke with irritation – It is not about the weather

Catarina looked at him. Outside was dark grey.

Catarina

Yes

When I am in London I feel like I am sitting at the bottom of the sea. In one of the places where there is no seaweed and there are only fish without eyeballs.

Catarina laughed. She said his name. She put her forehead on his shoulder and made a sound.

The next week, applications for the permanent government job in São Paulo opened and Pedro put down his name. He spent three months in the public library in Vauxhall studying for the exam. Some days in there he heard kids speaking Spanish and Portuguese. He almost lifted his head. When the day came Pedro sat the exams in a quiet room, with three other men in suits at the Brazilian consulate, the sounds of Regent Street behind them.

By November 2015 Pedro had passed the public exams and left. He packed his two large suitcases and sat with them on the Piccadilly line to Heathrow. The train pulled itself overground just ahead of Hammersmith station. As it passed through Ealing, Acton, Hounslow, Osterley, Pedro watched the ancient modern grey city for the last time. The tube was all people with large suitcases. He held on to his. Catarina had tied ribbons around their handles the night before. He had said he wanted to talk to her. She had said to him that he should shave and wear a proper shirt with a collar to go through security. She took a shirt from his case and ironed it. He shaved. He didn't like her telling him what to do. She had said she worried for him, that was all. They had not discussed the future. Pedro stared across the carriage. The tube was full of tourists. He could tell they were tourists. A woman spoke in French to her child, an Asian couple checked a paper map. What did they think when they looked at him? He had not been a tourist in this city, had not been at home. As the tube slowed, he stood, pulling his coat around him. Heathrow Terminal 3.

He would spend two months at home in Recife. And in the new year he would move to São Paulo, a city that was bigger, more full of concrete, as corporate and as cosmopolitan as London, and begin his new job – a historic job for him, for his family, a job for life – as a judge specialising in corporate law.

Catarina breathed deep. She did not feel the way Pedro felt about the city. She had been standing in London in her mind since she had been a child, reading books set in Europe since she was a child. There were all kinds of answers to old questions here, so many things that she wanted to touch and know. She could not help it; she did not miss her family, she did not even know if she would miss Pedro. He had said to her, This will be hard, long distance. We should talk about how to make it work, long distance, and she had said yes but also she had changed the subject until the time had passed and he had left. Exhale

Catarina watched the season turn from summer into autumn. The dry leaves fell around her onto the earth. Red and yellow as subdued colours, like she had never seen them.

That Autumn, Catarina was alone for the first time in her life, and it felt to her like a threshold. All this quiet. A new city as old as history. She felt a lightness in her body. She wrote for hours in the library. Words came to her like water. Decisions were easy. She would finish the new academic term and then she would move into a new apartment in the new year. She would do groundbreaking research. She would make herself a new London life. She would throw herself into the city. Every event, every exhibition, every evening lecture; she would fill her life with new words and new people. In December she messaged twenty-five different people on the spare room site, including a girl with a Brazilian-looking surname and purple hair.

Around her, outside the windows of the library, red and yellow fell, from the sky, settling on the ground. Hours later, on her way home, she would walk over the loose, dismantled firmament.

There was a rhythm to the flat in Mile End that February. Coffee and a mug on the counter in the mornings. Melissa and Catarina each took the tube WESTBOUND an hour apart into the west end of the city. Packed Central line underground trains passed through the station minute on minute. Melissa never got a seat; Catarina never got a seat. At lunchtime Melissa ate sushi or tupperware pasta with Femi and Catarina ate falafel wraps and sandwiches from the supermarket. In the evenings Catarina worked late in the whale belly bowel part of her brain; she went to public lectures and when she got home she read or skyped Pedro. In the evenings Melissa went for drinks with Femi and Marc at the tiny ancient pub. On the evenings when she could escape, she went on dates with people off apps, showering at the gym beforehand. When Melissa got home she cooked and scooped up in the crumbs Olivia had left on the glass table during the day. Occasionally, Julieta left or entered her room.

That term Catarina began teaching classes on the Introduction to Modern Latin American History course for undergraduates. She taught groups of baby adults mostly from England, fifteen at a time in a classroom in the new part of an old building. She made them answer the module questions that Professor Henrietta had chosen.

What can memory studies contribute to the study of the past in Latin America?

What can urban history tell us about the history of neoliberalism in Latin America?

What can the history of commodities teach us about the achievements and limits of Pink Tide governments?

What can the history of sexuality tell us about the nature of authoritarian rule in twentieth-century Latin America?

What can the study of state formation teach us about the Estado Novo?

What can environmental history approaches tell us about Cardenismo?

What can the Colombian experience teach us about the nature of collective violence?

What light can labour history shed on the impact of the Great Depression in Latin America?

Did Sandino help create an 'imagined community' in Nicaragua?
What can a focus on race and ethnicity tell us about the Chaco War?
What can studies of the Good Neighbour Policy tell us about the character of US-Latin American relations?

Overdue library books piled on her desk in Mile End and this made her feel at home.

They both noticed, an hour apart each morning, how the park began to fill with new rich redder and disrupted soil, which men in council uniforms, wearing thick soil-covered gloves, thrust their hands into. The fountain in the park began to shuhslosh with flowing water.

When they were both in the flat, Melissa told Catarina about her hook ups and Catarina listened with her nose wrinkled without blinking. Melissa asked Catarina non-invasive questions about things with Pedro, wondering privately if they ever sent each other explicit photographs and concluding that yes otherwise how else could it work. They ate at the table or on the sofa. Melissa made food and Catarina washed the plates and pans and she would have wiped the surfaces but Melissa did this as she cooked. Melissa asked Catarina for the vegetarian feijão recipe. Melissa watched a video online of a Black woman in a white skirt making vegetarian moqueca. Sometimes Femi came over, and he ate with them. Even at the end of the day Femi always looked sharp and he always brought pudding or beer. Sometimes he slept on the L-shaped sofa instead of going back to his parents' house in Norwood. They went for drinks near the office with Marc and drank pints that Marc paid for and Marc told them again about the time that he had met Colin Powell, and Catarina argued with Femi about US politics, Catarina using words like Regime Change and Coup and Neocolonialism and Femi using words like Democracy and Intervention and Incentive until she got breathless and he relented and when Catarina was in the loo he would say to Melissa that No of course he agreed really, he was a social democrat really, his family was from an ex-British colony don't forget, what else was he meant to say when Marc was there and Catarina's PhD was in fact very interesting to him and he admired the clarity of her passion, her deep

46

knowledge of the history, her moral rigidity. When Catarina talked about Brazilian politics they listened. What was impeachment, how did it work, why did it matter, the English translation of pedalada and Lava Jato, which both had literal meanings as well as their principal analogical metonymic meanings. When she spoke about Brazil no one contradicted Catarina – not even Marc – and sometimes her voice cracked and it sounded like she would cry.

One night in the rain she had turned to them, to face the three of them, Marc standing at her height and Femi and Melissa taller than her although she was standing on the kerb and they had their feet in the street, and Catarina had said the name

LAURA

My aunt, I never met her, she disappeared – we thought she was disappeared, killed, her body dumped in a mass grave – during the dictatorship. For five years she was gone. When she came back she was different. She had been tortured.

The three of them were quiet. Rain slipped from the sky down their bodies onto the street.

Melissa listened and at night she read news articles on her phone. She read a Wikipedia page called 'Military Dictatorship in Brazil' and then squinted at another one called 'Ditadura militar brasileira'.

Catarina only sometimes asked Melissa the story of herself. Where her family was from and what had happened; she let Melissa talk about South London but never asked why she had left or how her family had ended up there or what part of Brazil they were from. She wondered sometimes if Melissa knew. Catarina noticed when Melissa played Brazilian music – sometimes followed by tracks from the *West Side Story* soundtrack – but Catarina did not comment.

They could not hang up paintings or paint the walls of the flat because the landlord did not permit it. One day Melissa came home with a small plant. It had a jagged, zig zag pattern on its upright leaves. She was not sure why she had bought it from the flower stand by the station.

When Catarina saw it she said –

You know this is from Brazil? It is called Espada de São Jorge. It has come from our continent, like me and like your mother.

Melissa put it on the glass dining table.

The next week Catarina came home with a plant from the stall by Goodge Street station. She said –

It is called Costela de Adão.

She said –

I will put it in the bathroom because it likes humidity.

And that night Melissa planted chilli seeds into a pot, placing them by the windowsill, saying, They need heat and light the internet said.

She bought a tiny two-shooted hanging plant with six small green leaves in a pot, which she hung in the balcony.

The label says its leaves will turn purple in the summer, Melissa called, while hanging it up.

When the bulbs in the park hatched in March they formed a yellow curving path along Mile End Park, like the Yellow Brick Road in *The Wizard of Oz*. A week later blue flowers broke and then pink and then lilac. Wearing leggings and a hoodie, Melissa began to run outside.

Daisy moved in the bed like a waking person. Like a waking person, Melissa pressed her nose against Daisy's white shoulder.

Ach. God. Daisy drank from the pint glass by the bed and handed it to Melissa. Melissa drank.

Fuck I'm hungover.

Daisy stood up, took a towel from the floor, and left the room.

She'd gone without her glasses on. Melissa put Daisy's glasses on her own face but they made everything too small. Melissa reclosed her eyes. Her contacts were still in.

Melissa sat up on the pillow. It was a dark and untidy room. The window wasn't facing the sun and the grey sheets and a tall dark wood wardrobe darkened the white walls. The house was Victorian. It didn't have double glazing. Melissa wondered how much Daisy paid for her room; she would guess at least £750/month. This would have been the dining room. Melissa felt the cold in her forearms and her feet.

Daisy had stuck postcards from exhibitions, and what looked like one small poem, on the wardrobe. Melissa couldn't read them properly from the head of the bed so she knelt forwards, palms flat on the duvet. She recognised one postcard – it was a Georgia O'Keeffe, the white and blue petal vulva painting. The other postcard was a photograph of a woman on her side, hands out hair out, in black and white. On the floor of the room there were several pairs of trousers and shirts, and dungarees hung over a chair. Kneeling forwards she read the poem, arranged like two lines of prose:

on wild nights who can you call home? Only the one who knows your name.

Melissa reached for her phone.

The door opened.

Daisy came in with wet hands and red wet cheeks.

God I'm so hungover – she spoke with a fake-drama hand on her forehead, and a grimace.

Mmmn.

Melissa took the towel that Daisy held out for her.

Thanks. Which is your toothbrush? Is it okay if I use it? she said.

Yeah. It's the blue one

Daisy's bathroom was up a set of stairs and dark. The corners of it were dirty. Melissa pulled the light on. There was a no fuss upmarket moisturiser by the sink. There was, in a plastic cup, the blue toothbrush, which had wet scrunched out bristles. Melissa drank from the sink tap and then she sat on the loo and peed and brushed her teeth. She felt a small anxiety in her chest. She got in the shower and washed the sweat off herself, washed her hair. After she dried her body with the towel, she put the moisturiser on her face.

They had had sex, around 1am in Daisy's house near Dalston Kingsland station. They had undressed very fast and then everything had taken too long, they were both drunk, and Daisy never opened her mouth to kiss and Melissa had only wanted to taste her mouth just a little. After forty minutes or so Melissa sat up apologising saying –

Sorry. It's my antidepressants.

But, in the earliest part of the morning when there was just the lightest grey outside the curtains to let them know that it was morning and they had slept the night together, Melissa had leant herself (exhale) into Daisy's back, her nose on her shoulder skin and Daisy had pulled Melissa's body into her. There was no looking then, no kissing on the mouth; they weren't waiting or working for anyone to come – they had been asleep until then, were still a little drunk – and Melissa held her mouth against Daisy's shoulder. If she had bitten into it, would it have caved, soft and sky pink like a guava

Twenty minutes later Daisy would say YesYes I love that, I love it, Melissa thinking Yes Oh this is it open hold close gasping legs around me

When Melissa came back into the flat she could hear voices in the living room. The daylight had been dark. Her head was not clear but a little fuzzy. The voices were fuzzy. She listened. She pressed her body against the kitchen / living room door. She heard an older woman's voice. She heard an older man's voice. She heard Catarina speaking.

The very inside of her chest caught against her ribs like the skin beneath a blister.

She went into her room and closed the door. She could hear the voices. She could not hear the words but she heard the sound of Portuguese. An older woman's voice. She took off her boots and took off her last night clothes, she turned her bedroom light off, she put a towel round her body, she walked up the stairs and got into the shower and let the hot water fall around her ears and block the sound of Catarina skyping her family.

They went on another date, still in the winter. The weather was watery and Daisy wore a black band in her blonde hair and put little black cat flicks in the corners of her eyes. She told Melissa she was finding getting a proper job in curation hard. She said something Walter Benjamin something John Berger and also Susan Sontag? and Melissa said, My flatmate loves Susan Sontag.

They tried to kiss in the street (awkwardly) under the railway bridge in Bethnal Green but kept being interrupted by teenage boys on bikes.

So they went down a side street and tried again although it wasn't really working felt clammy.

Nevertheless they went back to the not double-glazed room in Dalston and had sex where they both came, eventually. Afterwards lying on her back, her glasses on the bedside table, Melissa asked simple questions like

What else do you like? What makes you come?

(Daisy had touched Melissa with her fingers, light and hot)

Boldly, she said –

I want to see you make yourself come

Daisy shut her eyes, white belly half under the white sheets, and said, I want to do that too.

Melissa never texted Daisy after that and Daisy never texted Melissa.

When she told Catarina this, sitting on the L-shaped sofa, Catarina screwed up her face and laughed and said – But didn't you like her Mel? And she was nice no? Pretty? Liked Jeanette Winterson?

Melissa shrugged and laughed. Yeah she was great. She was alright. It's not that deep really.

At night Melissa felt a deep relief at being alone in her bed. She drank a glass of water. She made herself come. Once and then very quickly again after. She felt shame that coming to the thought of Daisy was so much easier than with the actual breathing body of her.

The morning Melissa told Femi they were going to a protest outside the Brazilian embassy, he said – What's the point?

Melissa frowned at him behind her glasses.

We're protesting the coup

The *coup*?

Yes

We being you and Catarina?

Yeah

What do you know about what's going on in Brazil Mel

What do you know? I've been reading

Femi closed the laptop. Protests are not an effective tool for change Mel.

What about – what about the War in Iraq?

Exactly. Biggest protest in British history – didn't change a thing. Policy, lobbying, influencing, now that's the answer

Melissa leant back in her chair. She looked around the white office.

Well I'm going

Femi nodded. Good luck. Stay safe.

The protest on the Cockspur Street pavement was small. The Brazilian flag hung flat and dark green from the rain on its pole over the street. It was windy and the sun had gone down by the time the protest started. It wasn't really clear when it started. For fifteen minutes they knelt on the pavement trying to light candles but the wind blew out every single one. A small group of older white-looking people stood together with pre-printed placards. A smaller group of younger not-so-white-looking people stood holding flowers. They took turns at the megaphone, both groups speaking first in Portuguese and then in English. Catarina and Melissa stood in the middle, freezing. Catarina took a turn, reading from her phone. She read a text that Pedro had sent her. Cars made noise behind her on the street. When Catarina finished an older woman shepherded the group into position. They posed behind a banner that read –

they raised their fists. Melissa raised her fist. They shouted –

NÃO AO GOLPE

Melissa's heart began to beat fast. Somebody took a photograph. The small crowd stirred and music began to play on speakers that had been mounted onto a supermarket trolley. Melissa's heart was moving fast. She recognised the music. She hadn't heard the song with the lyrics about the construction site in god knows how long. Two women in fleeces began dancing. A policeman parked his motorbike. There's nothing happening, sir, somebody said.

A person holding flowers approached Melissa and Catarina. She was wearing a purple puffer coat down to her knees. She blinked.

Are you coming to the meeting? she said. It's about to start.

The meeting?

Yes. In the university building. It's about to start.

They said nothing.

Usually they're not in the university buildings but we couldn't find anywhere else tonight.

Melissa and Catarina looked at each other.

The person holding flowers and, as it happened, two tangerines and a banana led them down the West End side streets through Leicester Square and Chinatown, round the back of Soho Square, almost past Melissa's office, almost past the British Museum, to a door with a University of London plaque. A security guard looked up at them and pointed at a visitors' book.

Sorry – the person with the flowers said, and lowering her voice – You don't have to put your real name.

Melissa looked at Catarina. She watched Catarina sign herself in as Catherine Smith in her curly Brazilian handwriting. Panicking, Melissa wrote down six capital letters, the name GLÓRIA.

The three of them walked down the university hallway.

The person with the flowers looked back at them and smiled, opening a door into a huge teaching room. As she stepped into the room, Melissa froze.

There were at least a hundred people gathered there, people who might be women and people who might not be women, everyone except for men, Melissa guessed. They were sitting on the floor, apart from two people sitting in wheelchairs, talking while shuffling themselves back into a rough circle. Someone had a baby on their lap. They were all kinds of people there. Young people and older people and people who could have been any age. People with pink hair and people with ginger hair and people with thick heavy black hair and people with locs and people with no hair. Nose rings and hijabs and biker boots and cleavage and long skirts and all kinds of hands and backpacks and handbags and moustaches and lipsticks and earrings and sports bras. Melissa could feel her jaw drop. She recognised some of them. A girl from uni, another one from Olivia's old work, someone with the face of a girl called Meena from her class at secondary school.

Melissa and Catarina looked at each other. They sat in the circle.

The person holding flowers stood up and so did the person next to them. They looked at each other. They clapped their hands. The clock above them said 8pm exactly.

Ready? Phones off. They spoke with loud and smiling voices. Let us begin.

On the way home Catarina was almost singing.

Let's walk through the park, she said when they emerged from the mouth of Mile End station.

Spring was breaking across the trees in tiny green buds that looked orange under the streetlights. The sounds of a saxophone. Cherry blossom fell too early on the ground, also orange. They followed the lilac, blue and yellow flowers down the park towards their flat.

Tell me about your mother, Catarina said.

Melissa looked at her.

Finally, she opened her mouth to speak.

AMEN CORNER

(1993–2011)

Baby Melissa never cried. Sleep, her mother said, and she would.

The night she was born St George's Hospital in Tooting, South London, was overfull. The trees in the suburban streets surrounding the hospital were overfull, the air was too hot, too humid.

It was August 1993. The wards should have been empty, relatively speaking, seasonally speaking, but it was a hot hot night and people were collapsing of dehydration all over the city.

In the minutes after Melissa was born Glória was alone. She closed her eyes. Small hot ribs against her palm. Outside, a sweet bin bag smell rose through the hot night air around the hospital and the surrounding streets.

Baby Melissa never cried. Sleep, her mother said, and she would.

In winter, after her husband left after the altercation in the bath which had been loud enough to wake the neighbours, a policewoman asked Melissa's mother the following questions:

a
b
c
d
e
f
g
h
i
j

k
l
m
n

To which Glória, worried that her English would not be good and correct enough, replied

Yes
No
Yes
Yes
No
No
Yes
No
He has left
Yes yes here is my passport.

Glória was holding her baby. (Jiggle jiggle.)

Right, the policewoman said.

It was hard to know exactly how old Jean and Janine and Jasmine who lived on their street were. They'd been on the cul de sac called Amen Corner since their houses had been built in the craters left by World War Two. They were old enough for their husbands to have died at a *die-able viable* age a while ago (apart from Jean's husband who, as if dead, never left his armchair). They had accents; they had come from somewhere not there some time ago on ships and boats and planes.

When the policewoman came round to ask questions they were each in their own living room.

Oh I was about to put the kettle –

Just about to make a brew!

How many sugars is yours, Officer?

In answer to the policewoman's questions, Jean said –

Oh yes I've known Glória and her husband since they moved to the street – oh it would be about two years ago

Yes I wanted to help her out, so I put some notices up saying call this number for a cleaner, in the church and play centre you know while she got her nursing qualifications here

She was already pregnant, the most glowing look, it always is

In answer to the policewoman's questions, Jasmine said –

Oh Tuesday? Oh Wednesday? The neighbours heard it? Well I am her neighbour and I didn't hear No no I heard nothing

There was an altercation you say? Good riddance to him then, I say

Gosh

In answer to the policewoman's questions, Janine said –

Yes

Oh yes. She often leaves the baby with me when she is shopping or out cleaning houses

And yes that is right her paperwork is all in order, quite in order yes.

Gosh

That winter was cold, and the dark came in the afternoons.

For two weeks they slept at Jasmine's where the heating was on. Jasmine kept the plastic covers on her chairs. All the white of all the walls was covered in photographs of her children and grandchildren.

In the cot next to the bed, Glória listened to her daughter's baby body breathe.

And then
And then

As delicately (and as surely) as the white lilac nights had turned to black, the cold air thawed and the days linger lengthened into the flower-crowned spring again

Here was a beginning

At school they called her Mel.

Mel

Her mother loved it

Mel

means honey

meleca

meloso

All the children in her class lived in the streets surrounding the school.

Anna, whose mum was French and had been a dancer

Aisha, who watched Hindi films instead of Disney and whose grandma lived with her

Chiara, who had had a trampolining birthday party in Crystal Palace

Ahmed, whose mum didn't speak English and fed them ketchup on pasta

Dean, whose mum was really pretty and really really young

Jamal, whose dad sometimes picked him up from school

Shanice, whose skin was the same colour as Mel's but with different hair

Travis, whose tired-looking mum never wiped his nose

They all lived on the roads that ran parallel to hers, that came off the main road where the big brick Victorian school building rose up the hill that led down to the corner where the buses to Tooting Broadway left from.

In assembly they didn't sing hymns – only at Christmas time and then Ahmed and Aisha had to sit outside the hall. They sang 'Yellow Submarine' and songs from popular musicals

Shanice's mum asked if Mel would like to come over after school for tea. Shanice's mum made them curly pasta and grated cheese. They lived two roads across, on another cul de sac, number 17.

One time Anna's mum had come into the playground wearing sunglasses and a scarf all up to her nose and her cheeks chapped red and Janine, who had been picking Melissa up that day, said, Well but sometimes it is better to have no husband at all eh my darling? Janine ripped out a page of Melissa's exercise book and wrote her phone number on it. The next week Mr Higgins said that sadly Anna had left the class. Her family had gone. Moved house.

At the weekends they got buses.

333

57

127

355

All the buses went from the roundabout to Tooting Broadway. They went to the leisure centre for swimming or to the market to do the shopping. In the market, stall owners tilted their heads and asked them – Punjabi? Gujarati? thinking that they might have good light-skin genes, or imagining a paper-skinned English husband or rest of a family at home. To this Glória would take her bags of fruit, holding them to her chest and laugh and exclaim – No-o! No husband. We are from Brasil! You know Brasil?

In the summers, Glória would open all the windows and play the songs she had used to listen to back when she was young. In the summers, sitting on the sofa, Melissa would watch her mum's small steps around the living room and she had used to step step also, at her knees. This song, this sound, it is the sound, Glória had said to her.

When they went swimming, Glória wore a green bikini, which the English women at the leisure centre found provocatively small. A woman that size in a bikini that size! It showed her belly round and her breast weight. It showed the scars on her legs. The stringy bottom part showed all of her bum cheeks, which had the texture of tiny waves, like the sea from a distance.

(Here was a beginning)

One August morning, the front room windows were open and the white net curtain was hanging still and burning in the window.

Aunty Janine knocked on the door, her head in the window, Put the news on Glória Put the bloody news on. Two minutes later Aunty Jean knocked on the door and Aunty Jasmine. It's awful God So awful

Can you believe

I can't believe it

Meu deus

Her mother was crying with her face in her hands

Não dá pra acreditar filha

That is one way to end a marriage

Princessa Diana

Filha

Diana

Can you imagine

Meu deus meu deus a car accident

The news rolled on, showing a photograph of a black car that didn't look like a car any more. Melissa imagined if her mum had been in a car like that and started crying too.

That afternoon, 31st August 1997, was Melissa's fourth birthday party. The little paper invites had said *Start: 3pm.*

The kids from school who weren't on holiday with their families were in Janine's garden. Janine's corner house had the biggest garden and also she had all that squash in her cupboard that needed to be drunk. Glória and Jean had blown up balloons and they lay loose in the garden between the children. Glória stood in the doorway in sunglasses originally from New Look. Jean and Janine and Jasmine sat inside cutting cake and laying out napkins and drinking tea.

In the garden, under the sun, a blonde girl called Eliza ran around the circle touching their little nitty heads:

Melissa

Derek

Travis

Ahmed

Rahel

Mohammed

Duck Duck Duck Duck Duck GOOSE

Aisha

Jenny

Ellie

Dean

Jamal

Duck Duck Duck GOOSE

Glória stood in the back doorway holding a tray of brigadeiros wearing sunglasses looking at the TV which was rolling pictures of a black car that didn't look like a car anymore. She had been crying into the brigadeiro dish and inside Janine had her hands on her cheeks and Jean and Jasmine were shaking and shaking their heads

Mel's mum is crying, Aisha whispered.

WHY is your mum crying Mel? Dean said.

I know! Jamal stood up on the grass authoritatively – It's cos Princess Diana died

Princess Diana died in a car crash

In the middle of the night when we were asleep Ellie said

In Paa riss

Dia narr

Crash!

How did

What

But

Who is

That is so SAD

The news rolled on into the evening after they had eaten the brigadeiros and Victoria sponge cake and the last kids got picked up late by their apologising mothers, and Melissa, who knew the alphabet by that time, saw the letters again and again on the telly Diana Diana Diana

Before it could get dark, Glória jump grabbed her purse and in her other hand her child. *Chega. Vamos.* Holding hands, they got the bus to Tooting Broadway station, where Melissa's mum bought a bouquet of pink roses from the flower stall for £3.50. Melissa had never seen her mother buy flowers before. Glória asked Melissa if she would like to hold the flowers and Melissa said, Yes, quero. They sat on the tube and moved, quiet and rose-bearing, into the centre of the city.

On the leafy side of the centre of the big hot city, which was full but still, moving but slow in the heat, Melissa's mother laid the roses on the edge of the flat mass of flowers and plastic which spread like a new threshold from the palace gates, hot and advancing like the surface of Pompeii stopping only at the feet of the living.

There were thousands of people there, there were thousands and thousands of bouquets and cards, people on their knees.

Melissa's mother, wet face and sweating, knelt on the ground.

Nothing ever happened in August. People lingered waiting, looking down and into the sky, people had brought their children, it was August children didn't have to be at school, the daylight lasted, the hot day was still living, lasting, long

When Mel was six and seven and eight she started getting homeworks.
Long sheets of spellings like

    september

    october

    november

    december

which Glória read slowly like

    ought

    thought

    through

    night

    slight

    light

    might

Even in August, even in August her mother didn't trust the British summers, Put on your casaco before you go out, she had used say.

Melissa's first friend was Ruth.

The first time Melissa saw her, Ruth had just turned eleven and Melissa was ten. Ruthie had a mousy brown mushroom-type haircut and grey colour eyes. She was carrying a child-sized tennis racket.

In Glória's voice Ruth was Ruthie; there was only one word, a homophone.

Ruth Curtis
Ruthie Curtis

Ruth Lily
Lily pad
Ruthie Lily-pad Curtis
Roo
Ruh ooh th-eee
Ruth

There was only
once and
only
always only

Here was a beginning

To start with Melissa thought that Ruthie did not have a dad. And then she thought that Ruthie was embarrassed of her dad for some reason and kept him hidden. In Melissa's world, through which Ruthie moved as if it was the only world, having a dad was weird. And having three grandmothers who lived on your street and rarely mentioned their husbands was normal.

But, of course, Ruth had a dad. He wore a blue suit like a uniform. The shirt and tie colours changed: salmon, light blue and beige. His name was Roger.

When Vicky dropped Melissa off in their burgundy seven-seater for the first time and Janine opened her door, Vicky had said, Are you the grandmother? peering inside. You've got such a lovely home, you must be right inside the catchment area for Beatrice Webb Secondary School. It's why we moved here, our youngest two –

Janine had looked straight ahead into the road. She sighed. My son went to Beatrice Webb before it was called Beatrice Webb, you know.

In fact, Jean, Janine, Jasmine and Glória did know about catchment areas. And, yes, their cul de sac was safely within it.

Vicky and Roger approved of Melissa. Vicky and Roger approved of Glória. Melissa would hear them say so around the kitchen island in the evening as she hovered by the fridge. Over a glass of Merlot, head leant back, Roger said –

To arrive in a city with nothing, to go from hospital cleaner to hospital nurse –

Vicky turned the stem of her glass in her hand. A single mother, it must be hard –

Roger interrupted – Glória represents – I don't know

Vicky looked at him, tucking her daughter under her arm.

All that is good and possible about – England – London – multiculturalism

Her daughter at the same school as our daughter

Receiving the same education as our daughter – Roger drank – Well if that isn't success, what is?

Mmmn.

Ruthie squirmed in her mother's armpit.

The first time Ruth came over it was beginning to get windy on the cul de sac on the hill. Glória picked them up wearing a puffer jacket, holding a smaller puffer jacket and a scarf.

It's so cold querida! I brought this jacket for you.

It's not cold, is it *Ruth*?

Glória held out her arms and Ruth stepped into them. She wrapped the scarf around Ruth's cheeks and neck.

Glória watched them run to the end of the road. Melissa said – My auntie Jean lives here. And here is my other auntie Janine's house. And this is my aunt Jasmine's.

And And

And this is my house. Mel faced it, as if for the first time. It stood at the turning tail of the cul de sac. They sat on the little brick wall in the front garden, waiting for Glória. Ruthie looked behind her, at the white net curtains and the well insulated-looking windows.

Glória left them on the sofa with their shoes off watching TV. She hung up their jackets.

In the kitchen, she put a cassette tape in the stereo. She pressed play. She moved her weight from foot to foot in her slippers, from her toes to her heels, from her toes to her heels.

She turned –

A child had appeared in the kitchen.

Please may I have a glass of water please?

Glória looked down at Ruth. Brown blonde hair. They stood together in the kitchen. Glória touched Ruthie's mushroom head and handed Ruth her water in a plastic green cup. Ruth looked up at her as she drank.

What is the song playing?

Águas de Março, it is by Elis Regina. It means –

Melissa spoke from the doorway – It means the waters of March

And, as if prompted, the line came from the little speakers on either side of the cassette drive –

São as águas de março, fechando verão

78

Melissa continued, accompanying the sound from the cassette player – The waters of March closing the summer

Ruth frowned – The summer

Glória opened her mouth.

Melissa kept going – It's wood, it's stone, it's the end of the – path? It's the rest of the –

Glória interrupted – Tree.

Melissa looked at her – It's a bit lonely

Yes – é um pouco sozinho . . . it's a bit alone. Resto de toco is a tree, a tree that is dead –

A stump

Glória continued – It's a crack of glass

Melissa continued – A shard –

It's life it's the sun –

The soul –

No não – It's the night, the death, it's a bow, the hook –

Melissa said – The lace, the hook

They paused. The music came again. Glória raised her eyebrows.

Melissa began again –

It's the wood in wind
The fall of the
It's a mystery profound (deep)
It's wanting not wanting

Melissa looked at Glória. Melissa spoke –

It's the windy wind
It's the rainy rain
These are the waters of March
Closing the summer
It's the promise of life
In your coração

Leaning on the counter, Glória looked at Melissa. The music stopped. Ruthie looked into her friend's face. She looked at Glória.

You must have a dad, my mum says everyone has a dad – Ruth said on the monkey bars in the playground.

No – Mel had replied, jumping to the soft floor. I've got three grand-mas instead.

And it was true. At 3.15pm Jasmine was there, waiting outside the stone arch exit of the school building with all the mums of all the other kids in year 6. Her hair in a white plait to her bum. And the next day Jean was there, holding biscuits, and the next day it was Janine, grabbing Melissa's hand, saying we've got to get home, I've left something on the stove, and then stopping to talk for twenty minutes to a teacher who asked her how her son was doing.

And Glória noticed Ruth's big-eyed always enthusiasm for Melissa. Her want to share and show all her things, to be together with her, to ask her questions without taunting. Glória noticed how when Ruth came into their house on Amen Corner she wiped her little winter boots on the mat and said it smells nice, and how often she said that she wished she had three grandmothers like Jean, Janine and Jasmine.

The first time Melissa came over, Ruthie had just been given permission to walk home from school alone. As Ruth turned her new key in the door, she looked back at her friend. Melissa's bowl cut hair hung around her ears.

This is my house.

Melissa stood beneath its tall Victorian façade – red brick, bay window, white cornices.

Your house is so nice.

Ruth turned the key in the lock and they stepped into the hallway.

Through the corridor through the glass door at the back of the open plan kitchen and dining room, Melissa could see the tense grey canvas of a trampoline. As they ran up the stairs, Ruth swung the whole weight of her body on the banisters; Melissa did the same, her feet deep in the green carpet.

Ruth's bedroom was at the top of the house. The ceiling was gabled and a recently painted lilac. There was a skylight. Her bed was in a corner, raised like a bunk bed but with a desk and chair in the place of the lower bunk. The bed and desk frame were silver, and a silver ladder led to the bed itself.

In another corner of the room, there was an IKEA dresser piled with paperclips and hairbands and in amongst them little oyster rounds of blue sparkling pink shining eyeshadow.

They stood in the middle of the room. The house was silent. Ruth looked directly at her.

I hate my older brother, Jonathan.

Melissa nodded.

And my little sister Freya is annoying.

Melissa nodded again, looking at the dresser.

Ruth widened her eyes. Do you want to see something secret? You can't tell anyone.

I won't

Ruth retrieved a box from the back of the second drawer of the dresser.

Ruthie looked towards the door. She shut it, and then she climbed the silver stairs to the bunk, box under one arm. Melissa followed her.

They sat opposite each other, heads bent below the sloping ceiling. Ruth lifted the lid.

The lipstick was an other worldly indigo.

She never wears this one. She hasn't noticed it's missing.

Melissa looked up at Ruth.

Can I put it on you?

Ruth leant forwards and closed her eyes.

Melissa took the task seriously. She moved her right hand slowly and with light pressure she aligned the edge of the lipstick with the edge of Ruth's mouth. Her lips were thin. She traced Ruth's mouth shape, and began to turn it a bloody, intergalactic colour. She pushed the melted surface of the nightlit universe across her new friend's mouth. The rich dark made the rest of her face look pale.

In literacy and numeracy they sat together on the little child-height table.

potential
essential
initial
substantial
partial
torrential

In the summer, the week before they finished primary school there was a fight in the playground. I can take you I can take you. Jamal didn't break Travis's nose but it was bloody. Jamal was excluded, missing the last end of term assembly. Miss Williamson said to him, in front of everybody, I am so disappointed you and your mother will be so disappointed in you and everyone, including your new teachers at Beatrice Webb, will be so disappointed in your behaviour when I tell them what you have done.

Shanice, whose mum was moving house, was going to the girls' school in Wandsworth with the red uniform. Aisha and Ahmed were going to the Islamic Centre in Tooting Bec. Travis was going to the boys' school in Wandsworth. Chiara and Ellie would be going to private schools in Dulwich. Jamal and Max and Ruth and Mel would go to Beatrice Webb.

It's the lace, it's the hook
It's the wood in the wind
It's the wanting not wanting
It's the life, it's the sun
It's the night, it's the death

É a lama
É a lama
It's the mud, it's the mud
É a lama
It's the mud

Melissa knocked on Jean's door after school hoping for biscuits or ice lollies and found her mum asleep on the sofa, her walkman and her travelcard on the table. She was still wearing scrubs. Jean cut Melissa a slice of cake. When her mother woke up they walked twenty metres home and fell asleep in the same bed.

Beatrice Webb Secondary School was huge. The biggest school in the borough. It spanned two sides of a small residential road. On one side was a three storey Victorian building – this had once been a separate school with another name – flanked by four glassy purpose-built blocks, full of bunsen burners, stools and whiteboards. At the centre of the Victorian building was the headmaster's office and a library. On the other side of the road was a music building, a languages building and an assembly hall. Porter cabins covered in stucco scattered themselves around the playground, filled with more stools and more science textbooks. At the bottom of the field behind the playground there was a sports hall.

Nothing in the school was child-sized, except some of the children, some of them still tiny in their pretend adult clothes; the tables and the chairs were adult-sized, the older students wore their adult bodies in their adult-sized uniforms. On their first day police stood outside the school in the street.

Melissa stood in the assembly hall with two hundred other eleven-year-olds. Her blazer was stiff around her wrists, her shirt was stiff against her chest, her tie bright blue and black. She and Glória had gone to the school uniform shop in Tooting market where Glória had got her a pleated black skirt and pair of black trousers, both a size too big. Baby you are growing, her mother had said.

Melissa stood small in her big uniform. Her skirt was tucked into her waistband all the way around and she touched the fold. She looked around the assembly room. Ruth was two rows behind her. She exhaled.

A man in his early twenties in a suit read their names from a sheet. Melissa stood. He took them up concrete stairs to a classroom with high Victorian ceilings and bars over the windows. Handwritten poems about World War One crowded the wall displays. The two-person desks were arranged in rows, facing the front of the room. The man in the suit said each name again, each time pointing at a different chair, until every child was in their place.

He cleared his throat.

I am Mr Cross. Call me Mr Cross or Sir.

He cleared his throat. He reached for a pile of small ring bound notebooks on his desk. Take one and pass them on. These are your homework diaries.

Hands in the room shuffled.

And, he took a tray out from his desk, here are your ID cards. You'll use these to pay for lunch. You can put money on them at the card machines in the cafeteria. If you need to pay in a cheque from your parents or for free school meals you can fill out this form.

A small white plastic card landed on Melissa's desk. She held it and looked at her miniature face. She scratched it with her thumbnail.

A voice behind her whispered – I look like shit.

Me too

Mr Cross did not look up.

Mr Cross said her full name. Please step outside the classroom.

Thirty-two bodies inhaled.

Now.

Melissa did what she was told. Her chest was so tight and she felt her throat turn dry.

I will speak to you shortly Melissa.

Mr Cross shut the classroom door and turned to address the other students.

You are 7C. And C is very good because A is the top class and K is the bottom. Overall there are nine classes in year 7. Overall there are 1800 students at Beatrice Webb.

You must always tuck your shirts in.

You must always do up your top button.

There were thirty-three kids in 7C

Max
Ruth
Melissa
Anastasia
Alfie
Lucas
Meena
Zarah
Ellie F
Sam
Tom
William
Jonny
Ella
Sophia
Amy
Frances

Hannah
Vinay
Sophie
Ben G
Caitlin
Roshani
Abiola
Ellie D
Charlotte
Annie
Theodore
Ben T
Rebecca

Leila
Ben K

Harry

There were five one-hour periods per day, apart from Mondays when there were six. On Monday, Tuesday and Thursday mornings they had form time with Mr Cross when he made them read in silence. And on Wednesday and Friday mornings they had assembly with the rest of year 7. Every week they had five English lessons, five maths lessons, five science lessons, tech, ICT, French, Geography, History, Religious Studies, PE and PSHE.

Year 7's two hundred students divided themselves into four groups – the neeks, the Asian crew, the (mostly) Black crew and the (mostly) white kids. The (mostly) Black crew included a couple of white kids and the (mostly) white crew had a couple of mixed-race girls with white mums. Ruthie belonged to the (mostly) white crew and there-fore so could Melissa. Hesitating, the mixed-race girls had invited her to their sub crew. She's just Brazilian, someone had shouted. But Mel and Ruthie were their own twosome, sealed like tupperware. Between lessons they walked with Anastasia and sometimes Abiola. Melissa lis-tened to Ruthie as she spoke, dropping her Ts like Roger had told her not to do. When Melissa and Jamal saw each other in the corridor they nodded, saying each other's names.

In history, Ms Ellis taught them about the Cold War. Ms Ellis said there had been two *poles* in the Cold War – the capitalist USA and the communist USSR, or Soviet Union. Ms Ellis said that the Soviet Union had committed many atrocities and killed many people. And whereas the Soviet Union had been power hungry and taken over its neighbours the USA had provided its neighbours with aid. Ruth was drawing in the back of her exercise book. Abiola put his hand up. Ms Ellis reflected that killing one's own people was somehow so much worse than kill-ing others, as the Nazis had for example. Melissa leant to look at the drawing. Ruth whispered in her ear. Abiola kept his hand up. Ms Ellis frowned. Yes?

That's not what happened.

Ms Ellis looked at him.

Abiola what do you mean? Ms Ellis said.

As soon as Glória came in from work, taking off her shoes and jacket by the door and putting on her slippers, Melissa told her that Vicky had decided that Ruth was old enough to go out without an adult during the daytimes. Glória frowned. She held her jacket in her fingers.

I won't go anywhere alone, I'll always be with Ruthie.

Where will you go?

Just shopping

Her mother frowned.

Melissa looked at her mother

I don't need money though mum, like it's just to hang out

Glória tilted her head.

Melissa kept speaking – Ask Jean, Janine and Jasmine what they think, they'll say it's okay, I'm sure

Glória hung up her jacket. Melissa followed her into the living room, where Glória sat on the sofa, rubbing her eyes. She looked at her daughter.

Okay but querida, you must always stay with Ruthie. Don't go anywhere on your own.

I won't –

Promise me

I promise

On Oxford Street tourists held rectangular shopping bags like people in movies. Melissa wore skinny jeans and Ruthie wore skinny jeans and Vans. The street air was hot and loud and dirty and the buildings were so large. Adult bodies pushed them into walls, and they pushed them back. Ruth's mushroom hair lifted off her neck in the wind.

By their fifth or sixth visit they strode with purpose up and down the Topshop aisles of neon thongs to the bright yellow nail polish and green lipstick aisles. Melissa took two Barry M testers out of their plastic holders and painted black eyeliner wings onto her face. Ruth put on a leather jacket, adjusting her fringe in a little mirror. They walked apart from each other. They communicated without words via eyelidded looks, tuck chin nods, finger to finger squeeze

under sleeve

deep coat pocket

slip in bag

curled in a hand

earring under tongue

side pocket

Oh yes there are um – one, two, three and *four* items here

As she came closer to the glass entrance Melissa whistle hummed looking straight ahead at the north entrance of the station on the street. Two paces behind, Ruth pretended to answer a phone call on her flip phone. Ruth smiled at the guard.

They ran down into the tube entrance –

Oh

my

god

Surfacing, panting, on the other side of the intersection. Melissa put her hands into Ruth's pockets. The whole time on the bus home a Panic At the Disco pizzicato playing in the background of her mind.

That summer Ruth invited Melissa on holiday. Jonathan who was two years older was allowed one friend, and so was Ruth. Freya, who was only six, was not. Altogether they filled the seven-seater; Melissa and Ruth sat in the back, sharing headphones. They drove six hours to the Curtis' cottage right at the edge of the sea in a place called Cornwall.

Can you smell it? Vicky said as they turned into the drive. Her eyes were shut. Can you smell the salt in the air? I used to come here with my brothers during the summer holidays – we used to stay in the house down there, can you see –

Roger jerked on the handbrake.

Vicky where are the keys?

Before Melissa left Glória had been anxious. She had pressed three ten pound notes into her hand.

Is this enough money? Does Vicky need money for food?

No no, Melissa had said.

Tá bom. I washed your green jumper.

But later Melissa heard Glória, awkward but clear, asking the same question into the landline. Vicky on the other end repeating, Oh. *No.* Don't worry about it Glória.

Femi was Jonathan's friend from school. He was tall and slim. Nigerian family. He and Jonathan played rugby together; Femi did debating. Femi had had to learn, better and faster than Melissa, how to speak with a mouth of drawling *ohhs* and jarring *arhhhs*. Femi dressed nice, had known to bring a new clean pair of wellington boots.

At dinner on the first night in the little cottage, Roger interrogated Femi –

Now what do you think of this war, Femi

Femi didn't blink.

I actually support it Roger

You do?

Yes. For the people of Iraq. Femi bit into a piece of bread and looked Roger in the eyes. Saddam is a tyrant, don't you think?

Well! Well as a matter of fact I agree with you. But – Roger, spoke with a full spoon of soup in his hand – But you'll have a hard time convincing *Vicky*

Femi turned to her. He made no attempt to convince Vicky.

I just – Vicky shrugged her shoulders – I just wish there was a way around any war with Iran, Afgha—

Iran! Iran! Roger rolled his eyes and Jonathan laughed.

Oh Vicky! Roger held onto the table. Don't be *stupid*.

Femi smiled at Vicky.

Softening, patting her, Roger said, It's alright.

Two hours later they closed the cottage door and then the cottage garden gate behind them. In single file they walked into the setting sunlight, down a dirt path –

Jonathan

      Femi

           Melissa

                Ruth

with bracken and soil smells on either side. The sea crushed itself into rocks below them.

Femi made eye contact with Mel, widened his eyes and smiled.

Earlier that day Ruth had seen a lighter fall out of Jonathan's pocket and quickly said, I will tell mum if you don't take me and Mel with you. So here they were.

Jonathan took them down a grassy side path down the cliff just above the rocks just above the sea. The sea was loud and angry and Melissa didn't like to look at it. It was too big. The horizon of it was too big. They sat at the place where the grass met the rocks. Melissa turned her face away from the sea to look at Ruth. Ruth stuck her tongue out like a lizard. Melissa stuck her tongue out too. Behind her her hair, spread upward by the wind, was purple. The sky was purple.

Femi peered over Jonathan's shoulder.

Why's it bent like that Jon

Shut up you're fucking bent Femi

Jonathan pulled out the crumpled spliff, still dry in his curled hand, and put it in his mouth.

That winter Ruthie turned thirteen. Vicky asked them to babysit. She left an oven pizza on the counter. She and Roger were going to a charity auction at Jonathan's school. Melissa watched her as Vicky prepared to leave the house. She had little emerald drop earrings in and the powder over her face was unsettled, making her skin look dry and thin like tissue paper. Melissa wondered how old Vicky was. Vicky turned to face them in the hallway –

Don't stay up too late.

We won't!

Mwah! Vicky rubbed her hands on Ruth's upper arms and tapped four awkward fingers on Melissa's right shoulder. Roger was already outside, holding out the key and unlocking the car remotely.

Vicky, we're going to be *la-ate*.

Call us if you need anything, the number's on the fridge –

They slammed the stained glass door behind them.

Ruthie looked at her friend.

They made the pizza, which came out underdone, and fed two slices to Freya, who was wearing pink pyjamas from Boden with llamas on. The three of them sat together at the kitchen island on stools. Melissa crossed her ankles. She looked at the black kitchen reflection in the French windows, finding the image of her own body in the glass. She listened to the sisters talk.

Have you had your bath?

Yes.

And remember to brush your teeth.

Uh huh I will.

Ruth raised her eyebrows and poked her sister's plate – Why don't you finish that second slice, hm Freya?

Freya looked at Ruth and put the crust in her mouth.

Melissa crossed her ankles. Outside was totally dark.

Freya go to bed.

Freya frowned.

Now?

Yes. Me and Mel are going to watch a film, so go to bed.

Can I stay and watch it with you?

Ruth looked at Melissa.

No.

After Freya climbed upstairs, Ruth and Melissa loaded the dishwasher. They went into the TV room. They closed the door, listening for the metal to hit into the groove. Click. Ruthie drew the curtains. Looking at Melissa, her hands against the cream sofa cushions, Ruth pulled a VCR tape from the cupboard.

This one – this one – has proper sex in it

Mel nodded

In a car

A *car*?

She gets naked

Naked?

Totally naked

So you can see her –

Everything

Everything?

Except her – but boobs you see her boobs

Melissa nodded.

Ruth pushed the tape into the slot. She pressed fast forward and they heard the plastic flutter. The movie squiggled on the screen.

They're getting on a boat, Ruth said, She's rich but she's actually not rich. Her mum made her get engaged to an actually rich guy.

Melissa nodded.

Ruth pointed to a new character on the screen.

He just won a ticket on the boat too but for third class. He's an artist.

Melissa nodded. The film squiggled forward to the sea.

She hates her life so she is trying to kill herself by jumping off the boat but he – yeah there he is – but he talks her out of it – he says to her that the cold water will kill her even if she can swim.

Cold water?

Yeah. The boat has to go through the Arctic.

Melissa nodded. Ruthie stopped talking. Melissa waited. Kate

Winslet drank a beer and rose onto her toes. At triple speed Kate Winslet collapsed, her hair moving up, out.

Without a word Ruth pressed play. Melissa's hands pushed against the wooden floor.

The film played at normal speed but it felt like slow motion. As if in slow motion, Kate Winslet removed a thin black and yellow kimono. In a room with wood panels. She was holding a necklace. She lay down on a sofa. Naked, Kate Winslet held eye contact. The camera panned down her body (white, perfect, round)

I believe you are blushing –

Melissa breathed

In an old car, one that looked like a horse and carriage, in the belly of the boat, Kate Winslet put her hands under Jack's arms and pulled him into a booth with leather seats. She held her body over him.

Ruthie squeezed her hand

Kate Winslet's hair touched his face, stuck to him.

You're trembling – Kate Winslet said.

That night they climbed into the lilac bed in the lilac room but left the light on. Melissa sat with her legs crossed and so did Ruth.

Dean and Shanice did kissing in primary school

With tongues –

With tongues

Melissa considered.

Ruth tilted her head.

I don't want to get it wrong –

No me neither

When I do it for real –

Me neither

It was Ruthie's suggestion. Ruth closed the door. Melissa took her glasses off. Ruth cleared her throat. Outside the skylight was shining black.

We should close our eyes –

Ruthie nodded.

Ready?

After thirty seconds they pulled away. Breathless. It was warm like egg yolks.

It's so – slimy

Melissa looked serious.

Let's try again.

oysters

Once upon a time Furzedown, Tooting, had been a Quaker village, built in the shape of a kite, five or six miles from London. That's why there are no pubs there, or so Janine said.

Now red buses rode down the big roads of SW17 on each side of the kite, east to Streatham, south to Mitcham, west to Wandsworth, north to Balham and Clapham down down to the big river centre of the city. Red double decker buses rode down Roman roads built two millenniums before. There's a new mayor, a man from the Labour Party – A bit Red for my taste, Roger said. The mayor's office gave every child in London free bus travel as long as they didn't drop out of school. At first they stormed onto the buses without making eye contact and if they got called back they said, Driver I swear I'm only thirteen! By 2005 they had filled out the paperwork and got the little blue cards with their photo on, called oysters.

After that – they could go anywhere. I don't do postcodes I do bus routes, Anastasia said. No one had ever moved more freely across the part of the surface of the earth that was that city, which became their city, opened for and to them.

The winter after the summer Melissa turned fourteen, they summoned one hundred teenagers to the south bank with the click click click of a public Facebook event created at Janine's computer.

Melissa looked at Ruth before pressing publish.

Do it! Ruth said.

Anastasia nodded.

They took turns logging into their accounts and inviting people. Girls from 10A and 10B and boys and Anastasia's friends from the other school in Streatham and the year above from the school in Putney.

At 8pm Mel and Anastasia and Ruth got on the bus with the other girls from school. They sat on the top deck at the back. Adult passengers looked away from them.

Sitting on the top deck of the 155 bus, they drank from a Glen's vodka bottle. The bus drove down the length of the Northern line, past Stockwell and Oval and Elephant up through the city, which in that moment was their city. Anastasia knew where to go. She led them past the station. She led them to the river, which moved fast and close to their feet. She led them past the landmarks and theatres and the scary emo kids in the state park to a small patch of grass lined by bushes and new build flats. On the building above them they read in bright red neon letters

O
X
O

The night fell and fell around them. Boys in skinny jeans arrived. Girls in T-shirts worn like dresses arrived. Side fringes and Mayfair Supercuts. No one was cold. Ruthie and Anastasia stood in the dark, at the edge of a circle. Anastasia had seen the boy she liked. Ruthie put a cigarette in her mouth and Melissa lit it. They looked around themselves at all the people and all their drinks and sounds and hands – they had done this, they had brought them here.

A man in a dressing gown on a balcony shouted –

That's it. I've called the fucking police

Twenty minutes later blue lights flashed through the bushes from the street. The sound of a radio. A door slamming. Ruth, who had a little drugs – just a quarter of a gram of mdma – in her bag took Melissa's hand. She led her, running, away from the others through the little bushes to the riverbank. Adults strolled past them.

Act normal.

Okay

We are adult women now, okay?

Melissa looked over at her, smiling at her.

We've just been to see a play at The Globe where we had a couple of glasses of wine and

Ruth giggled.

Ruth readjusted her posture in the shape of an adult woman. She wanted to touch Melissa's purple shining hair, all the yellow white from the hanging lights moving off it. They blended in like tourists strolling by the river, the tide full and moving close to their feet as they leant over the iron balustrades at its banks.

The school bell rings and they look at each other. In the ten seconds before the wail spreads through the corridors and classrooms Melissa turns her head towards Ruthie. Strands of brown mouse hair reach up with the intake of her breath. Behind her the window shows the empty sunlit road. Melissa starts putting her pens and her maths book into her bag and Ms Chatterji opens her mouth to ask her *what* she thinks she is doing. But the bell rings, and Ruthie turns to face her.

The road is full of uniformed ununiform bodies, thronging. Tall and small and pock-marked and voluptuous with crew cuts and side fringes – and wedged between them teachers with lanyards and on that afternoon a policeman and a policewoman. It is not hot yet, but bright with season change sun. No wind. Teenagers leak from the buildings as if one molten substance spreading across the road, blazers in their hands or falling off their shoulders, top buttons undone, the corners of their shirts tied above their belly buttons like Britney Spears.

Mel and Ruthie stand in the middle of the road with Anastasia and a girl from 10B called Tabitha. Mel and Ruthie wear trousers but they've put lipgloss on and hold their phones in their hands. Ruthie's is an iphone with the screen cracked. Anastasia's chewing gum, roll up in her hand. Tabitha has a nose piercing. Anastasia asks –

Are you going to Lucas's later?

They nod

Cos we're gonna go to another party first

What party

Where

Near Herne Hill. It's Tabitha's boyfriend's friends. Dulwich boys. It's gonna be rammed

A male teacher waves at Anastasia's midriff. He shouts – Have a little dignity!

Ruthie wrinkles her nose

She's got loads of dignity, thanks

What about Lucas's

Lucas is always having parties isn't he

Melissa moves her head to the side.

Come with us

Melissa and Ruthie look at each other

You can go to Lucas's after. It's just one bus

Melissa and Ruthie look at each other

Ok yeah.

Yeah

Cool.

Text me –

They get strawberry laces and snakes at Budgens. They eat them in the park by the school.

Ruthie looks at the sky –

They sit at the round metal tables with the metal stool attached whose surfaces are scratched with names and initials and tags. Small children climb a climbing frame ahead. Melissa presses a rizla flat on the table surface and spreads a pinch of tobacco along it. Ruthie watches her. Mel licks the cigarette to seal it and holds it out.

Here

Ruthie puts it in her mouth. She takes a lighter out of her pocket.

Are you not having one

Melissa leans back, stretching a strawberry lace between her teeth and thumb and index finger.

I'll have some of that

She closes her eyes

A woman by the slide is waving at them.

Ruthie holds up her left hand and waves back at the woman, stretching her right hand out behind her back, her fingers meeting Melissa's and transferring the roll up.

How are you? she shouts back. Whispering – It's Freya's friends' mum

Let's go to the track.

Yes

They walk down the road, blazered bodies on bikes whizzing past them and whistling

Fuck off –

Fuck off –

They walk to the path at the edge of the woodland where Tooting Common proper starts. They walk off the path into the trees by the athletics track. The mud floor slides against the bottoms of their school shoes. There is no one else there. They sit on a tree trunk, feet in the sludge earth. Melissa relights the rollie. They pass it between them. Melissa throws the butt into the bushes.

Don't do that –

Sorry.

Let's have a proper smoke now?

Yeah

Melissa pulls a grinder out of her pocket and a long rizla. Ruthie watches her as she moves the paper between her fingers and thumb and licks it.

Do you remember playing spin the bottle here?

Yeah

So stupid

Gross

Can't believe I kissed Tariq.

And Lucas

They look at each other.

Ruthie leans back into the tree trunk. Melissa puts her forehead against Ruth's knees.

At Janine's house they eat biscuits. When she opens the door they lean down and bring her into a three-way hug and she says –

I know you want to use the computer but before you go upstairs come to the kitchen, you must be hungry

Oh yes please –

Aw yes Janine –

Sit down sit down girls

She reaches to get them plates

And tea?

Yes please

Yes please

She puts custard creams and bourbons on the table.

You're growing girls

Not anymore

Not really Janine

Don't be silly you'll grow till you're eighteen

Um

Melissa my dear you may well laugh but

Mel dips the biscuit in her tea, the bottom half floating to the bottom of the mug.

In Janine's spare room they go straight on Facebook. Melissa sits in the chair and Ruthie sits on the single bed whose brown flowers bedspread matches the curtains.

Here's the party that Anastasia was talking about

Click on attending

No

No

Fucking ugly

No

He's alright

Nah

This one's fit

Looks a bit like a – what are they called they're in the lion king

Lions

No

Timon and

Hippopotamus

No

Meerkat!

A meerkat.

What about this one?

Perci-val?

Ruthie is laughing, back against the flower bedspread.

Melissa snorts. She closes her eyes, then opens them. She looks at the clock on the computer.

I promised my mum I'd be there when she got back.

Ruth nods, rolling over, standing up.

Melissa's key turns in the lock. Clunk. They stand in the silence of the corridor with the lights off. Ruthie takes her shoes off and Melissa takes her shoes off. Melissa does the washing up in the sink and Ruthie dries and puts the plates away. Melissa puts a load of laundry into the washing machine. Ruthie pees with the door open. Melissa chops and fries onions and garlic and chillies. Ruthie boils pasta. Melissa adds meatballs and tinned tomatoes. Ruthie gets two bowls and two forks out. Melissa holds out a spoon of sauce and blows on it so it isn't too hot and puts it in Ruthie's mouth and asks Ruthie if it needs salt and Ruthie pauses and says yes just a bit. They sit on the sofa and watch *The Simpsons* and eat the pasta from the bowls. Outside is dark blue streaked with white. Melissa closes her eyes. Melissa leans her head against Ruthie's shoulder. Ruthie pulls the blanket over them.

A key turns in the door.

Hello?

Hey

Querida?

It's us

Ruthie

Hello

Glória is wearing an outdoor jacket with a taut rainproof hood. She unzips it.

Girls it smells good in here. Did you cook?

Ruthie points at Melissa

Glória smiles. Glória whispers – She is asleep?

Ruthie nods.

Glória takes off her shoes. She's wearing scrubs. She moves her shoulders backwards in a circle, standing straight. Glória looks at her daughter. Outside is dark, inside is warm. She can't believe the size of her. She wants to laugh out loud because it is not believable to her. Long like an adult, sleeping like a child.

They meet Anastasia at the off licence on Mitcham Road around 10pm. Anastasia goes in alone, three fivers held tight in her right hand. She's wearing black Primark heels and mascara and a long black coat.

After five minutes she comes out holding a carrier bag, blue plastic stretching under the bottle weight.

Anastasia you always get served

Yup

They sit on the granite part of the pavement, their feet on the street. Anastasia crouches between two cars and pours half the coke onto the tarmac, and then the vodka into the coke bottle. Cold vodka spills onto her fingers. Fuck. Melissa rolls a cigarette and lights it. She leans back. Anastasia pours slowly, gaze on the bottle heads. Without looking up she says

Can I bum one Mel

Yep

Ruthie puts her hand on Melissa's arm. She shivers.

It is so dark.

They get to the double-fronted house a bus ride east of Herne Hill before midnight. It has that sound like a party. It's bigger than Ruthie's house and the furniture is darker wood. Tabitha opens the door greeting them with kisses and when Anastasia goes to find her boyfriend Ruthie says

Let's explore

Taking Melissa by the hand

They go up and up the stairs, wet shoe soles on the light blue carpet, spilling coke with vodka on the light blue carpet past three landings up to the highest, gabled bedroom. It is so quiet there. Ruthie opens the window and lets the night in. Ruthie turns –

Mel? Where'd you go

There's an en suite

The en suite is off-white tiling with dull rose pink towels. Mel opens the cupboard above the sink. She pushes her hand across the cupboard shelves and pill bottles and creams and toothbrushes clatter into the flat square sink

This sink doesn't have a fucking plug

The water goes down the sides
What
My mum's friend has one like that
Melissa opens a small pot of hand cream and puts it on her hands and wrists. She sniffs.
Whose room do you think this is?
Ruthie shakes her head.
Doesn't look like anyone sleeps here
Do you wanna go downstairs?
Hold on
Ruthie drinks from the bottle until there is just an inch left
Finish it?
Mel nods.
They sit on the bed. The window is open. The night comes in.

They go into every bedroom (six). They open every kitchen cupboard for booze. White wine in small slender bottles (Riesling) and deep brown satin whisky with ice from the fridge. They eat crackers and put them in their pockets and let people push past and around them. Melissa says can you see straight, cos I feel sick and Ruthie says have a beer it's basically water Ruthie says let's go talk to some people and Melissa says Nah and Ruthie says, let's go let's go let's

They announce themselves with aplomb barging into bodies in a group of boys wearing Jack Wills and popped collars, Ruthie has just reapplied her lipgloss, they start to talk Anastasia is there too boyfriend behind her body like a tree
Uh huh
Uh huh
Nah

I'm Anastasia's
Uh huh
But
I'm here with Anastasia, and Tabitha
Really
Yes

(smash)

Who broke a glass
Where did you get
Who invited you here
Are you talking to me
Mel –
What
Don't
Tabitha pulls Melissa away from the Henry or Mark or Charles saying What are you doing Mel
He started on me
What are you talking about
Are you saying I'm lying
Come here
What
Come in here Mel Let's talk to these people Mel

After thirty or twenty or forty or seventy minutes Ruth reappears from the back of the garden doing up her jeans with a Ralph or a Hugo or a Joshua, his dirty fingers thick wet
Melissa pulls her into the house.
She opens a door on the second floor. Fuller, with bath salts and children's toothpaste
Ruth locks the door. She holds out her hand.
Look what I got.
Ruth shimmies down her pants.

Melissa bends and inhales, finger against one nostril. The blue flesh thrill. She turns her head from Ruthie and opens the cupboard above the sink. She drops packs of pills into a dry square sink. She slowly pushes her hand across the top shelf stuff falling everywhere and then she stops

She holds out two little plastic lipstick tubes and puts them in her pocket

YSL, Mac

The N3 to Lucas's house moves slowly through the white and blue streets.

Lucas runs down the middle of the street; they hear him yelling. Lucas's eyes are shut. There is a sapling in his arms, roots splayed just above the ground, soil chunks in a train behind him. Max criss-crosses him, also running, in the middle of the street, a train of black soil behind him, a magnolia sapling pressed against his chest, flowering. Still moving they throw the trees up over their heads, SMACK into the tarmac. A rain of soil. Panting, Max runs into the nearest garden, reaching his hands around the base of a small and potted bay.

The front door is open. The top of the road has that sound like a party. It's like the show *Skins*. No lights. They know the song playing. Sophie from their class leans back into the front garden hedge, skirt riding up her thighs. The front door is open. In the corridor, people tussle around them, kissing and grinding and shouting in the kitchen, the light is fully on and bright, Lucas is being sick in the kitchen sink and filling it with red bile and pasta chunks. Everything in every cupboard has been eaten. In the garden it's raining. They know the song playing – Mel takes Ruthie's hand and pulls her to the living room where Amelia is dancing on the sofa bending down low and strange couples are kissing full bodies reaching up onto each other's bodies and Ruthie pushes herself into Mel, not facing, and Mel touches her fingers on Ruth's lowest ribs in the dark, and Mel feels the yes yes grind of her waist and the yes of her waist and they move like that Ruthie's hands not on the floor but close and Tariq is whistling and other people are whistling and clearing a space around them and Ruthie's hair touches the floor as she presses into Melissa more fully and more fully and then no one is watching

when Ruth rises Melissa puts both her hands on Ruth's bare forearms and Ruth turns inside her embrace – here – no one is watching them a kiss like in a movie

This is a story of

The night sky is   purple

(Tell us)

Six feet move in the living room between the table and the sofa on Amen Corner – watching *West Side Story* and singing that they liked to be in America

Clapclapclapclapclapclapclapclap

They watch a film, they fall asleep, they wake on the sofa. Soft light. Warm and pell mell limbs. They brush their teeth, one toothbrush. Lights off. Pyjamas. Fingers in fingers. A bedroom the colour of the summer night. Exhale. Touching limbs. Limbs pell mell. Warm faces. Eyes shut. Warm breath. Dusk on the rooftops.

There are two types of kissing –

One kind makes your insides dead and cold with nerves. You do it with boys that you don't know at parties. This kind of kissing can lead to boob cupping and fingering and hand jobs and blow jobs and sex.

The other kind of kissing – Ruthie moves her hand, leans forwards – it's the kind of kissing you do in spin the bottle, or the kind of kissing that two girls do to turn boys on – it doesn't count. This kind of kissing doesn't lead to anything.

It was the year after Britney shaved her head. The year that Amy Winehouse started turning up late to shows and then not turning up to shows at all. Roger said there had been a crash, and Femi said there had been a crash and Gordon Brown said there had been a crash. It was the year that whole parts of the UK flooded in August. Rooftops at the waterline and dogs standing on floating cars. That summer the grass on the common drowned.

There was a rumour that Lucas who was well built with a tight eight pack torso and short cropped blond hair had given head to a boy from another school. When confronted Lucas switched, Who's fucking saying this Who's fucking I will Fuck them up I will Fuck them up, kissing his teeth, loosening his school tie his chest taut

Two days before her sixteenth birthday Melissa walked down Amen Corner with the rain in her eyes. She turned the corner to the road with Beatrice Webb on it. Her hands were in her pockets. She moved the soft part of her fingers around her ID card, which she had never lost or got replaced. The week before she'd seen Shanice for the first time in two years and let Shanice cut her ponytail off. Her head felt light, taller. She could see people gathered in the road. Teachers in their weekend clothes. Her feet were sweating in her trainers.

She would open her results and go home. And call Ruth who was at the internet café at a resort in Corsica. And open Ruth's results and read them to her. She judged the distance between herself and the school gates. She looked behind her and lit a cigarette. She felt the smoke in her warm wet throat. Jean had called the weather muggy.

Melissa's results were good. Ruthie's were bad.

In September, at the start of the next school year, one week after Melissa's sixteenth birthday, Mr Cross called her aside and handed her a form.

Bring a photocopy of the documents on this list and get your mother to sign the form, he said.

After that Melissa got £90/month from the government to go to her lessons and go to them on time.

Melissa left the money, occasionally all of it, often half, in cash on the kitchen table. That winter they kept the heating on. Glória hated winter. Janine, Jean and Jasmine's tupperwares filled the cupboards. Biriyani and rice and peas and a cottage pie. Jasmine's son had just had a baby, she was thinking of moving away. Melissa was home more in the evenings. They watched *West Side Story* and every time Glória cried.

Two shifts a week Melissa worked in Sainsbury's in Tooting Broadway. She saw Ms Eastham the English teacher in there at the weekends with her boyfriend. Ms Eastham and her boyfriend always said, hi, how are you doing Melissa are you doing okay, apart from when they didn't see her because they were using the self-checkout machines.

Glória noticed her daughter had stopped going round to Ruth's. Glória noticed that Melissa cooked less, studied all the time. Glória watched her. Glória thought about her all the time. She held so many hopes and anxieties for her. Melissa went to the library with a girl called Ivy who Glória gathered was from a Vietnamese family who lived in Streatham. Melissa had messaged that friend of Ruthie's brother, the one who was so gifted academically, when she'd got the surprisingly good results. One time when Glória picked up the house phone, a girl called Olivia introduced herself. Hello, I'm Olivia. May I speak to Melissa, please? she had said. Olivia and Ivy are in my maths class. They joined Beatrice Webb for sixth form, Melissa had said.

When Glória saw Vicky in the street Vicky talked to her just like before. Vicky rolled her eyes – Ruth is always out, always chasing boys, never studies! Refused to come skiing with us at half term! I don't know what do to with her. You must have the same problem.

Glória moved her head in a vague way. Vicky looked older, she thought.

Glória waited to hear the answer that she thought would come from Melissa. I know how it feels to be heartbroken, she wanted to say. There are so many things I want to tell you too. But Melissa, her English child, never spoke to her mother about Ruth. And it maybe it wasn't so bad, Glória thought. Melissa's other friends were nice. And Glória liked to see her daughter quiet with her textbooks open at the kitchen table in the evening. Femi, who was such an ambitious young man, had decided to take Melissa under his wing, giving her all kinds of advice, saying that she was exactly the kind of person who should be going to a top uni and had she considered the STEM subjects? Glória felt relief to see Melissa fill out her forms for university.

Every night Glória wondered where the time had gone. There were so many things she wanted to tell her daughter.

In her final year of school Melissa's friends told her that she had to come with them on the march. They said –

Melissa aren't you angry?

In assembly, the head of year 13 said – You must not bunk. This does not change anything. For those receiving EMA, you will be marked missing.

In Maths, Ms Allen-Holder told the whole class that they should go.

Olivia went. Lucas went. Anastasia said she might go and even stood by the gate but then she didn't. Ivy did not go. Melissa did not go. Ruthie did not go, Melissa was almost sure.

After school, at Janine's house, Melissa went on Facebook to see what Femi was saying. She saw that he had posted two days ago explaining that

1. There was no evidence that fees are a deterrent to students from Deprived and Disadvantaged Backgrounds
2. Really, why should people who don't go to university subsidise those who do?
3. Perhaps we should all consider how the proportion of the population going to university has grown in the last thirty years and whether that is, in fact, sustainable or, indeed, desirable.

He tagged his location as his own prestigious university.

At home that evening Melissa sat watching the news on the sofa with her mother. Placards and shouting filled the screen. Two boys with bandanas over their faces kicked a glass door in.

Melissa blinked. Melissa looked at her mother.

Glória was nodding.

Are your friends there?

Melissa moved her head to the side.

You did not go?

Melissa shook her head.

Obviously not mum I'm here.

Glória sighed.

You are very sensible Melissa.

Yes mum.

When I was your age, I was always on the streets.

Melissa looked at her mother.

OYSTERS

Melissa didn't understand the oyster metaphor in its total sense. She knew what it meant, teachers were always saying it, their expressions a little condescending, a little excited for her. You can do what you want, where you want – go! The phrase invoked the full expanse of the round and rolling, horizon-edged world; *there are more things in heaven and earth,* the Shakespeare display board in Ms Eastham's classroom said. Ms Eastham gave her books set in North West London and she read them at lunchtime in the library. Mr Cross asked her to stay back at breaktime and asked her where she was applying for uni. Femi helped her write a personal statement made of words like Ethic and Ambition and Extracurricular. They went through five drafts together on Facebook messenger. And it had worked. But oysters? She had seen oysters in cartoons; they were wet and soft like inside-skin, exotic and expensive, revolting-looking, their shells open and opening, like roundels of makeup casing.

In August 2011, Melissa turned eighteen. On the other side of the city, on the other side of the river, in Tottenham a man called Mark Duggan was shot by the police. There were riots all over London and riots all over the country.

Clapham Junction on fire.
Streatham on fire.
Kids arrested over bottles of water
Kids arrested over TVs really big TVs

Melissa recognised the boys on the streets and the middle-class girls' mothers, offering each other lifts in their space wagons. She saw Jamal at the bus stop and he had nodded at her

At night in her adult body in her mother's bed, she smelled her mother's smell

They had had seventeen nearly eighteen good years together that was true
Seven lucky unlucky years at Beatrice Webb

(What was this the story of? What was this the story of What)

(Tell us)

Baby Melissa never cried. Sleep, her mother said, and she would.

SOHO

(2013–2014)

Glória died in February
  Right in the middle of the English winter that she hated.

On the morning she died she had been at home.
  Glória was about to eat a toastie on the sofa. No one else was home.
She was wearing slippers. Her mobile phone was in the other room. She
put her feet up. Her heart stopped beating in her body.

Melissa came home late. She was coming from work, still in her uniform.
The bus was empty and she sat with the soles of her trainers against the seat
in front. Headphones in. Walking up the hill and turning into the cul de
sac she hummed to herself. It was dark and it was quiet on Amen Corner.
There were no stars and no moon and all the lights in the street were off
apart from the one at the front of her house. The living room light was on
behind the curtain. Yellow and white. She had a woollen scarf around her
neck and her mouth. She breathed into it and the inside of it became damp.
She took her key out of her pocket and felt the metal cold against her cold
fingers. She turned the key in the lock and leant into the door. Click.

Melissa called 999.

  Can you tell us your postcode and address
  Can you tell us the number you are calling from
  Can you tell us the patient's name Is she your mother
  Can you touch your mother's neck or wrist (do you know the place)
and call her name

  Mum
  Mum
  Mãe

The paramedic had said –

Who do you need to call?
Do you have a phone?
Who will you call?
Do you have credit on your phone?

She called Femi, who came to the hospital, immediately. Femi had said on the phone, Jesus Christ. Wait for me. Wait.

A year and a half earlier, Melissa had accepted a place at a university in East London. It was a good university. Door to door the commute was an hour and a quarter – bus, tube, tube. She was one of five women out of a cohort of two hundred on the Computer Science course. She spent the daytimes at lectures and seminars and doing shifts at the supermarket. She was nineteen. She took an optional module in Philosophy. Jay the manager tried to make sure her shifts and her seminars didn't clash, and in exchange she pretended to be stupider than she was in conversations with him. When she had an afternoon to herself she sat outside on the campus lawn. She rode, for the first time, a train line called the Overground. On the map, it was the colour orange. She did not know if it had always been there. Freshers' week events had been in clubs in Dalston and Hoxton and Shoreditch; she'd never been to Dalston and Hoxton and Shoreditch before. At the start of her first year she had watched the other eighteen-year-olds retch up cider with blackcurrant cordial. None of them smoked properly. They had seemed too young to be real. Most of them were virgins. Someone invited her to crash in halls and she said no. She went home. Sobered up on the night bus. The road signs looked different in East London. The Victorian houses were flatter. The roads were thick with tower blocks. Every schoolchild in Britain knew that the East End had been bombed to shit during the Blitz, and here she was, finally, winding through the midnight evidence of it.

When she had an afternoon to herself she lay on the campus lawn. Back against the grass. Book open on her belly. Eyes shut.

The ambulance didn't put the siren on.

Femi arrived at St George's Hospital twenty-five minutes after her, his bike helmet still on his head. He had been at his parents' house. She was sitting on a chair in a corridor. White and beige and well lit like a good NHS corridor. Easy to clean. He approached her with wide eyes.

There was a room. Glória's body was lying in it. Melissa felt horror in her mouth. Femi asked the doctor questions. Melissa looked at Glória.

Could she leave the body?

What would happen?

What would happen?

Could she leave the body?

The doctor said her name and Melissa turned her head.

She woke up in Femi's parents' house. The light came in the window like a scream.

Mel
Yeah
Yes

Mãe

Ivy arrived. Olivia arrived. They had been ringing her phone. Brr brr brr. Femi spoke to them. You need to go home, Femi said to her. She felt embarrassed in front of Femi's parents who she didn't know. His mother was a doctor. His mother made her breakfast which she couldn't eat. He didn't have any siblings. His house smelled like him. His mother looked like him. Their house was in Norwood, next to the cemetery. Femi and Melissa took a taxi to Amen Corner. The taxi driver asked them the reason for their journey, any special occasion? Ivy and Olivia were standing in front of the house in puffer coats. It wasn't cold on Amen Corner but the sky was angry. Melissa didn't know where her key was. Melissa started crying. She'd never lost her key before. Can you ask a neighbour? someone said and at that moment Jean appeared, eyebrows pencilled in, walking stick at her hip and Melissa had to tell her what had happened, and Glória died all over again.

Inside the house they were silent. White net curtains. TV remote between the sofa cushions. Someone opened a window. Dishes in the sink. The heating on. Olivia had never been inside. Bathroom light on. Ivy had never been inside. Femi had a list of documents to find and a plastic pouch. Bank statements. Birth certificate. Where are your mother's papers? he said. Is there somewhere she keeps – where she keeps them?

Ivy ran her a bath. Melissa got into the water without locking the door. They offered to stay with her. To watch a film on the sofa. To make dinner. To make breakfast. The sun set. Nighttime came like a scream under a hand. No sound.

When Melissa had started university in the East End of the city Glória saw her less. Glória herself was working. Day shifts and night shifts at St George's Hospital, where she was an ICU nurse. Sometimes people died on her shifts and sometimes they were friendly to her and sometimes they said they would prefer to be treated by a proper nurse, a British one, it wasn't their fault they couldn't understand what she was saying. At the end of her shift she would put on her coat and walk through the hospital car park and get the bus home where Melissa would be sat at the dinner table, typing or reading a textbook. Her daughter wore her hair cut around her ears, like a boy, like the young women Glória had used to know. One day Glória would retire. When the autumn light fell over Melissa's hair, it looked purple.

In Brazil it was normal for children to live with their parents and study in their city and stay living there until they married, if they ever married. It had not been what she had done. Her daughter cooked and she did the shopping. Glória cleaned. Melissa called the council for her and helped her with the bank. Glória wondered if this might be their life, here. Melissa could have whatever freedom she wanted, Glória wanted to tell her that. There was so much she had not managed to tell her.

Glória knew that in England it was common for children to attend university away from home. And she had never asked her daughter to stay. It was a good university. Her daughter was learning things all kinds of things. She would have access to the sort of salary that would allow her to have whatever life she wanted. Although when Glória looked back she thought that there was nothing so bad about what they'd had.

Her mother's mobile phone was locked. So was the filing cabinet with the documents that Femi needed. Melissa couldn't find the key. They stared at it. Do you have a screwdriver? Yes. Melissa fetched it from the cupboard. She faced the filing cabinet and pushed the screwdriver between the top edge of the drawer and the cabinet edge, opening it a centimetre. The metal of the screwdriver bent the metal of the cabinet.

The documents were neatly arranged. Some she had seen before – the ones from Lloyds Bank and Wandsworth Council. Other she had not – birth certificates in Portuguese. Old documents in Portuguese. Expired passports.

Femi stared at one and then another, putting some into the plastic pouch. He read through a letter with the Lloyds logo. He looked briefly up. He held the plastic pouch of papers in his hand.

O2 might be able to unlock the phone.
He looked down at it. He held it flat on his hand like a living thing.

Femi
Yeah
I don't know how to contact my family in Brazil

They had the funeral in the church up the hill by Melissa's primary school. The sunlight was bright that morning and it had been raining so the tarmac on the hill was bright too. Ivy told Melissa that she could wear sunglasses if she wanted to, but she didn't have to. Ivy said wear black if you want to but you don't have to. Olivia gave her a lit cigarette on the road outside her house for the walk to the church. Femi had got there early. Anastasia touched her shoulder with her shoulder. People gathered outside and then they sat inside. Everyone looked exactly the same but also everyone looked so old. Jamal's mum was there and Ahmed's mum and Shanice's mum and Travis's mum and Mr Cross and Jean and Janine and Jasmine, their grey hair rising from their heads.

In the church Jasmine stood. White sari around her body. She spoke –

I have had many sisters on Amen Corner

I have had many sisters

No no I know what I will read, Melissa said to Femi. I know what.

She stood at the pulpit, the altar behind her. She had never seen her mother pray or go to church. She had seen her mother cross herself. The room smelt old and like the earth and like a cave. She did not know the priest. She was wearing a skirt and the waistband dug into her stomach.

It was an old church made of stone and inside it the carpets were red and all the pews had purple cushions on them. Melissa had never been in this church before. It had been there for a hundred years.

(breath)

These are the words of a song called 'Pedaço de mim' by Chico Buarque. This translation might not be right

(breath)

Oh, piece of me
Oh, distant half of me

Look away from me
because yearning is the worst torment
it is worse than forgetting
it is worse than paralysis

Oh, piece of me
Oh, exiled half of me

Take your signs with you
Because yearning hurts like a ship
tracing an arc, bit by bit,

and avoiding mooring at the pier

Oh, piece of me
Oh, ripped out half of me

Take your shadow with you
because yearning is the reverse of giving birth
yearning is tidying the room
of a child who is already dead

Oh, piece of me
Oh, amputated half of me

Take the rest of you with you
because the pain of yearning throbs
like a stab
to a limb I've already lost

Oh, piece of me
Oh, adored half of me

Wash my eyes
because yearning is the worst punishment
and I don't want to take with me
the shroud of love

Adeus

59.

On the beach, by the sea, sitting in the sand

She said this

Here, with you, it is as if there were no dictatorship

As if the dictatorship did not and had never existed, nor torturers, nor conquistadors, nor explorers, nor mines, nor mining companies, nor imperialists, nor the United States of America, nor the Portuguese, nor the Portuguese language, nor Portugal, nor Brazil, nor whites, nor slavery, nor master's house, nor slaves' quarters, nor smallpox, nor kings, nor princesses nor emperors

O que será que nossas filhas dirão de nós?

Quer saber o que é que aconteceu? Quer mesmo?

Não vou contar a minha história. A história da minha vida antes de chegar aqui não existe. Sempre morei aqui. Sempre existi.

60.

Once upon a time –

  (it is 1968)

A young woman, brown skin brown eyes and hair in cachos stands inside a church in a place called Olinda, in a church that was built whenever it was built by the Portuguese but this one not bedecked with gold. She's holding pamphlets that she printed the night before on the mimeograph in the small town where she lives. She's travelled all night and all day to be there. She waits for the speeches to begin. X, who will become the governor of Minas Gerais, is there. Y, who will become the Minister for Agriculture, is there. Not that they know this, not that anyone could have known it, at the time. The woman who will become president thinks about stealing a car on the other side of the country, not that they could have known it at the time.

In the summer of 2014 Melissa moved into a flat with a balcony with three women she didn't know. There had been no time to do a viewing. Wandsworth Council was taking the house on Amen Corner back. When it turned out Ivy's new graduate job as a management consultant meant she could be Melissa's guarantor on the estate agent forms Melissa had cried.

Femi had got her the job which had meant she could move into the flat with a balcony. He had been working with Marc for nine months with the job title Communications and Research Assistant when Marc asked him if he knew any developers. Someone young and reliable and smart – and *cheap*. Femi said yes without hesitation. The next day he made Melissa shower and brought her into the white office. It was six months after her mother had died.

On the escalators to the street outside of Tottenham Court Road station, Femi said to her, Don't say this is your first job.

And she said, It's not.

And, Mel, you've got to educate yourself, know what's going on a bit. Watch PMQs every week. Read *The Economist*. Listen to the *Today* programme on Radio 4.

Marc sat Melissa in the glass room at the back of the white office. He asked when she could start. He said he could pay her £130 a day and waited for her to negotiate. Melissa nodded and looked at Marc. He slapped his thigh. Well that's that! Melissa pressed her lips together.

Melissa went into work every day in the white office off the Soho end of Tottenham Court Road. Beneath them diggers were carving out the earth, expanding the tube station for Crossrail. The office was an old shop front, to its left there was a dark, fancy-looking Korean restaurant and on the right there was a tiny and ancient pub. Melissa sat at a plastic table near the back of the space, next to Femi. She had a second screen, which Marc had paid for. There was a medium-sized palm tree by the door which it was Melissa's responsibility to water.

In the white office, on her new second screen and a laptop that she had bought two years earlier with a grant from the university, Melissa did back end stuff. Marc was a great believer in the importance of back end stuff, although he did not understand it. On her second day at 10am Femi gave her a task that took her three hours. Marc billed the clients for a day of her time, and what Marc billed for a day of her time was three times what she was paid for a day of her time. She didn't have a contract.

Stay busy until 6pm, Femi said.

On the 3rd of the following month £2600 was deposited in her bank account. It was the most money that she had ever had access to.

Femi had told Marc that Melissa was still finishing her degree and would sometimes need to take an hour or two, here or there, to work from home or do a piece of paperwork or coursework. But she'll get the work done, Femi had said. Marc, who did not work regular hours himself – he liked to go to the gym, grind his own coffee beans and then read the paper in the morning – had said I want to see you both at your desks when I arrive in the morning. I need you in at 8.30, Femi, in case any clients get in touch.

At the end of her first month at the white office Marc turned and put his arm around her shoulder. Melissa! Oh Melissa (sigh). Working with you is so *easy* it's so *easy, ah a dream*. Last project I worked on the developers were out in *Sri Lanka* and it was just a nightmare let me tell you –

She closed her eyes

Melissa knew Femi thought Marc was full of shit but then again according to Femi everyone was full of shit, and it was hard to get a job in politics these days. And Femi believed Marc could help him, that Marc would one day make a phone call that would change everything; and Femi had always been ambitious. One lunchtime, over katsu curry in Soho Square, Femi told her the story of how he'd met Marc. Femi had invited him to be guest speaker at a Labour students' event at his university three years before. Marc's lot were more or less out of fashion by then and he'd appreciated the opportunity to relive the golden years of his career in his old student haunt – the place where power had first appeared within his reach. Marc had got way too drunk in the pub, stayed there till it shut telling Femi that *he didn't know how things used to be*. Femi, is that your name? You have no idea. Privately, Femi had agreed – all Marc had had to do was not fail his degree and turn up in Westminster. Wasn't like that now. Not for Femi despite his education, and internships, despite – everything else.

Whether Marc thought Marc was full of shit was less clear to Melissa. It wasn't that he didn't really have Cherie Blair's number on his phone, it was that they never talked. It wasn't that he hadn't been interviewed by Gordon Brown's biographer, it was that they hadn't used any of his quotes; his name wasn't in the index. All his anecdotes were ten or fifteen years old.

We're a consultancy, an agency, Marc said. A communications policy PR strategy online media consultancy agency. Who also do websites. But for good bloody causes! He slapped the table. That's what makes us different. And, leaning wistfully in – The secret sauce is introductions. Not something you can charge for *per se*. Somewhat ineffable, knowing who to bring together and creating that moment that gel that –

Marc handled the clients until the contracts were signed. When they arrived he would gesture at Femi – his young bright thing – and Melissa – a young woman coder, no less! And from Brazil! Via South London! It's like the United Colours of Benetton here! Clients were always friends of friends – he'd had a long career – people he'd worked with in Downing Street or his wife's friends from the BBC or even people he'd known back in his student days. Sometimes they saw the small wiry body in its signature tight fleece through the glass front of the office and came inside just to slap him on the back and ask him how the fuck the last ten years had treated him. Still eating out on '97? Once they were in the office, once he'd taken their coats, he'd ask, *sotto voce* with a tilt of the head, whether Femi or Melissa would make tea. How do you take yours? He'd ask the guest. And they'd talk in the glass booth at the back of the office where there was a sitting desk and two chairs from Habitat. Later, touching Melissa on the back, he'd apologise – Sorry about that. Sorry to ask you to get tea. If Femi had got the tea he said nothing. A woman called Sabine who only existed via email did the payroll. When there was website stuff Melissa did it. A lot of the time clients wanted websites. Melissa made the simplest possible websites using templates. She very rarely used any of the skills she learnt at university. Occasionally she did other online tasks for Marc like finding out people's email addresses and who they knew that he might know. Femi did everything else.

How much money was coming in, and where the money came

from was also not clear. This office must be fucking expensive, as Femi had said. Melissa said couldn't it be their main client, Marc's younger brother, who had made it big in the dot com boom by creating and selling software to estate agents, or their other client, the car company running the international carbon capture competition. Melissa said, maybe Marc was just loaded? Femi shook his head, there was no way, he said, as Marc told them endlessly, he'd gone to the local grammar – first in his family to pass the eleven-plus! – in Sussex or Surrey or Suffolk. He had made his way up from nothing – Marc said this putting his hand on Melissa's shoulder – from *nothing*. Not like you eh Femi, Mr Public School?

Every day at 5.45pm Marc asked – Drink?

More than half the days they went to the tiny pub, hunched under its old wood inside arch or outside on the Soho pavement. Marc and Femi would argue about politics. They spoke over each other and said things like Be reasonable! *Be reasonable!* They disagreed about David Miliband, the Euro, Ukraine. Melissa smoked cigarettes. Occasionally a friend of Marc's or a client would be there and she would light her cigarette then stand in silence, looking at the street.

When she hadn't gone drinking Melissa went to the gym after work. The gym she went to was a 1970s leisure centre. It had a swimming pool and badminton courts. Melissa ran or cycled on the machines; sometimes she swam. She never listened to music and did not have a gym playlist. The gym exit opened onto Shaftesbury Avenue. It was the first time in her life she had had a gym membership. At the start of each month she bought a Zone 1–2 travelcard for £120, her whole body clenched as she typed her pin into the machine.

Over the course of the year Melissa began to build a list of all the points on which she disagreed with Marc –

That people without jobs were lazy

That people with 'mental illnesses' were lazy

That people who weren't proud of being British were ungrateful

That people who smoked weed were lazy

That Muslims, who should be organising anti-terrorism protests, were lazy and/or ungrateful

That immigrants who didn't speak proper English were lazy and ungrateful

That the IRA were pure evil

That the economy was like a household budget

That, overall, things were getting better

That this – London, Soho – was not the real England

And the Tories would win the next election

Melissa sat at the back of the white office. Headphones in. She stared at the screen. When she woke up she listened to podcasts or the radio. On the street she listened to podcasts. On the tube she listened to podcasts. She listened to a podcast series about the Russian Revolution, two podcast series by comedians, a podcast series about US politics, two true crime podcasts and three different news podcasts. There was always another podcast. The voices of the hosts became familiar. By the end of 2015 it had been a year and a half since she had listened to music.

They called it counselling, not therapy. Their first meeting had been in an institutional building on a backstreet between Stepney Green and Mile End near Melissa's university, four months after her mother had died. Melissa turned into the building in the sunlight. In the waiting room she looked at the other patients. A tall and too skinny-looking girl filled in forms. An older man in glasses checked his phone. Everyone was quiet. Melissa stared at her lock screen. A woman in a cardigan appeared from behind a closed door.

Melissa?

Yes

I'm Jane.

Melissa nodded.

Did you find us okay?

Uh huh

Jane led her up a set of stairs. Jane's hair was grey and she wore a lot of rings. She looked somewhere between forty-one and fifty-three years old. They entered a small room. There were two armchairs. Jane smiled at Melissa and indicated that Melissa should sit. Melissa looked around. Between them there was a table with water and tissues and a small clock. On one wall there was a watercolour print of a bird in blue and white. Above the bird was written in watercolour writing – *You inspire me with your determination and I love you.* Melissa cringed. She looked away from the watercolour. On the other wall the street passed quietly behind a blind.

Jane looked at her.

Tell me, she said, why you've decided to come.

It was May. The trees were in full leaf and fresh in the long park down the road. The fountain in the park was on. Slush slush slush. Jane wanted her to talk about growing up. Melissa didn't understand what there was to say. Your father is also missing from your life, Jane said. Melissa frowned. He was never really there. Jane nodded. Do you have a stable place to live? Well What about friends Well We might need more than ten weeks, Jane said. We don't have more than ten weeks Melissa said, the university only offers ten for free. Then let's discuss rates after that, Jane said, her hands in her lap. Jane smiled at her. Tell me what you can afford.

At the end of the ten weeks, Jane asked Melissa if she would mind meeting on Thursday afternoons in Canary Wharf. Melissa said, Sure.

Canary Wharf – the words were grey to her, perhaps because of the colour of the glass or the river there or because it was on the Jubilee line. It was only when she separated the word – Canary – that it came back to her in her mind. A bird, yellow like a pastel.

The address was One Canada Square, which turned out to be the Canary Wharf building itself. Melissa arrived at the reception, sweating. There were security barriers and uniformed guards and receptionists on all sides of the lifts. Melissa stood in front of the counter. She pressed her fingertips into the counter surface. A woman said –

What company?

Um 'Jane'? It's not a company Uh

What is your name?

She was given a temporary key card and instructions to go to lift C.

Mel's ears popped in the lift up. She emerged on the 37th floor against a sheet of glass overlooking the Millennium Dome. Jane led her into the centre of the building to a room with no windows. There was a textile print on the wall.

She stepped out of the door of the white office onto the wet street like she did every Thursday at 2pm. White sunlight in her eyes. Someone was peeing against the wall of the building opposite. Down the escalators at Tottenham Court Road to the Central line EASTBOUND platform. The tube swung around her. She got off at Bank and walked through the station. Stepstepstep. Bank station is cursed, she thought, dirty and curling, labyrinthine like a videogame. She reached the end of a tunnel where she was met by two downward moving escalators next to each other. Their tiny metal tongues charged at her then dived.

Mel took another dirty tunnel and then another, her feet carrying her underground. She got on the tube and sat down. The tube carriage was small, suburban. It might have been the lower ceiling of this carriage, the black and grey square seat patterns, the smaller windows. Home. The announcement came

This is the SOUTHBOUND Northern line service to Morden via Bank.

The closing doors began to beep. She lunged forwards. The closing doors trapped around her shoulders. An automated announcement rang

Please do not obstruct the doors. This can cause delays to the service.

The doors released and reopened. She felt the shame of a Londoner who causes delays to the service. She felt the flat hard of the platform (BANK) under her trainers. She stood with her back against the curving platform wall. The tunnel air moved fast and hot in the wake of the train. She looked at the tracks.

She arrived at One Canada Square late and sweating.
I'm sorry, she said. I was lost.
Jane nodded.

How Femi had made sure Melissa got therapy so fast when she had no money –

No don't go to the NHS. Tell student services you're suicidal.
Suicidal
If you tell them you're suicidal they'll give you an appointment fast
Say I'm suicidal
When they ask you how depressed you are tell them you think about it – not that you've tried but that you're thinking about it
Suicidal
Trust me
Yes
Otherwise you'll spend nine months on a fucking NHS waiting list

Olivia and Ivy and Femi kept saying, go to the doctor. Ask them for meds, maybe. When someone moved out of the flat with the balcony in Mile End, Olivia, who had just got a job doing night shifts for the news, moved in. She brought a green carpet for the corridor and two blue velvet cushions for the sofa. After she had moved in, Olivia asked Melissa again if she had gone to the doctor. They were sitting on the L-shaped sofa.

No.

Olivia paused and looked at her.

I can't go to the doctor until I've registered at a new GP.

You're not registered anywhere now?

I'm registered in Amen Corner

We could go back —

Melissa shook her head

I would go with you – we could stop by your aunties' houses, what were their names —

No No No

I don't want to go back there to the road where

Okay okay – just the GP then, just once, it'll take half an hour —

Melissa looked at the wall and then the floor.

No.

Why don't I call them and make an appointment and then

Melissa shook her head.

Okay. That's okay. Olivia climbed to the other end of the L-shaped sofa. She put her arms around Melissa's shoulders.

When Olivia registered herself at the GP surgery by the park, she registered Melissa too. So, a year after moving in to the flat in Mile End, a year and a half after her mother died, Melissa filled out the forms and registered with the GP and booked a doctor's appointment.

The doctor prescribed her an antidepressant called Citalopram. The doctor said, it won't work straight away. Wait it out. You might get other side effects at first – diarrhoea, excitement, dizziness. Call us if you think you want to stop. Wait two weeks to see results.

She carried the pills around for days without taking them. Went to work just listening to the rattle of the packet against her keys in the small pocket of her backpack. Every day it was sunny. Burning. She felt heartbreak rot through her chest.

She took the first pill before work. She was standing in a Pret with Femi holding a latte. People pushed past them.

It's not even a big deal

No

Of course not

Everyone's on them

Yeah.

Just serotonin init

Uh huh

He looked at her.

They won't work for two weeks – I was – I was on them for a while at uni

Yeah?

Yep

Melissa looked at him.

Yeah. Don't stop taking them though Mel.

I won't.

She cut a pill out of its spot with her thumbnail, and put it in her mouth.

At 11am she got diarrhoea. She ran to the loo in the office. She sat with her head in her hands. She got up and made herself a cup of tea.

Femi sidled up to her. Are you alright?

She looked at the wall and whispered – I'm fucking buzzing

Yeah?

Feels like mdma

Femi smiled at her.

Yeah

Femi laughed.

I'm so fucking high

He clapped her round the shoulder and she leant into him. He smelled warm.

Enjoy it.

The next day was a Thursday. Ivy texted Mel to say that she could meet for twenty minutes, between 12 and 12.20, and Marc was out for a lunch meeting so Melissa left the office earlier than usual on her way to therapy.

Ivy asked to meet outside her office building. Melissa stood there. Hands in her pockets. Men in suits walked past her.

How long have you got? Time to eat?

Yes. There's a falafel van over here

Okay.

I've got these too. She handed a half-packet of Doritos to Melissa, who started munching them.

They ate their falafel wraps sitting on a patch of grass by the station. Ivy pulled at her blouse and wafted her chest.

It's fucking hot today

Yeah. Melissa lay with her back on the ground. She squinted up at Ivy. Ivy put her wrap down. She picked something out of her teeth.

Can't believe this cost £7.50

Melissa made a sound.

You know what is actually the best lunch around here

What

Waitrose

Yeah?

Yeah, they handmake the sushi. You can get a whole dragon roll for £4.50.

We should have gone

Ivy coughed.

I can't go into the shopping centre

Really?

She shook her head.

Why

Well

Ivy rolled her eyes.

I've been banned

What

Well

What the fuck

For shoplifting

Oh my god how could they accuse you – that is so

No well. Ivy swallowed, she lowered her voice. The thing is that – Ivy pushed the Doritos packet into a ball in her hand – I actually was shoplifting.

Melissa looked at her.

I don't know – Ivy shrugged.

What happened?

I got cocky

Uh huh

The security guy thought – I must have been wearing a big coat or something, not had much makeup on – and he said Oh lady are you okay? You're gonna be banned from Canary Wharf shopping centre complex. And I said I can't be banned, my gym is here. And he said your gym is here? looking all confused. And I said yeah Equinox. And he said you work around here madam? And I said yeah I said I work at PW fucking C. And then he noticed my shoes and stuff.

What were you stealing

Sushi.

Melissa inhaled. From Waitrose?

Ivy started picking at her nails. The fucking thing is that I've stolen all sorts from that Waitrose, linen bedsheets, the lot

Melissa sat up. Wait what

It started with pâtés and camemberts. I used to bring them home to Will for dinner

Wait but

I don't know why

Melissa put her hands over her face.

It's just too easy. Airports are the worst – the only limit is the liquid maximum. On our last mini break I told Will to meet me at the gate cos I was loading up – Mel stop laughing – I think it's an illness, I've got a problem – it's not funny. I feel really ashamed. I need help for it

Mel

Tears were coming down Melissa's face.
　　Fuck. Sorry sorry
　　She put her hand on Ivy's hand.

Ivy looked at her.
　　Did you ever used to shoplift?
　　Melissa paused.
　　Yeah. All the time at school. Mostly makeup with this friend I had back then, do you remember that Barry M stuff
　　Yeah.
　　Do you remember um Ruth? With her
　　Ivy nodded.

The packet said –

Some young people have thoughts about suicide when first taking an antidepressant. Your doctor should check your progress at regular visits. Your family or other caregivers should also be alert to changes in your mood or symptoms.

The doctor had already told Melissa this. Melissa had sent a picture of the text to Femi and Ivy and Olivia. The doctor had said – Sometimes it is the case that antidepressants suddenly give a person the energy to – to hurt themselves – before they properly change the person's desire to die. A sort of mania. Call us if that happens. Don't stop taking them.

The next day or the next day or the next day was a Friday. Melissa woke without her alarm and looked at the street from her bedroom window. A rubbish truck reversed down the road. The smell rose up and up, dirty and sweet. She could hear voices shouting and the sounds of full bin bags crushing against each other. She took a shower and in the shower she felt each single drop of water against her shoulder skin like hail. She brushed her teeth. She made coffee and toast. She drank the coffee. She buttered the toast. She ate it looking out at the street. Bright. Kids in school uniform.

On her way to the station she put her headphones in. She listened to a ready made Spotify playlist. Kids in school uniform. She ran down the steps to the tube platform two at a time. She touched her oyster card onto the reader and strode through the open gates. She got to Tottenham Court Road early. Bought herself a coffee.

At 5pm Marc put his hands on Femi's shoulders.

Drink? It's time for a drink don't you think? God knows when the weather is this good on a Friday it's a crime to stay in the office isn't it?

Melissa closed her laptop.

They stood in the street. Pints?

Yes

Yes

Estrella Guinness

Yes

Marc stepped inside the pub. Melissa lit a cigarette.

How you feeling?

She shook her head. Pretty fucking wavy

Yeah?

Yeah.

That's great.

She nodded. She looked out at the street.

Did it rain?

Yes at lunch.

The streets are shining
Femi looked at her.
What you doing tonight Femi?
Tonight?
Yeah. Let's go out!
You wanna go out?
Yeah! I wanna dance
Femi exhaled. Just some girl from uni's birthday drinks
Can I come?
Sure. It's down the road.
Ok let's load up on drinks here then
Femi laughed.

Marc returned. Melissa said to no one in particular – It's a beautiful evening
Yes! Melissa you're on good today form I must say
Melissa shrugged.
I love summer
Marc moved his hands in the air.

Yes there is something about London in the summer isn't there, Melissa
August especially, everyone's on holiday, the city's quiet, tube's empty
Oh yes –
For sure.
I remember god I remember I used to come to this very pub when I was your age. What you do you lot do now go on 'dates'? Well there was none of that then. You used to snog a girl and then she was your girlfriend if you called her, if you remembered her phone number, if you were lucky and she wanted to be – oh but you have no idea. You know I used to come here – when I first moved to London – oh Soho was the most exciting place – look at it! – not like it is now. You have to imagine – underground clubs everywhere, gay bars of course, always open late, the AIDS crisis, beautiful women.

Oh beautiful women, and in summer wearing almost nothing – it was the late 1980s you know what the 1980s were like – or I suppose you don't but we used to come here and dance and get trashed, right when I'd first graduated – I was sick once on Soho Square and you know me I can take my alcohol, but it was the 1980s and back then everything was a party, everything you have to understand – even now I mean look at it – it has a romance a promise a seediness a Londonness – you know it's something no one can escape, you know it's the neon of it. Where I grew up in Surrey there was no neon – bet there isn't any in Tooting either. You know there is a Tracey Emin quote – Tracey she was big in the late 90s I used to see her at things always drunk of course – there is a Tracey quote and it goes like this

Marc stepped back into the street. He spread his arms and hands like wings. He paused.

Ahem –

Neon is emotional for everybody

I think that's quite beautiful. Don't you agree? Neon is emotional for everybody –

Melissa lent forwards. Yeah! Cos it is right

Femi nodded. He looked at Marc and then at Melissa.

Oh absolutely Melissa

Marc stepped back onto the pavement and touched Femi on the shoulder. Femi you wouldn't believe all the things I've seen here over the years. (Femi looked at Melissa.) All sorts of drugs of course. But even last year – you were here weren't you – it was a hot day and a very attractive woman bent to pick up something she'd dropped, a 50p coin I think – it was just over there. She was wearing a turquoise colour dress. It was a sweaty evening, everything was sticking. She squatted to pick it up and just that moment a black cab ran over her fingers. Broke all ten of them. Poor woman wasn't even drunk. I got her a whisky of course. Speaking of – who'd like another?

It was the year Ebola happened and all the snow and Scotland didn't leave the UK. It was the year that Peaches Geldof, whose little sister Olivia had known because she'd gone to one of the private schools in Dulwich, died. She died of an overdose which was ruled not to have been a suicide. That year Soho looked bright. It leaked rainwater. Sex workers and sex shops and women kissing; unnamed restaurants that didn't take bookings; private members' clubs and GUM clinics and tourists; cheap noodles and expensive noodles. Big theatres and little theatres. New entrances to Tottenham Court Road tube. Greek Street and Dean Street and tall people who could have been models smoking on the pavement. The nighttime coming. Marc wasn't wrong. Neon for streets and streets and streets.

Let's go out – Melissa said

It was the birthday of someone Femi knew and they were three drinks in already when they got to the pub on Old Compton Street which was too full, all its windows open onto the street.

Katie! Give me a hug. Many happy returns! What can I get you to drink

Hello

Hi

Hi yes, me and Mel have been friends for years –

It was August and the pub was full and hot with people who didn't know each other and hadn't worked full working days; it was all the people Femi had gone to uni with gathered in weird and untested groups, interspersed with other unknown people who worked nearby; everyone wearing unbuttoned shirts, no tights.

Ellen is in Portugal with her work friends. Anjali is at her sister's wedding.

Mel stood for a moment on the pavement. Around her people smoked cigarettes and shouted to each other. Two men in patent high heeled boots walked by arm and arm. A woman with two designer handbags. Girls who looked like teenagers. Everybody sweating lightly. The teenagers looked at her. Femi had disappeared. Melissa ground her heel into the uneven pavement and turned on the spot to face a woman with a tidy fringe and brown eyes.

Hello

Hi

Are you here for Katie's birthday?

Yes.

I'm Tara

Hi – Mel had looked at Tara – I'm looking for my friend who knows her, there he is

Femi there you are

Mel Mel – Do you want a drink? Let me get you a drink

Melissa followed him inside.

Later, three drinks later, Mel was outside smoking. A rickshaw cyclist with pink lights around the seat pulled a couple down the road. The rickshaw was playing music. The cyclist was sweating.

Tara came outside.

Hi

Hello

Mel?

Yes. What was your

Tara

It was warm and light and busy on the street

How do you know Katie?

We work together

You're a teacher?

An art teacher. I teach mostly year 7 to 11

Oh

Yep

How's that

I love it.

Melissa looked at her phone. She could hear music. Tara didn't get any cigarettes out.

Tara looked at her and smiled.

I just spent a month in Barcelona. School holidays are great of course.

Yes

Melissa looked at her.

So are you new to London?

A year

Will this be your first Carnival?

No – I went last year

Did you like it

Yes.

Tara had done a joint honours degree – Spanish and Philosophy. She wanted to know what languages Melissa spoke

Only one really – But
Tara told Mel that she loved her job. The school I'm at is in Balham, do you know it?
Melissa nodded. Yes I know Balham. It's near where I grew up
Yeah?

Melissa felt an urge to leave the conversation. She could hear music. She moved her body a little on the spot. Hard boots against the pavement. Drunk shouting came from down the road. Two men in tight white T-shirts with French accents asked her the way to Leicester Square and she said –
It's that way.
Melissa paused.
But you don't want to go there it's a shithole
The two men stared at her.
Tara smiled.
As the two men walked off, Melissa looked at the spot where the men had stood. She blinked.

Would you like a drink Tara? I'm getting myself one
Yes
Ok.
Ok
Inside the pub Melissa inhaled. Femi came up behind her
Melissa Mel you met Tara
Yep
You're in a good mood
Where are you going Femi –
Femi followed her out, holding her drink, drinking from it.
She rejoined Tara on the pavement, handed her her glass. Femi turned to face them, putting an arm around both of them bringing

their faces close together. Melissa grimaced. He was about to speak but Tara interrupted him – Who is going dancing? Mel?

They ended up at a shitty bar down the road. It was cheesy and carpeted. Full of older camp men and somehow also Mexican themed and charging entry on the door.

What is this place? Melissa said to the night to the street

Do you remember Femi when we used to drink just get a couple of tinnies that's what we should do now, that's what we should do now

But everyone was already inside. Melissa stood on the pavement. She looked down Greek Street. All around her neon lit up the darkness. She stumbled into the dark bar.

Inside, her feet started to move. She knew this music, a bit. Shots? Yes. Sticky dancefloor. She closed her eyes. She moved her hand, reaching for the soft of a waist

She didn't know
what to say
how to touch a stranger's breasts, with open palms or

And, if she said –

   you're so wet

would that be too – pornographic?

In the end in the end after how many years it happened like that
in the night
in a bedroom she didn't recognise

Tara had looked back at her when she had turned her key in the door.

My flatmate's asleep, she had whispered.

Tara's flat was at the top of a tower block. As they had crossed the river in the taxi Melissa had leant back and covered her eyes with her fore-arm. In Tara's bedroom she looked out of the window; there were no streets, just the purple sky

Come here, Tara had asked her.

Inside herself she heard herself.
Ruth
Ruthie curtis
Ruthie rooftops

in her mother's voice there was only one word, the homophone – *Ruth*

Melissa had felt sure that Ruth would find her, for years and years after the funeral had passed, she had been sure Ruth would call her, text her, Facebook her, write her letters or emails or send her a package or even a parent, Vicky, striding in with emerald drop earrings

She had felt sure that Ruth would be there on her doorstep. When she climbed the stone steps of her building in Mile End, jumping up them two at a time, almost every evening she was sure Ruth would be there, waiting. She could see her – *Ruth* in the door frame; *Ruth* sitting on the floor back against the front door; *Ruth* caught in the rain her mouse brown hair wet and humbled

She felt sure Ruth would appear – because Ruthie was always in this city, somewhere in this city, a GPS mark on some street, some bus, some tube, somewhere that was not – or was almost – where Melissa was. In every step she took onto a tube carriage, every turn she took down the street in central London, every Soho bar she walked into, every party, every event, every single room Melissa expected her to appear, smelling of the perfume with the cloves

She had asked Femi what happened to Ruth. One afternoon after work. Femi hadn't made eye contact. He'd said Oh he didn't talk much to Jonathan these days but he'd heard she'd gone on a gap year with that boyfriend, did Melissa know the one, did she remember, the one from before, he was a piece of work truth be told a bit of a cunt, and then they'd both gone up to Manchester, and well he didn't talk much to Jonathan these days, no he didn't talk much to Jonathan these days.

Melissa had no memory of the six months after her mother died.

The university let her take two terms off. The terms she was meant to be writing her dissertation and sitting exams. They gave two options – to take a year out and submit her dissertation and sit the exams in a year or to get an automatic pass in the exams and coursework and graduate with a 2.1. She had been averaging a high 2.1 so far with 60% of her coursework done. Femi wrote the email saying yes to the automatic pass because taking a year out would have meant no student loan and no free emergency university counselling service. Jean and Janine and Jasmine had been coming round with food in tupperwares but Melissa was a grown up now and they were getting old. Wandsworth Council took the house on Amen Corner back.

Tell them you're suicidal.

Melissa had no memory of clearing out the house on Amen Corner, no memory of saying goodbye to Jean, Janine and Jasmine.

In August 2015, around the time of her birthday, a year and a half after her mother died, Melissa stood over the river. She had come from the North side, looking South. She stood on the bridge that goes to Covent Garden from the IMAX, the one with the low white railings.

Melissa felt angry. She felt so angry she couldn't speak. Her whole body angry, like the colour white. When Melissa's mother died, Ruthie had not come to her

How could time keep passing like this? Become August. And all the things, every thing that had happened, the last time they had spoken, every tiny thing and the tiny days and tiny weeks keep passing and passing

how could time separate them like this?

Her mother moved all around. City lights. Light pollution. Neon in the sky.

The tide was high. She felt the swaying edges of the moving river, the push of the tide. Melissa leant her body over the bridge in the rain. Cold river. Black water. The river crashed and slushed against itself. She leant over the water, her chest against the railings. High tide. The river spat onto her face.

Come in, querida. The river said.

MILE END II

(2016)

Before the night tube started, which was in August 2016 – later than planned due to strikes by transport workers concerned about their working conditions – if you were from South London and you went to a party in Tottenham you used to have to wait till 6am to go home. The bus took two hours and a minicab cost £50 plus. Before the night tube, before uber, it was go home at midnight or go hard. Like arrive at 1am, take mdma, or ket and mix it with coke, and dance with strangers for three hours straight then smoke a spliff with strangers and dmc with strangers then fall asleep on a sofa cushion on the floor or have sex with a stranger under a cold duvet in an upstairs bedroom, people opening and closing the bedroom door, and wake up, right before the light came, mouth dry, and walk to the underground, stepping over cherry blossom on the tarmac as the sun rose, and wait outside the station with the workers. The first Victoria line train was always packed and so loud. It crashed down the tunnel; it took you to the other side of the city, SOUTHBOUND, home.

On that first night, when the person in the long puffer coat led them from the Brazilian embassy on Cockspur Street through Soho through Bloomsbury to the meeting (remember? the night when the lamplight in the park turned the grass and the almost closed daffodils the colour orange), they spent two hours sitting on the floor leaning into the circle of people gathered that night in the university building.

Catarina sat cross-legged on the floor. Her knees touched then retreated from the knees on either side of her. There were backpacks and bike helmets and wet coats everywhere around them. A baby made a sound. Every kind of face. They could have been in Olinda, Catarina thought, except for the double glazing on the windows and water pooling on the window glass, except for the dark and rain outside. She looked beside her at Melissa, and the person next to her, and the person after and the person after, each leaning forwards, called into the circle like the sea called on by the moon.

The person in a puffer coat holding flowers and a tangerine looked out across the room. She smiled and took an iphone in a Hello Kitty case from her pocket. She spoke –

Let's read the founding statement.

The person in the puffer coat looked up and out. She spoke –

We are women and gender non-conforming people

She passed the phone to her left.

A woman with a blonde fringe held the small iphone in her hands. She spoke –

fighting for liberation and planetary justice

She passed the phone to her left.

A person with bantu knots held the small iphone in their hands. They spoke –

For centuries
hetero patriarchal capitalist imperialists have ruled over the people

They passed the phone to their left.

A person in a leather jacket held the small iphone in her hands. She spoke –

using violence to dominate, exploit, and extract from the people and the land

She passed the phone to her left.

A person with a baby in their arms held the small iphone in their hands. They spoke –

But
we are many

They passed the phone to their left.

A woman who looked only fifteen years old held the small iphone in her hands. She spoke –

We fight together: alongside our sisters, our siblings

She passed the phone to her left.

A woman with the side of her head shaved and golden earring held the small iphone in her hands. She spoke –

and our ancestors

She passed the phone to her left.

A woman with white hair in a raincoat held the small iphone in her hands. She spoke –

by any means necessary

She passed the phone to her left.

The person who looked like Meena from Melissa's year 7 class held the small iphone in her hands. She spoke –
because none of us

Black
brown
poor
disabled

She passed the iphone to her left.

A woman in blue hospital scrubs held the small iphone in her hands. She spoke –

migrant
woman
non-binary
gender non-conforming
trans
queer

She passed the phone to her left.

Catarina held the small iphone in her hands. She spoke –

are free
until all of us are free

She passed the phone to her left.

Melissa held the small iphone in her hands. She read the words on the screen twice in her head before looking up into the room. She spoke, raising her voice to the size of the room for the second word —

We

SHOUT

the names of the dead

Melissa's hands were shaking as she passed the small iphone to the person to her left. A person who looked fifty-five years old held the small iphone in her hands. She bellowed —

to remember

Immediately, the room spoke back to her, words echoing from every direction, forming, somehow a chorus —

Pinakin
Rubel
Christine
Sheku
Seeta
Amy
Jill
Sarah

Melissa heard next to her Catarina shout —

LAURA

Melissa opened her mouth and shouted also —

GLÓRIA

And then the room went silent. Somebody stood to give an update about a place called Rojava. The meeting began.

Melissa felt her chest wrench. It was a kind of panic, an unbinding of the ribs. She wanted to stop the reading of the statement. It was so earnest and so sure. A chorus broken into parts. Like she'd heard in school or in a church. If Marc could have seen her in that moment, he would have laughed.

Later, when they got off the tube, they saw the spring breaking across the trees in tiny buds in green that looks like orange under the street-lights. Cherry blossom fell too early on the ground, also orange. They followed the lilac, blue and yellow flowers down the park towards their flat.

Let me tell you about my mum, Melissa had said.

That night in their flat Catarina made a list of words

    quero

    desejo

    wish

    want

    desire

She took all her books off the bookshelf. She opened them all. She felt awake; suddenly, urgently clear and sure and real.

Melissa left a half cafetiere of hot coffee on the glass table in the kitchen / living room next to the plant called Espada de São Jorge. She did this after inspecting the monstera plant's new leaf, after pulling two brown leaves from the spiderwort plant on the balcony, the cold air touching her washed face for the first time that day. She touched the tip of the ball of her index finger against the spine of the new leaf, which had not yet uncurled. She took a tupperware of spaghetti from the fridge and put it in her backpack.

She descended the steps to Joseph Street two at a time, the sound of the soles of her shoes echoing in the open-air stairwell. Children on the street swung their bookbags over their heads and shouted at each other. She listened to 'Desperado' and then 'Consideration' and the sounds of them filled the residential streets all the way to the park and to the high street.

Two thousand commuters poured into the open mouth of Mile End tube. All the young professionals who had come to the area to live with strangers in flats built for families tapped their oyster cards. They poured down the stairs, hard shoes clip clopping on the hard steps to the WESTBOUND platform where they swayed, clutching each other without touching each other, the legs of their black work trousers and the sleeves of their overwarm coats leaning right and left against each other.

Melissa stood at the end of the platform at the back of a cluster of commuters formed in the anticipation of where the last set of doors would open. A train rattle crashed down the tunnel, bright eyed. It slowed and the last set of doors opened a step to the left of where the cluster had gathered. Together they shifted sideways. The tube doors opened and no one got off the tube. A person in a suit clambered into the corner by the door. A woman pushed herself, handbag first, into the curve under the doors. They closed over her face. Melissa stepped forwards, the train pulled away, and more people joined the cluster, pushing from behind her. She stood with bodies on all sides of her. She recognised the shampoo brand of the woman who stood in front of her. She breathed in. The smell of cloves. A train rattle crashed down the tunnel, bright eyed. It slowed and the last set of doors opened a half step to the right of where the cluster had anticipated. Melissa half stepped to the right. She saw in front of her, behind the window glass, a man standing in the middle of the carriage reading his book, elbows askew. One person got off the tube and the three people in front of Melissa pushed themselves onto it, including the woman with the shampoo hair. Melissa was lunged forwards from behind. Someone shouted Move Down the Fucking Carriage and the bodies around her tensed. The man reading his book in the middle of the carriage did not look up. The tube doors closed. Melissa stood with her toes only the length of her shoes away from the platform edge. She looked down. She looked at the rails. She turned her head to look down the tunnel. She could see the eye lights of the next train. She heard the crash of it. She breathed in.

The tube doors stopped directly in front of her. She put her feet on the carriage floor, in the small space cleared by the open doors. She took off her backpack and held it between her knees. She grabbed onto a ceiling rail. She leant her body back over the person behind her. Sorry Sorry, she said. The tube doors closed. The bodies in the carriage held together.

Femi sat in his chair in the white office eating cereal. She saw him through the glass. She watched him frowning at his laptop screen as he spooned cornflakes into his mouth.

Mel.

Femi.

What you doing?

Reviewing socials for the launch of that tool they made – the one for the child refugee charity

Where Marc wanted to make it look like a bomb dropping on your house?

Yeah, the one using Google streetview

Yep. They emailed yesterday evening to say they want to launch today to make the most of the deaths in the news.

Melissa nodded. She opened her laptop.

They decided it wasn't in bad taste in the end?

I guess

Melissa nodded. She spoke while looking through her glasses at the screen.

I don't understand why they don't just criticise the government

Femi rubbed his eyes. Cos they get their funding from the government

Right.

And people who voted for the government

Right

Melissa frowned at the screen. She moved in her seat.

Have you checked the donate journey Mel

No but let me do it now.

Thanks. Femi closed his eyes. Do you want a cup of tea?

Yes

He stood. He put his hands on his head then stretched them to the ceiling. At that moment Marc came through the door of the white office.

Femi! What are you doing yawning? Tea break already is it? Two sugars, then.

He winked at Melissa. She looked at the wall.

At 6pm Femi was still on the phone to the client and Marc was leaning over his shoulder but they did not call Melissa over; she had done what she'd needed to for the day. They were discussing Facebook ads. Outside the window it got dark. Melissa sat at her desk until 6.30pm. She read the news in one window and whatsapped Ivy in another. Headphones in. She packed up quickly just in case Marc was thinking of suggesting a drink.

Melissa went to the gym with the exit that opened onto Shaftesbury Avenue. She listened to music and made eye contact with nobody. When a man came up to her and said, Let me show you how to use the leg press, she said, I'm alright. Afterwards, she moisturised and put on the fresh underwear that she had brought in her bag, including clean socks. She put her black jeans on and a new shirt. She ran her hands through her hair. She put her eyeliner on and brushed her teeth. She watched as the other women around her changed from their shower-blotched, jiggling bodies to the clothed bodies of business-women in suits and youths in heels and skinny trousers. She put on her boots and checked her phone. She checked it again. She zipped up her backpack.

At Tottenham Court Road station a man played the *Titanic* theme tune on the flute and she dropped a pound coin in his case. She checked her phone. She followed the signs for the Northern line, SOUTHBOUND down into the belly of the city below the sewers and the foundations of buildings. She stepped onto the Northern line carriage, smaller than the Central line carriage. As the train pulled away from Embankment station she closed her eyes, her chest twisting as they descended into the dark under the river, crossing from North to South.

At Oval she waited for the 36 or 436 or 185 bus. Because she was early she got off the bus at Peckham Rye and walked. She passed the Ghanaian aunties in their hair salons and African food shops and Iceland and McDonalds, past the white people wearing hippy clothes and white people wearing athleisure, peering into all their faces waiting to see whoever she thought that she would see without recognising anyone. She checked her phone. Melissa knew from her profile that Eleni was two years older than her and worked in fashion journalism. Eleni had suggested the restaurant. She had said, It's meant to be good, have you ever been? Do you like Iranian food?

Melissa scanned inside the restaurant through the window. She recognised Eleni sitting at a small table, wearing a yellow jumper. She felt an urge to run back up the high street, to send a message saying she was ill and turn off her phone. Eleni checked her phone. She was pretty, with lots of hair in curls. Next to her a couple fed each other meze. Melissa breathed in, pushed open the restaurant door.

Eleni ordered her beer with a Brummie accent. They fumbled around the questions Are you vegetarian Should we get food to share What do you fancy? The restaurant moved around them. Melissa waited. She looked around, waiting to see someone she knew, someone she had grown up with. Eleni asked her questions and she answered without thinking

I'm a software developer and Eleni said

I'm Greek Cypriot

Melissa looked up.

Eleni was nodding.

I mean Cypriot I believe in a united Cyprus but I grew up in Birmingham. I moved here a year ago. Do you know this area? Do you know South London?

Do I know it?

Yeah

I do. I grew up in Tooting.

Melissa paused.

Near the common, if you know it

It has that huge lido

Yeah –

Melissa looked at Eleni.

We broke into the lido when we were teenagers, once

No!

Yeah – we were fifteen or fourteen I think, it wasn't open because it was spring and it only opens in the summer, but I remember it was really hot and we were on the common so we jumped the fence and jumped in in all our clothes. We were so scared – Melissa swallowed, she was speaking too quickly – we were so scared but obviously no one – no one gave a shit

Melissa exhaled. She made eye contact with Eleni.

It was Eleni who said, two hours later, leaning forwards, knife and fork laid neatly together on her plate –

What are you feeling, next

Next

Melissa held eye contact.

Eleni nodded.

A drink? If

Yes.

They walked to the pub in the dark with their hands by their sides. The headlights of double decker buses going too fast down the road lit up the street. The neon of a kebab shop sign and a pharmacy sign. White people in Doc Martens and ripped jeans passed them. It was like her mother had always said, rich people always trying to look poor. Young people in long coats with home-dyed hair. Melissa did not look into their faces.

Eleni lived in one of those terraced Victorian houses with the coving above the door. The heating was on. Melissa took her shoes off. The carpet was green and Melissa felt it under her toes under her socks. Her room was on the first floor. She had a bunch of daffodils in a jar of water on her bedside table and photos of her family.

Melissa began making the words in her mind. *Sorry I might take a while, I might not be able to.* All around her beige pink beige forearms and the beer and water taste of Eleni's mouth.

Melissa opened her eyes.

Eleni.

Eleni looked at her.

Um sometimes I find it hard to come, the first time, with someone new

Eleni sat up on the bed. She touched her on the arm.

That's okay

Melissa nodded

I never come the first time with someone new either

Oh

Unless – she opened a drawer of the bedside table with the daffodils – unless I use one of these –

This one is a Hitachi magic wand, this one is like a tiny vibrating cushion thing, it curves into your hand sort of like an oyster or seashell, this one with the handle uses suction, this one is just a bullet

Oh

Melissa blinked.

On her way into the white office Melissa drank hot coffee that Eleni had made her from a flask Eleni had handed her as she left. On the bus and then the tube she read the Wikipedia page for 'Presidente João Goulart' and then the page for the 'Lipo', proper name Leandro, three-time governor of Pernambuco State. Every time the tube stopped at a station, she reconnected to the wifi, and the page refreshed. Between Embankment and Charing Cross she clicked on the Personal Life section. At Charing Cross it loaded.

When she arrived Femi was sat at his desk drinking coffee. Melissa showed him her phone.

Look at the surname. This is Catarina's Grandad

Femi scrolled. And her cousin is a Senator?

Melissa nodded.

They're like the Kennedys of Brazil

Sort of but like actually leftwing

Melissa read over Femi's shoulder. She put her finger on the screen. Read this, she said.

Femi cleared his throat.

His daughter Laura was a guerrilla accused by government forces – and cleared – of killing a member of the military police in a shoot out in 1968. She was a member of the illegal MCRB (Movimento Comunista Revolucionário do Brasil) and spent five years underground with another female revolutionary [citation needed] during the dictatorship until she was discovered in São Paulo city in 1974 and tortured, sustaining permanent injuries to her brain and legs. After the Amnesty of 1979 was declared she was reunited with her parents and four sisters in Recife. She died in a car accident in 1988.

Femi looked at her

That's Catarina's auntie

Fuck me

Melissa zoomed into the words *another female revolutionary* – Do you think they were

Maybe

The door to the office opened and a voice interrupted them from across the room –

What are you looking at? Tell me what is so interesting I must know

Femi looked at Melissa.

Just the football. How about that penalty yesterday! Did you see it?

There was a brightness – red – behind Catarina's eyelids. It held for less than a second. Until her mind located itself, began to tell her fingers, elbows, cheeks and toes and mouth: move. Eyes: open.

Catarina brushed her teeth while the shower water warmed. She flossed. She mouthwashed. Bright morning light came through the mottled bathroom window. She heard Melissa leave the flat, slamming the door twice to lock it. In the kitchen the counters were clean and there was a mug next to a cafetiere of hot caffeine. She poured herself coffee and made herself cereal with soy milk. A mug was such a large unit of coffee. She checked her phone for messages from Pedro. She checked her emails. She heard someone get in the shower. She had a missed call from her parents. She put her mug and bowl in the sink and left the flat. The morning rush had passed, and she sat down and read a book as the Hammersmith and City line train moved slowly towards Euston Square.

Catarina had been going to a different event every weekday night. 'Decolonising contraception: gender and medicalisation of racialised bodies' at the Student Union; 'Intersectionality 102: let's talk about class' with the University Feminist Society; 'The Half-Life of Caste: The ill-health of a nation', a lecture by Arundhati Roy at the Institute of Education. She had invited Melissa to one the week before called 'Indigenous genders of Latin America' at the Queer Studies Department but Melissa had said she had a date.

Catarina wrote down the new English words and phrases from each talk and repeated them to herself. She made a list of the words on her phone

Homonationalism
Afrofuturism
Social Reproduction
Queer kinships
Affect Theory
Black Capitalism

At the queer histories talk someone had been handing out fliers with the word Maricumbia and a guava on them. Catarina had said thank you and put the flier in her pocket. When she got home she put it on the fridge.

Catarina's teaching room was on the third floor, its windows at the treeline. She paused for a moment before opening the door. She smiled at her undergraduate students as they slouched in, and as they unpacked she looked at her notes and turned the projector on. She had spent the last two days preparing the slides and the readings, although she was only paid for half a day. She smiled at the shy girl who arrived first and sat at the back. She nodded at the two boys in Barbour jackets. A tall South Asian girl in trainers and her white friend with a nose stud sat down. She smiled at them.

They were in their first year. She had asked them to read Benedict Anderson. She thought back to the first time that she had read Benedict Anderson. But it was not the same, she had grown up with those ideas. She looked at her notes. She thought of her mother at her desk in the university. The heat and the whirring turning face of the fan in her office disrupting loose papers.

How are you?

The tall South Asian girl in trainers was speaking to her.

Catarina closed her eyes and opened them. I'm good.

The girl was looking at her.

I wanted to ask you – What do you think about the situation in Brazil? What do you think of Dilma

Catarina felt her hand move to her face. The room was almost full.

Catarina inhaled. She looked at her slides on the computer screen and then she looked at all their faces.

Yes. Perhaps, perhaps today we can spend the class discussing that.

After the class she went to the History Department office. Out of the window she could see over the roofs, over the river to the London Eye. She put her soup in a microwave reserved for graduate students and waited for it to heat. She leant against the window, looking out. When it was ready she sat down and opened her laptop to the *Folha de São Paulo* homepage. She began to eat.

Cat. Are you ready?

Matt, who was also in the PhD programme and had really been Pedro's friend, appeared at her desk. He was wearing a blue jacket with a round collar and grey jeans and Converse. He had a Tesco meal deal sandwich in one hand and a packet of prawn cocktail flavour crisps in the other. Matt spoke with an accent that he had told her was from Liverpool and was always changing his thesis title from *Anglo-American Neoliberalism in the post-Thatcher era* to *Post-Thatcherism: the Anglo-American neoliberal era* and back again and asking Catarina what she thought. Catarina had forgotten that she had agreed to go to a lunchtime panel in the Politics Department with him.

Catarina used a phrase she had heard Melissa say – Hold on.

She grabbed her coat and closed her laptop. As they walked through the buildings and down the stairs she tried another English phrase –

The weather is picking up, isn't it

Oh yeah

The lecture theatre was half full and the talk had already started. They settled at the back in the middle section. Matt ripped the sandwich packaging slowly. An older-looking man in front of them turned his head. Matt whispered to her –

So what's happening in—

Catarina interrupted – Your country is pretty fucked too huh

Well, yeah.

You think you will leave?

Matt looked straight ahead. No.

Matt turned briefly to her – I don't know –

She shifted forwards. She whispered –

Some people make the leftwing argument, Fortress Europe

Bollocks, there'll be no workers' rights if—

The man in front of them turned again.

Sorry –

She turned to face the front. She whispered without looking at him –

Pedro says he thinks you will leave. He says you underestimate the populism in this country.

Matt didn't look at her.

How is Pedro

Good.

He's a great bloke.

Catarina nodded.

Henrietta said you two spoke about the job going in Bristol.

Catarina looked at the front.

Hasn't Pedro got a permanent job in São Paulo –

The man in front of them turned his head.

Catarina looked away from Matt to the panel. She focused on the nodding heads and mouths of the people on the panel. She breathed in. She felt her chest and throat tighten and hold.

That afternoon she answered emails from students at her desk.

That evening she went to a talk by two poets in a bookshop. Afterwards she did what she had done the evening before and the evening before and walked down the tall tree-lined streets of Bloomsbury to Holborn station. She left a Pedro voicenote giving her thoughts on the lunchtime talk and asked him his opinion. She described the cold to him as she walked through it. She said she missed him, which was true. Larissa had posted photographs of her and Tia Lamis with their new poodle puppy on the family whatsapp. Catarina flicked through them. She messaged Larissa. Straight away Larissa began to record a voicenote back. Catarina listened to it while sitting on the tube. Larissa said that Tia Lamis was trying to convince Sônia to get a poodle puppy too, there was still one left in the litter, she thought it would be good for her anxiety but Sônia had said No no it would be too much work. So they were trying to get Miguel on board. But, on the plus side, Larissa said, at least she was not saying What Anxiety? That was the therapy Tia Lamis had convinced her to get. It is working, Larissa said.

Catarina locked her phone and put it in her pocket. The Central line was so small and dirty. It is the grimiest line, Melissa had said to her more than once.

As she walked from Mile End tube station to the flat she messaged her parents to say she was too busy to talk. She would see them on Skype on their regular slot on Sunday.

I am still in the office querida, Pedro wrote to her. She expected that he would make her a voicenote back at midnight, like he had done in the days before, and she would listen to it as she fell asleep. Pedro was always saying the same thing to her – I don't know about these gringos, Catarina, power always corrupts, even here PT made mistakes it is not sacrilege to admit this, they became too close to the big corporations this is the truth where were the environmental protections? What use is this theory without praxis, what do they know of the fifty Black kids killed every day in Brazil?

In the morning, she would listen and she would reply.

Catarina caught the smell as soon as she stepped into the flat, as soon as she opened the front door. It was a rich and salty smell, like the earth. The clocks had changed and it was the first time that she had arrived home to the flat at dusk. Sunset filled the kitchen / living room. It entered horizontally across the dining table across the L-shaped sofa to the kitchen units, turning them from yellow to red. Their plants were bigger than she remembered. The monstera lolled, almost black against the sunlight. The Espada de São Jorge was the size of a chair. She heard the *tsssss* of a pressure cooker.

You're making feijão

Yes

It smells really good

Yes I'm using the recipe you sent me. Did you say your mother made it?

No – no it was the woman who works in the house, Dona Flor

Say thank you

I will

Catarina took her coat off and her shoes. Melissa was playing music. She moved her weight from her heels to her toes, her heels to her toes. Catarina recognised the song.

It is not so cold outside

No

No –

Melissa turned from the stove

These plants are so big

Yes

They feel the season changing

Melissa nodded. This is what the internet says anyway. Also we must only water them when their soil is dry. Overwatering can be fatal.

Catarina nodded. She put her bag down on the sofa.

I was playing Femi this song at work today.

Catarina cocked her left ear, tilted her head – 'Terra'

I told him it means Land. Or earth? Even, soil

Yes

Catarina repeated in an English voice – Teh-*rah*

He thought at first I was saying Terror

Catarina nodded.

I said – Melissa looked at Catarina and then away again – I said what you told me, why the song matters, that Caetano Veloso spent time in exile in London during the dictatorship also and that that is important context, you know. He is talking about being apart from the land that he is from. About freedom.

Yes – Catarina sat down next to her bag – Yes but you know he is singing about a specific photo of Earth itself, the planet, there is a whole story of this song. Do you know the story?

No

Let me tell you. Let me look it up and check I am telling it right. Yes. Wikipedia says he was in jail in Rio de Janeiro in December of 1969 for saying subversive things at a concert with Gilberto Gil who also went to jail and then London for exile with him. In jail in Rio de Janeiro in December of 1969 Caetano Veloso was reading a magazine, and in the magazine he saw a photo of the Earth from space. It was the first photograph ever where you could see the whole planet and all the sky and stars around it. It was taken by the US spaceship Apollo

8. Then they went to London for exile the January after and stayed there until 1972.

Oh

Let me find the image.

The music continued.

Melissa stirred the pan. And now – is he singing about a woman as well? Or the earth is the woman? A naked woman. Falling in love with the naked earth woman?

Yes. Catarina nodded. The woman is the metaphor.

Melissa made a face. She rolled her eyes.

Catarina felt herself rile.

Melissa handed her two plates and Catarina arranged them on the table.

Catarina frowned. I guess –

Melissa handed her two knives and two forks and she laid them on the table.

Catarina felt defensiveness in her throat. She checked the feeling. She picked up her phone and stared at the lockscreen. She shifted forwards in her chair. Melissa had made her a whole meal. She opened her mouth. She felt herself begin to form intellectualising words. She felt so protective of – something.

The sun was in her eyes.

She looked at her friend's face.

Melissa sat down, she hovered over the pan with a pepper grinder before stirring it with a wooden spoon. She tasted it.

Ready.

Smells really good

Melissa served Catarina.

Melissa served herself, looking at the food. She spoke – I added a little vegetarian Worcestershire sauce

Worcestershire sauce? What is this

Hold on. Melissa stood up and opened a cupboard. She handed her a small plastic bottle.

Catarina shook a few drops of Worcestershire sauce onto the corner of her plate. She dipped the tip of her finger into it.

It is weird.

Melissa laughed at her.

Quietly they ate. The sunset filled the room and they turned no lights on.

As Catarina ate, she felt something inside her unbind. She exhaled.

I went to a talk today

Yeah?

It was some poets talking

Uh huh

They were talking about love

Yeah?

One poet quoted another poet called Anne Boyer, do you know her?

Melissa shook her head.

She said that Anne Boyer the poet says that romantic love feels like a place where you can have healing, where you can have so many possibilities

Melissa tilted her head. Her hair held around her ears.

She had a phrase I liked, she said it can feel like *a little communism of two.*

Melissa smiled. She considered the phrase.

Show me the image of the earth again

Catarina handed over her phone.

I like it.

I like it too

Receita de Feijão Vegano

Ingredientes

    250g de feijão carioca

    500ml de água

    3 colheres de azeite

    1 cebola picada

    4 dentes de alho

    2 folhas de louro

    1 colher de Worcestershire sauce, versão vegetariana

    Sal

Preparação

Deixe o feijão de molho por 12 horas.

Troque a água do feijão e bote o feijão para cozinhar com as duas folhas de louro na panela de pressão por meia hora ou 45 minutos.

Numa frigideira refogue a cebola picada com o alho em azeite até ficarem dourados.

Acresente a cebola e o alho ao feijão.

Acresente a colher de Worcestershire sauce ao feijão e misture bem.

Cozinhe por 15 minutos.

Melissa stood outside Café Nero at Liverpool Street station drinking a coffee from a disposable cup. Catarina ran towards her.

We are late!

They ran together, Melissa's arm outstretched, the coffee cup full and spilling on her wrist, to Platform 11 where the 19.41 Overground train East was about to leave. They pushed onto the carriage at the last moment and the doors closed against the back of Melissa's coat. Catarina squished herself into a free seat by the window. Next to her a woman in a yellow raincoat looked at her phone. Melissa, who stood in the aisle, read the woman in the yellow raincoat's messages over her head as she typed and retyped them. Catarina pressed her forehead against the glass of the window and watched the houses and the streetlights and the apartment blocks pass. Catarina pointed at two tall and retreating piles of light in the blue lilac sky and said to Melissa –

Those are the towers at the end of our road, I think.

They ran up the steps from the platform through the barriers onto the Upper Clapton road. It was dark. Car wheels spun through the dirty water at the side of the road and it spat onto their faces. The screen at the station said six minutes to eight. Catarina held a newspaper over her head to protect herself from the rain.

Do you know this area?

Melissa shook her head. She looked at her phone screen, wiping the rain off it with her sleeve. It says down here –

They crossed the road and turned onto a narrow residential street. The houses were tall with basements, and steps and stoops leading to their front doors. Through a bay window a woman served pasta into two pasta bowls using a slotted spoon. Two bikes swished past them.

It should be on the left here –

They turned and stopped in front of a tall church building. It was made of an old stone part with stained glass and a steeple adjoining a new square red brick part. A sign at the front read 'Clapton Little Angels Nursery'. Melissa tried to open the front door but it was locked. The lights were off. They listened for the sound of voices.

This is the address?

Melissa checked her phone.

Yes.

Melissa rechecked her phone.

She exhaled.

They stood together in the rain. The newspaper on Catarina's head began disintegrating against her thumb and fingers.

It's two minutes to.

Catarina shivered.

Maybe I've got it wrong. Let me load it again – hold this

Catarina took Melissa's coffee. Rain fell into the gap in the plastic lid. Catarina looked out at the narrow street. Someone walked in their direction. Catarina elbowed Melissa.

Look

The woman in the yellow raincoat walked quickly towards them and then turned suddenly down the side of the church. Water slid off her hood.

Let's go.

The woman in the yellow raincoat walked to the back of the church. She knocked three times on a fire door and disappeared.

When Catarina pushed against the door it opened. They stepped in, surrounded then by the sound of voices.

They settled, cross-legged, in a circle among fifty other people in a room decorated for children. A painting of a zebra with a tiny torso and face the size of a dinner plate was stapled to a display board above Catarina's head. The two people leading the meeting (not the same two as the week before) sat on tiny, child-size stools. When they clapped their hands, the room went silent. One hundred eyes turned in unison and a phone was passed from hand to hand and the founding document was read out loud. The circle exhaled. There was a rustling. The two people on the little stools at the front of the circle cleared their throats.

Ahem –

Listen –

They smiled at each other.

Today there is no agenda

Cheers came from the circle.

Quiet!

Wait –

Today we will be splitting into two groups PROPAGANDA and ACTION

Melissa and Catarina looked at each other.

Catarina followed a small woman with Amy Winehouse hair to a corner of the nursery room. She set two bulging tote bags onto the floor. Four other people with six other bulging tote bags and thirty people without tote bags sat with them.

The small woman with Amy Winehouse hair started to take things out of her bag. A knitting needle. Paint brushes. Blue paint and purple paint and red paint. Green paint. Big metal scissors.

Jenny did you bring the sheets?

Yes.

Excellent.

The small woman with Amy Winehouse hair looked up. She turned to Catarina.

I'm Meena. She/her

Catarina refolded her legs.

I'm Catarina. The same. Also she and her.

Catarina looked around. The woman next to her took off her yellow raincoat. Someone spoke –

Do you want to do the quilt with me again?

And we'll work on the banner.

Yes, let me grab the newspapers I got

Meena took a roll of fabric from one of the tote bags. She began to unroll it. She unrolled and unrolled it. It read, sewn and painted on in a deep purple –

S T O

And then traced in pencil –

P D E P O R T A T I O N S

They spread themselves out along the piece of cloth, taking up the whole centre of the room, tucking bits of newspaper under it and under themselves to protect the floor. Each letter was the size of a person. Catarina joined in, taking the newspapers from the bag someone had brought. *Evening Standard*s from the tube. The front page read 'Nightmare in Brussels'. Absentmindedly, she painted the prime minister's face purple with her brush. Somebody said –

All this shit is good for

A murmur of agreement came from the others.

Wouldn't wipe my arse with it

Catarina listened.

Somebody said, Is this your first meeting?

Me? No, I came last week

Ah

But yes I am new

Welcome

Welcome!

Welcome

Welcome!

Catarina smiled at them. She dipped her brush into the pot and wiped the excess paint onto the newspaper.

I am not a good painter—

That doesn't matter

Oh my god neither am I

How come you came to the meeting?

I was at a protest at the Brazilian embassy before with my flatmate and someone – I don't know if they are here – brought me and my friend

Oh

The Brazilian embassy?

Is that where

Yes I am from Brazil originally and we were protesting the political situation there

It's so fucked

Fucking awful

Catarina nodded. She waited for more questions but none came. She leant over and began to trace the left slope of the A. She moved her hand slowly. Catarina looked at each letter of the banner. In the day-time the room would be filled with children. Across the room she saw Melissa lean into another circle, full of intent. For a moment Catarina closed her eyes. On the floor at one corner of the banner there was a pile of fliers with a papaya on the front and one word: Maricumbia. They had come from someone's bag. Catarina took a flier and put it in her pocket. The sounds of someone's voice saying something in English and Meena saying something in English and all the discussions of all the people in the church that was also a nursery moved over her. Outside, she could hear the rain.

On the train and tube home Catarina asked Melissa what they had talked about in the ACTION working group.

Hacking the Home Office computers

Catarina looked at Melissa.

The week after the clocks changed, and all the magnolias and all the cherry trees in the bougie front gardens of London had blossomed and fallen to the floor – when the days finally began to get long, to linger – Catarina stood in the Homebase on Mile End road. She stood in the glue section. There were many different types of glue. She put two 500ml tins of an industrial-grade adhesive into her basket and then went to the rope section. She looked at the different types of rope. The picture next to one type of cord showed a picture of the cord attaching a car to a tow truck. She put three bundles of cord into her basket. She looked around. She approached a man in a Homebase T-shirt.

Excuse me could you tell me where the zip ties are

Zip ties are aisle 3.

Catarina put four packets of zip ties in her bag. She went back to the glue aisle and put another tin in her bag. The woman at the counter scanned the zip ties and the rope and winked at Catarina. Catarina paid in cash.

King's Cross station was full of families going on their Easter holidays. And families coming home. Police with guns. Thirty minutes before, fifty people gathered in a park nearby where a person in a long white skirt had told them what to do. And then they had dispersed. Meena and a tall person carrying a sports bag walked around the back past the canal and into St Pancras International. They filled the station. Browsing makeup in Boots. Holding suitcases in the queue for the ticket machines. A person in pigtails looking at hair clips in Accessorize. Three people in the queue in Pret. Someone else browsing the moisturisers in Kiehls. A woman with waving hair down her back and a woman with a fringe with two big suitcases going on holiday. As numbers on the clock moved closer to 6.45 a small and hardly perceptible current of the tourist commuter swell moved towards the international terminal gates. The station buzzed. Somebody played the theme from *Amelie* on the piano under the oyster bar and the Tracey Emin neon light sculpture that said *I Want My Time With You*. Catarina and Melissa stood in King's Cross under the big screens, wheeling a suitcase, looking for the train times to Newcastle.

The big clock struck 6.45 and suddenly the people who had been tourists and commuters began to link arms. Their suitcases fell open and placards, megaphones were taken out, and a 10ft banner was unfolded. The chanting began and the chain of bodies blocked the gates. Bundles of rope were passed to people with deft fingers. Tins of glue were opened and zip ties clicked into place. The banner blocked the gates. It read in lilac and deep purple

STOP DEPORTATIONS

The chanting began quiet and unsure at first and then became louder and clearer and bolder. It came from the microphone and people gathered in the chain, in call and response, arms linked and linked and linked. The chorus rang –

No human is illegal

No human is illegal

No human is illegal

Melissa sat down by the gates next to the two women with suitcases. Both wore golden necklaces, one read *Willow* and the other *Agustina* in cursive. They opened their suitcases and began to hand out the placards that had been inside. They held the final one in the air. The sign said:

YOU SHUT OUR BORDERS
WE SHUT YOURS !

Behind Melissa a white lady with dyed brown hair and grey roots holding tickets and a holdall asked a guard why she couldn't get through.

He shook his head at her and gestured at the scene.

Melissa heard Catarina's voice at the microphone –

Nenhum ser humano é ilegal!

Melissa opened her mouth and called with two hundred other voices in response

Nenhum ser humano é ilegal!

No borders! Catarina shouted.

No borders! they called in response.

Melissa looked around her, her mouth moved. She felt Catarina's voice and every single other voice all around her body.

On the way home that night, in the crash and warm dirty air of the Central line, Melissa said

Tell me about your family in Brazil, Catarina

RUA DO BOMFIM

(1989–2014)

Everyone had thought that Sônia would name the baby Laura. Vovó Olga had thought it, palm on her daughter's warm and new stretched stomach; Sônia's older sister, Lúcia, had thought it from her office in São Paulo; Sônia's other older sister, Lygia, had thought it from her office in Rio de Janeiro; Sônia's other other older sister, Lamis, had thought it from her apartment down the hill across the Zona Norte in Recife. Even Miguel, Sônia's husband, had thought it.

Miguel had been sure. Since the day that Sônia told him she had missed her period, he had in his imagination addressed their child *Laura*. During the months of Sônia's pregnancy, he and *Laura* did all kinds of things in his imagination. Her burped her. He held her. He changed her nappies, the first man in his family to do this. Through all the months of Sônia's pregnancy, from February to October of 1989, he waited for his wife to say the name. But she didn't. She stopped mentioning Laura. And once the baby was born, all the way from the hospital bed to the white gate of their house to their bed, she didn't mention Laura once.

Sônia picked a name that they had never discussed because Miguel had told her she should choose whatever name she liked. Two days after her caesarean, in their bed, in their skyblue house she looked down at the nameless baby and pronounced her, with only a small a question in her voice –

Ca
Ca
Catarina

The next evening, the phone in the wide house with the veranda rang. It rang through the living room, through the garden, through the bedrooms, through the hot hot street into the sugar stench of leaking rubbish outside.

Dona Dafne answered. She called to Sônia who came to the phone in a nightdress, the insides of her still unslipping, sewn together.

The voice on the phone said – Congratulations! Querida I am calling to tell you that we would like to offer you, Sônia, Professora Sônia, the permanent lectureship in the Literature Department. Parabéns!

It was news Sônia had been waiting for, had in fact planned her pregnancy around.

Sônia thanked Professor Antônio, the head of department.

He followed quickly with questions – How is the baby? How are you Sônia? We heard it was a difficult birth from Berta the department administrator.

Yes, it was difficult. But she is here, now.

What have you called her

Catarina

A lovely name.

Pause.

I am sorry we have taken so long to call you, but you know we have been unexpectedly busy.

Speaking from his office from the 10th floor of the university building, his hand on his face and in his beard, Professor Antônio said quietly –

There has been a suicide, another suicide. It was the early morning, Ignácio found her when he was setting up his stall. The police came and covered the body but the body was still there and the police were still there when students began arriving in the morning.

Sônia was silent, looking at the wall.

Que horror

That evening Sônia and Miguel ate dinner at the table in the kitchen, sweet pork and mashed manjioca and fried fish in front of them.

Sônia looked at her husband, she said –

There was another suicídio Miguel. From the fifteenth floor, not the eleventh like last time, in the madrugada, the man with the soda stall found her. A student of course. Antônio had to call her parents. Her parents don't live in the city, they're very religious, he said. Seventeen years old. I marked her paper last term on I forget what module, I forget what the paper said but

(breath)

but Professor Antônio said that her parents refused to believe that it was a suicide. He told them it was in all likelihood a suicide, but still they told him, No it must have been an accident, and began to say What a tragic accident May God Protect Her Soul although everyone knows, Miguel, it was even in our day, the department building is the place where you suicide from. I don't know how many times – I don't know why there is not a wire mesh fence or—

Meu deus do ceu, Dona Dafne said, crossing herself over the pan.

In the weeks after Catarina was born everyone visited. Lygia and her husband and her two children and Lúcia and her husband and her two children and Lamis and her daughter Larissa and Miguel's parents and Miguel's brothers and their wives and their children. Her colleagues from the Literature Department. Dona Dafne made everyone lunch – rice, two types of beans, fish or beef and salad. Sônia sat on a stool in the shower. And the water fell all over her and the light from outside fell all over her, all white. Dona Dafne held Catarina.

Sônia went back to work after eight weeks. Miguel drove Sônia from their house in Olinda in his car for an hour and a half over the cobbles down the hill past the big church past the kids in the dirty sea across the bridge to Recife where the traffic stood still, and then inland and west to the university campus. She was still sore in her abdomen and the up and down of the car over the potholes pulled at her stitches. She held onto the inside of the car door.

Desculpa querida

Sônia shook her head.

Go slowly.

Miguel nodded. He could see the university buildings at the end of the road. When they got to the porter, Miguel stopped. Sônia leant across him –

Olá Henrique

Doutora Sônia, parabéns!

Muito obrigada Henrique

A little girl?

Yes

Que alegria. This is your husband?

Yes – Miguel

Congratulations sir

Thank you

Sônia exhaled.

Miguel followed the campus road across the big lawns with the orange earth paths and big trees. There were students everywhere around them. He felt nostalgia press into his chest and swallowed it. He said –

The campus is a classic of Brazilian brutalism, tropical brutalism, it integrates two battling forces: the inevitable advance of human civilisation and the inevitable return to nature.

Sônia was wincing.

He slowed the car outside a fifteen-story oblong tower block. A huge jacaranda tree grew in front of the first five floors as if to guard them, its roots hanging from canopy to asphalt. Miguel continued –

Although of course the philosophy and human sciences building was constructed like this – each discipline on its own floor – by the dictatorship to prevent dialogue between the subjects, a fascistic principle at its core, the violent limitation of knowledge and of intellectual freedoms—

Sônia exhaled – It is where the girl killed herself, this building

Miguel lowered his voice.

That was very tragic.

He stopped the car in front of the Literature building. Sônia reached for her seatbelt, and he turned to face her. He reached for Sônia's hand with his hand. He kissed her on the cheek.

I will see you at 6.

Yes

He squeezed her hand.

Tchau Sônia

Tchau querido

When she got to her office Sônia dialled their home number straight away. The girl they had hired to look after Catarina – a niece or grand-niece of Dona Dafne – answered the phone.

Maria-Luiza?

... Doutora Sônia?

I want to speak to Catarina

What?

Just – put the phone up to her mouth

But

So I can hear her breathe.

Every day Sônia did this. Sometimes she did it four or five or seven times a day. She ran back from lectures to her office to call Maria-Luiza and sometimes she called back straight away after hanging up. She said Olá and Maria-Luiza knew what to do. She did not tell Miguel because he would feel sorry for her and this would make her angry and then she might say something nasty to him that she would regret. She did not tell Lamis because Lamis would tell her it was a mental disorder and that she should try talking therapy with a psychiatrist. Only Maria-Luiza knew and they never spoke about it.

Often, she got halfway through dialling her home phone number and stopped, terrified to hear Maria-Luiza's answer. TV static filled Sônia's mind, replacing every image she had of the future. Sônia was scared that she would not survive whatever Maria-Luiza said to her.

When Catarina was three years old Miguel and Sônia sent her to a little nonprofit school in Madalena in the Zona Norte of Recife. It was the school Tia Lamis had chosen for her own daughter, Larissa, and many of Tia Lamis' psychiatrist colleagues sent their children there also. Most of the parents were journalists or artists or teachers or academics who liked it because of its explicit adherence to the pedagogical methods of Paulo Freire. There were no exams and every day the children felt the sun on their heads in the garden or the sandpit and were told they could ask any question of any of the teachers at any time. Catarina did not play with the children her own age. She sat with a teacher, or alone, feet digging into the sand.

On Thursdays there was maracatú percussion and on Fridays story-telling of local folktales by a man with a guitar who explained to the children that Brazil was a culture with roots in Africa and Europe and the pre-colonial Americas and that they should take pride in this. And after school Dona Silvia, who cooked and cleaned and babysat for Tia Lamis, picked them up and walked them back to Tia Lamis' apartment where they could watch Disney films on their big TV and if Larissa had a friend over Catarina would hover near them or sit at the table looking at Larissa's homework.

Tia Lamis and Larissa lived in an eighteen-storey apartment block with a playground. From their fourteenth-floor apartment Larissa could see when the other children who lived in the apartment block were on the climbing frame or swings.

By eight years old, Larissa could identify them by the tiny tops of heads. Catarina, who was six, stood next to her, on her toes. Larissa pointed –

That's Julia, that's Isadora, that's João and that's Mateus.

Larissa grabbed Catarina's hand. She called to the kitchen –

Dona Silvia, we are going to the playground, Julia is there and Isadora

Dona Silvia was cooking –

Come back in ten minutes exactly please, food is almost ready.

Catarina let go of Larissa's hand. Her chest began to twist.

Larissa opened the apartment door and called an elevator.

Catarina stood in the doorway to the apartment. She kept her feet on the inside.

Larissa leant forwards to push the lift button with her nose.

The lift doors opened. Larissa looked at her. Coming?

Catarina shook her head.

She watched the lift doors shut and felt her ribs untwist.

She listened for the sound of the phone.

Catarina and Larissa were eating at the little table in the kitchen when Tia Lamis came home. Tia Lamis got two plates from the cupboard and sat down next to them. She gestured to Dona Silvia.

Dona Silvia sit down with us sit down, none of the formalities, please

Dona Silvia sat down.

When Tia Lamis asked what they had done that day and Larissa told her that she had gone to play with her friends in the playground, and that she had come back after ten minutes for dinner.

Dona Silvia interrupted — *twelve* minutes.

Catarina watched Tia Lamis.

Tia Lamis smiled and carried on eating. She opened her mouth to speak.

Has João's hair grown out? That haircut his mother gave him was very uneven.

At that moment the intercom buzzed.

Tia Lamis stood.

It will be your mother and father.

Tia Lamis had two ex-husbands and a terrible dangerous habit of driving alone in the dark while smoking, which was why Sônia had told Catarina she was never to get in the car with her. Tia Lamis always wore big busy patterned dresses with comfy sandals. Tia Lamis and Larissa's apartment had a living room, two bedrooms, an office, a kitchen, three bathrooms and ex-servants' quarters, which were now a small laundry room. At night, from the balcony, you could see the lights of a thousand other balconies, and during the day, between two buildings you could just about see the sea. The living room had a big sofa and big television for watching movies on VHS and novelas. And in their kitchen here was a jar full of chocolates that Larissa was allowed to help herself to. Larissa's bedroom was so full of toys there was barely space for her bed. Tia Lamis let her have all the pink Barbies that Sônia would not allow Catarina to have.

It was Tia Lamis who had the pictures of Laura on the table in the living room. Who had so many pictures of her face always looking like her sisters, always young-looking and in black and white – apart from in one photograph, in colour, Laura, holding baby Larissa.

Tia Laura. Your mother was always her favourite, Tia Lamis had said, smiling, when she caught little Catarina looking at it.

Sônia continued calling from her office landline, wherever Catarina was, the school receptionist getting to know her daily excuses and made up reasons well. She continued teaching at the university. Miguel continued to work as an engineer for the Pernambuco state government. Maria-Luiza moved south with her boyfriend. Dona Dafne left and moved to Natal because her son had had a baby and they hired someone new and after two years she left and they hired someone else and after three more years they hired someone else, a woman in her sixties, called Dona Flor. In 1994 Sônia and Miguel voted for the Workers' Party; in 1998 they voted for the Workers' Party and in 2002 they got the government they had been hoping for.

vanishes heavily

Catarina was the only child of her parents, Sônia and Miguel. Born in October 1989.

Professora Sônia was the last of five daughters
  Laura (dead)
  Lúcia (Rio)
  Lygia (São Paulo)
  Lamis
  Sônia

The story was that the paternal grandparents of the five daughters, Catarina's great-grandparents, had come from a small town in the interior of the state of Pernambuco in the Northeast of Brazil. Sugar cane land. (And before it had been sugar cane land the small town had been rainforest, home of the Pankará.) This was where the sítio was, where the family still gathered for New Year's Eve and other family celebrations, the sítio that their old friend, the grandpa-looking man, Wagner, looked after for them. Wagner who they paid well and spoke to like long lost family, who had watched Sônia and her sisters and her cousins grow up, whose sons and younger brothers Vovó Olga had watched grow up herself.

Over chocolate and sweets on the sofa in her apartment, Tia Lamis told Catarina and Larissa that Vovô Lipo's side of the family had been lawyers and before that they had been landowners. Tia Lamis said that Catarina and Larissa's great-great-grandfather had come over from Portugal in a boat. The story goes, Tia Lamis said, ashing her cigarette, that he arrived in the South of Brazil and moved North because that was where the land was cheap. The story goes that he died suddenly of a heart attack and only then did they discover that he had a second family in the South. A travelworn woman had arrived at the funeral claiming to be his wife, brandishing letters from him, a marriage certificate from the registry office in Santos, São Paulo, and two adult sons dressed immaculately in black tailored suits. Or so the story goes.

Tia Lamis said that Catarina's great-grandfather on the paternal side had bought a small farm because farmland in the Northeast was cheap. There were so many fires on the sugar fields in those years. Tia Lamis did not say what he had done with the land or whether he had bought, sold or owned people who were enslaved. Just that he had made the family rich. And his children sold the land to a bigger landowner, for sugar cane, keeping a small part of it for the sítio.

It was one of these sons, Catarina and Larissa's great-grandfather, Tia Lamis and Sônia's grandfather, who went to the city. He trained as a lawyer at the law faculty in Recife, set up by decree from Dom Pedro I himself, and when he was done he stayed in the city and bought a city house and married a city woman. And his two sons, Catarina and Larissa's grandfather, Vovô Lipo, and his brother, became lawyers too. And it was while Vovô Lipo and his brother were studying to become lawyers that they had met Vovó Olga, a small woman descended from Litvak Jews, schoolteachers who had fled Russia in the pogroms at the turn of the century. Vovó Olga was the only woman in the law faculty, although she never got her diploma because in her third year of law school she was pregnant. Oh, it was very scandalous at the time, Tia Lamis said, and if you ever ask your grandmother about it she will simply pretend not to hear you.

Vovó Olga and her husband brought up their daughters discussing the law and the constitution and the meaning of justice at the dinner table. Vovó Olga read Marx and Engels and Hegel and José Martí and corresponded with women's groups in Cuba. Their house was a dusty mess of spider plants and schoolwork and the five daughters – Laura, the eldest, who at sixteen had cut her hair off and insisted on smoking cigarillos just like her father; Lygia and Lúcia, who were so good at exams and loved to quarrel; Lamis, who Vovó Olga had decided to give the Arabic name, made collages and was in the children's theatre group; and Sônia, the baby, caçula, Vovó Olga's most beloved accident. Everybody knew us, everybody, Tia Lamis said.

Vovô Lipo, father of the five daughters, had been a lawyer for the sugar cane workers' unions. And then he had been the leftwing mayor of the town in the interior where the family sítio was and then the leftwing governor of the state of Pernambuco. Sugar cane land. In his memoirs Vovô Lipo says that he had never been a communist although he had certainly been described as a communist by the opposition and, to some people, that had been the selling point.

Vovô Lipo would be the leftwing governor of the State of Pernambuco three times. As history books say, in 1962 he was elected by a coalition of rural sugar cane workers, urban workers and the leftwing bourgeoise of which he was himself a member. Vovô Lipo's great promise was land reform and literacy. Workers, who were at that point tenants of the sugar cane landowners, wanted to own their own land. They wanted to work their own land. After five hundred years of serfdom and slavery and early deaths and beatings and eating dirt to try to die (approximately: generation after generation after generation after generation after generation after generation after generation after generation after generation after generation after generation after generation after generation after generation after generation after generation after generation) they wanted their own land. No masters and no slaves. And they wanted education. More than half of Pernambuco was illiterate. There were fires over the sugar cane fields.

When Vovô Lipo became the new governor of the State of Pernambuco he was strong in his body; thick limbed and thick furrow-browed and thirty-nine years old. For two years, he governed with his sleeves rolled up and, for the first time in the history of the state, union leaders stepped into the governor's palace. Feet on the marble. The landowners called him a communist.

Meanwhile, across the continent, 1000 kilometres south and 2000 kilometres inland the president resigned. This was a surprise to Vovô Lipo and a surprise to Vovó Olga and surprise to the vice president, a man known as Jango, Vovô Lipo's personal friend, a man the newspapers also called a communist.

To Vovó Olga's disappointment, Vice President Jango was not a communist. Nevertheless, as she listened to his inauguration on the radio, Vovó Olga felt a love of her country rise in her chest. She looked at her daughters and felt her incredible good luck to live in that time in history, to have children who she loved in that country that she loved and that could only get better.

Jango promised land reform and he promised literacy. And literacy for the people meant the people could vote. The people descended from the five million enslaved Africans who had been kidnapped and brought across the Atlantic to cut sugar cane and log rainforest trees and clean and cook to make the country rich. The people who remained of, and had descended from, the Aikanã, Aikewara, Akuntsu, Amanayé, Amondawa, Anacé, Anambé, Aparai, Apiaká, Apinayé, Apurinã, Aranã, Arapaso, Arapium, Arara, Arara da Volta Grande de Xingu, Arara do Rio Amônia, Arara do Rio Branco, Arara Shawãdawa, Arara Vermelha, Arabóia, Araweté, Arikapú, Aruá, Ashaninka, Asurini do Tocantins, Asurini do Xingu, Atikum, Avá-Canoeiro, Awa Guajá, Awa Isolados, Aweti, Bakairi, Banawá, Baniwa, Bará, Barasana, Baré, Bororo, Borari, Cabeceira do Rio Camanaú, Canela Apanyekrá, Canela, Ramkokamekrá, Cara Preta, Chamacoco, Charrua, Chiquitano, Cinta Larga, Dâw, Deni, Desana, Djeoromitxí, Enawenês-nawês, Fulkaxó, Fulni-ô, Galibi-Oiapoque, Galibi-Marworno, Gamela, Gavião Akrãtikatêjê, Gavião Kykatejê, Gavião Parakatêjê, Gavião Pykopjê, Guajajara, Guarani Kaiowá, Guarani Mbya, Guarani Ñandeva, Guarasugwe, Guató, Hixkaryana, Huni Kuin, Hupda, Ikolen, Ikpeng, Ingarikó, Iny Karajá, Iranxe Manoki, Isolado do Igarapé Tapada, Isolados do Tanaru, Isolados Akurio, Isolados akuriyó do Rio Mataware/Alto Jari, Isolados Amauaka, Isolados Bananeira, Isolados Cabeceira do Rio Camanaú, Isolados Capot/Nhinore, Isolados Cabeceira do Rio Acre, Isolados da Cabeceira do Rio Cuniuá, Isolados da Ilha do Bananal, Isolados de Mão de onça, Isolados do Alto Jutaí, Isolados do Alto do Rio Canumã, Isolados do Alto Rio Humaitá, Isolados do Alto Rio Ipitinga, Isolados do Alto Rio Jatapu, Isolados do Alto Rio Panamá, Isolados do Alto Tapajós, Isolados do Alto Tarauacá, Isolados do Amajari, Isolados do Arama/Inauini, Isolados do Auaris/Fronteira, Isolados do Baixo Jatapu/ Oriente, Isolados do Baixo Rio Cauaburis, Isolados do Bararati, Isolados do Cautário, Isolados do Igarapé Alerta, Isolados do Igarapé Amburus,

Isolados do Igarapé Bafuanã, Isolados do Igarapé Bom Jardim, Isolados do Igarapé Cravo, Isolados do Igarapé do Anjo, Isolados do Igarapé do Natal, Isolados do Igarapé Flecheira, Isolados do Igarapé Inferno, Isolados do Igarapé Ipiaçava, Isolados do Igarapé Lambança, Isolados do Igarapé Maburrã, Isolados do Igarapé Nauá, Isolados do Igarapé Pacutinga, Isolados do Igarapé Papavo, Isolados do Igarapé Patiá, Isolados do Igarapé Pedro Lopes, Isolados do Igarapé Preto, Isolados do Igarapé Recreio, Isolados do Igarapé São Pedro, Isolados do Igarapé São Salvador, Isolados do Igarapé Taboca do Alto Tarauacá, Isolados do Igarapé Tabocal, Isolados do Igarapé Tapada, Isolados do Igarapé Waranaçu, Isolados do Igarapé Xinane, Isolados do Iriri, Isolados do Iriri Novo, Isolados do Itaquaí, Isolados do Ituna/Itatá, Isolados do Jandiatuba, Isolados do Médio Jatapu, Isolados do Parauari, Isolados do Pitinga/Nhamunda-Mapuera, Isolados do Pontal, Isolados do Rio Amapari/Alto Oiapoque, Isolados do Rio Bóia/Curuena, Isolados do Rio Cachorro/Cachorrinho, Isolados do Rio Candeias, Isolados do Rio Citaré, Isolados do Rio Coari, Isolados do Rio Coti, Isolados do Rio Cuniuá, Isolados do Rio dos Peixes, Isolados do Rio Esquerdo, Isolados do Rio Fresco, Isolados do Rio Iquê, Isolados do Rio Itaquaí, Isolados do Rio Jamanxim, Isolados do Rio Jaminawá, Isolados do Rio Kaxpakuru/Igarapé Água Fria, Isolados do Rio Maici, Isolados do Rio Parauari, Isolados do Rio Pardo, Isolados do Rio Pedra, Isolados do Rio Quixito, Isolados do Rio Tapirapé, Isolados do Rio Tea, Isolados do Rio Tenete Marques, Isolados do Rio Uaupés, Isolados do Riozinho do Alto Envira, Isolados do São Pedro, Isolados dos Iguarapés Presído e Jurutí, Isolados Hi-Merimã, Isolados Ingarune, Isolados Kaidjuwa, Isolados Kanamari, Isolados Karapawyana, Isolados Katawixi, Isolados Kawahiva do Rio Pardo, Isolados Kayapó Pituiaro, Isolados Kayapó Pu'ro, Isolados Korubo, Isolados Masko, Isolados Mengra Mrari, Isolados Mihua, Isolados na Serra da Previdência, Isolados na TI Arara do Rio Branco, Isolados na TI Aripuanã, Isolados na TI Xikrin do Cateté, Isolados no Igarapé Tiradentes, Isolados no Norte da TI Zoró, Isolados Parawa u, Isolados Priripkura, Isolados Piriti, Isolados Pu'ro, Isolados São Tomé, Isolados Sapanahua, Isolados Surucucu/Kataroa, Isolados Tupi Kawahib, Isolados Yakarawakta, Isolados Yanomami,

Jamamadi, Jaraqui, Jarawara, Javaé, Jenipapo-Kanindé, Jiahui, Jiripancó, Juma, Ka'apor, Kadiwéu, Kaimbé, Kaingang, Kaixana, Kalabaça, Kalankó, Kalapalo, Kamaiurá, Kamba, Kambeba, Kambiwá, Kanamari, Kanindé, Kanoê, Kantaruré, Karajá do Norte, Karapanã, Karapotó, Karipuna de Rondônia, Karipuna do Amapá, Kariri, Kariri-Xokó, Karo, Karauzu, Kassupá, Katuenayana, Katukina do Rio Biá, Katukina do Rio Biá Kamanawa, Katukina Pano, Katxuyana, Kawahivo Isolado do Rio Muqui, Kawaiwete, Kaxarari, Kaxixó, Kinikinau, Kiriri, Kisêdjê, Koiupanká, Kokama, Koripako, Korubo, Kotiria, Krahô, Krahô-Kanela, Krenak, Krenyê, Krikatí, Kubeo, Kuikuro, Kujubim, Kulina, Kulina Pano, Kumaruara, Kuntanawa, Kuruaya, Kwazá, Macuxi, Makuna, Makurap, Manchineri, Maraguá, Marubo, Mashko Isolados do Rio Chandless, Mashko Isolados do Rio Envira, Mashko Isolados do Rio Iaco, Massaco Isolados, Matipu, Matis, Matsés, Maxakali, Mebêngôkre Kayapó, Mebêngôkre Kayapó Gorotire, Mebêngôkre Kayapó Kararaô, Mebêngôkre Kayapó Kôkraimôrô, Mebêngôkre Kayapó Kuben Kran Krên, Mebêngôkre Kayapó Mekrãgnoti, Mebêngôkre Kayapó Metyktire, Mehinako, Menky Manoki, Migueleno, Miranha, Mirity-tapuya, Munduruku, Mura, Nadöb, Nahuká, Nambikwara, Nambikwara Alakatesu, Nambikwara Erihataunsu, Nambikwara Hahaintesu, Nambikwara Halotesu, Nambikwara Hoskokosu, Nambikwara Idalamare, Nambikwara Ilaklore, Nambikwara Kalunhwasu, Nambikwara Katitawlu, Nambikwara Kithaulu, Nambikwara Latundê, Nambikwara Mamaindê, Nambikwara Manairisu, Nambikwara Manduka, Nambikwara Negarotê, Nambikwara Qualitsu, Nambikwara Sabanê, Nambikwara Sararé, Nambikwara Sawentesu, Nambikwara Sayulikisu, Nambikwara Tawandê, Nambikwara Uaihlatisu, Nambikwara Waikisu, Nambikwara Wakalitesu, Nambikwara Wasusu, Naruvotu Nawa, Nukini, Ofaié, Oro Win, Pankará, Pankararé, Pankararu, Pankaru, Parakanã, Paresí, Parintintin, Patamona, Paumari, Payayá, Pipipã, Pirahã, Pira-tapuya, Pitaguary, Potiguara, Puyanawa, Rikbaktsa, Rio Branquinho, Rio Coti, Sakurabiat, Sapará, Saterés Mawé, Siriano, Surucucu/Wathou, Surui Paiter, Suruwaha, Tabajara, Tapayuna, Tapeba, Tapuia, Tariana, Taurepang, Tembé, Tenharin,

Terena, Ticuna, Tingui Botó, Torá, Tremembé, Truká, Trumai, Tsohom-dyapa, Tukano, Tumbalalá, Tunayana, Tupaiú, Tupari, Tupinambá, Tupiniquim, Turiwara, Tuxá, Tuxi, Tuyuka, Umutina, Uru-Eu-Wau-Wau, Waimiri Atoari, Waiwai, Waiwai Karapawyana, Waiwai Mawayana, Waiwai Xerewyana, Wajãpi, Wajuru, Wapichana, Warekena, Wari', Wassu, Wauja, Wayana, Witoto, Xakribá, Xavante, Xerente, Xetá, Xikrin (Mebêngôkre), Xinane, Xipaya, Xokleng, Xokó, Xukuru, Xukuru-Kariri, Yaminawá, Yanomami, Yanomami Ninam, Yanomami Sanuma, Yanomami Yanomae, Yanomami Yanomami, Yawalapiti, Yawanawá, Ye-kwana, Yudja, Yuhupde, Zo'é, Zoró who had survived

(this is this is what happened)

There was a family story. Catarina had heard it in parts, from Tia Lamis, Tia Lygia and Vovô Olga, and from the history books.

On the night of the 31st of March 1964, the military surrounded the presidential palace in Brasilia.

That night the military surrounded the governor's palace in Recife.

That night Vovô Lipo was put in prison.

But that afternoon Vovó Olga had taken their children and she left the governor's palace. She took her children back to their family house and pulled off the dustsheets. And when the military came and when they asked her, guns in their hands, guns along the length of their torsos, if she was harbouring enemies of the state in her house, communists like her husband, she said to them that she would never tell. She kept her chin high and her voice did not shake. Her ancestors had survived worse. The military police stepped through her house. Boots on the tiled floor. Her husband was not at home. Her cook and her children were in their beds. Her youngest, Sônia, was five years old.

Seven years later, the military police came again. They asked her, guns in their hands, guns along the length of their torsos, if she was harbouring enemies of the state in her house. Communists like her daughter. Vovó Olga clenched her lips and mouth at the sound of the name. *Laura*. This time they hit her when she did not speak. Their rifle butts made bruises on her belly and her breasts. She said she would never tell. They pulled her out onto the street, where she did not trip over the cobbles. They shouted, Where is Laura? Where is your communist daughter? Terrorista. She clenched her whole body. She said she would never tell, and this time she shouted it. Every neighbour heard her say it and her two youngest daughters heard her say it from their beds. Every neighbour and her two youngest daughters heard the military police beat her in the cobbled street. Vovó Olga did not know where Laura was. Vovó Olga would have killed a man to know where in the wide and infinite world her eldest daughter was.

Vovô Lipo was not killed in prison. He fled for Paris, where he lived apart from his wife and his daughters for fifteen years. Vovô Lipo came back to Recife after the amnesty in 1979, which protected him from prosecution just as it protected the generals and the torturers. And, when state elections resumed in 1986, Vovô Lipo was elected governor of the state of Pernambuco for the second time. Sugar cane land. He rolled his sleeves up. He was a hero. His hair was grey. His wife slept in another room. The sugar mills had been industrialised, machines raked the earth. The unions weren't asking for land reform anymore. It was true now that everyone could vote, although not everyone was literate. 1994 he was re-elected again.

There were many history books about Vovô Lipo and some statues of him and one street named after him. And although none of his daughters ever ran for elected office, of his nieces two became leftwing politicians at state level, and one a senator; significantly, none of them were communists either.

And Laura? Laura had come back too.

Miguel was the last of three brothers
  Roberto Carlos (Canadá)
  Reginaldo (São Paulo)
  Miguel

And they were from the South. To Catarina's child ears they spoke with southern accents, crisp and proudly European with unlisped *sss* sounds spoken from authoritative, no nonsense lips.

There was no family story of how they had got to São Paulo, Brazil. All that Miguel could tell his daughter Catarina was what his father had told him – that back then the family had been poor. Their names were Portuguese but they had always been there; they were Brazilian. When she was old enough to ask for stories, Miguel repeated to his daughter what his father told him. Miguel's grandfather had worked on the coffee farms. He had not owned or bought or sold enslaved people but he had beaten them and by the time he was old he was no longer poor. He had hated Getúlio Vargas and loved the bandeirantes. His sons had moved to the big cosmopolitan city, São Paulo, where they had studied to become a lawyer, an engineer and a doctor. The engineer was Miguel's father, Vovô Rodrigo, or, as he was more commonly known, o Libanês. O Libanês had been tall with dark hair and had been given his nickname because of the large Lebanese population in city. While o Libanês was studying he took up running at the main athletics club in the city, the German club, which at that time (1938) was draped in swastikas. O Libanês was a talented track athlete and he was celebrated at the German club. His photograph was on the wall in the lobby of the club and this is what he pointed to when the club guards stopped him and asked him if he had Black or Jewish blood.

O Libanês met and married Vovó Alícia at the sports club social. Upper-class Vovó Alícia liked to tell people she was born in Lisbon. Like his father, o Libanês had three sons. And like his father, the coffee farm manager who had beaten poor Black people and retired rich, o Libanês had beaten his wife. Perhaps for being richer and lighter skinned than him, perhaps just because he wanted to. During the day, o Libanês the engineer built roads. For fifteen years his family moved to and from São Paulo, the big and brutalist city, and travelled Brazil building the motorway network necessary to transport trucks and tools and cars and men to the interior of the country and iron and coffee and sugar and gold out of the interior to the ports.

O Libanês's third son, Miguel, turned out soft. Liked his mother too much, cried when they cut his hair. Didn't like sports. O Libanês regretted that he had such a child and hated Vovó Alícia for producing him. He said as much out loud to her. And she said out loud to her husband that she hated him right back. She hated being away from her friends and their parties in the city, she hated the poor towns with dirt roads and dirty people he made her live in and she hated how in every new place she had to find a new maid, and the new maids who uneducated creatures who didn't know the first thing about making flan or the right way to wash silk and further to that they never followed her instructions. Miguel was five when his father asked him what time the clock across the street said, and Miguel replied, What clock? and his mother had slapped him on the cheek and said, Miguel don't be insolent, and Miguel had said, What clock? and his brothers had laughed at him and o Libanês had said, Oh not this again Miguel and Miguel had said, crying, No I really cannot see the clock. Miguel was seven when they realised he needed glasses. Miguel was sixteen when they moved to the North as o Libanês was overseeing a new infrastructure project, the Transamazônica, the road that would eventually connect Acre to Belém, that would open and know the dark heart of the country. Miguel was sixteen and two days when he decided he would never live in the South again.

Miguel agreed to study engineering but in Recife and not São Paulo, where o Libanês and his wife were returning. At university Miguel grew his hair. It was the 70s and skinny boys like him were in. He joined the student movement against the dictatorship because all his friends were part of the student movement and because the dictatorship was run by southern strongmen like his father. He let his southern accent slip and dissolve when he spoke. *Shhh.* He allowed his sentences to take the lilting rhythm of the Northeast and the pronoun tu. He met a polyglot literature student called Sônia, who was the sister of an infamous revolutionary and the daughter of a famous leftist politician who had been exiled in Paris – the kind of people his father believed should be shot. Sônia and Miguel began living together. He met her mother. In those years, when the dictatorship seemed to finally be ending and Laura was back, Miguel believed his wife was on the threshold of happiness.

In 1986 with their decent professional salaries, they bought a house. It was the most beautiful most Northeastern Brazilian house you could imagine. It was not in Recife, the port city with the university campus, but to the north over the rivers in the mangroves, in the old town, Olinda.

The house was on the hill. With one wall on the Rua do Bomfim and another wall on the parallel street. It was perhaps a century old and the veranda and the balustrades were crumbling. Woodworms had eaten the roof and it was about to cave in. Only a couple drunk on the hope and energy and optimism of democracy and sureness that things could only get better would have bought a house like that. A couple who had faced no tragedy that did not make them stronger, no grief they could not overcome. Forgiveness the size of the earth. Laura had seen the house, had spoken about it in the slow manner that she had, You should paint it blue like the sea and the sky, she had said. It looks like work, Lúcia had said and Lygia had agreed. Lamis thought they were crazy – they could have had an apartment with air conditioning and a garage for parking. But Miguel was an engineer and over two or three years he planned to rebuild it. And every wall would be painted white and every shutter, every beam, every wooden part of it would be painted blue. A house the colour of the sky that was always as blue and as bright as the sun could make it.

The garden still had trees – mango trees, palm trees, banana trees – and behind them the old veranda ran continuously around two sides of the building. This they would paint white. Put new wicker chairs there for hosting and drinking beers in in the evenings. The veranda was shaded by the roof, and from the shade you could see down the hill to the sea, and beyond that to the skyscrapers and the tower blocks of the city of Recife.

The windows of the house the colour of the sky had no glass. There were the blue shutters and above those there was a rectangle of air, and inside of that an iron strip twisted in an ornamental shape. The street sounds were always in the house, and the house sounds were in the street and the bedroom sounds were in the street, and the street smells and the street warm was always in the house and, each evening, the yellow street nighttime came into the bedrooms. The only separated part of the house was the basement. Perhaps they paused to feel some horror at the basement, which had once been slave quarters. They turned its cool and lightless rooms into the kitchen and a utility room.

They bought the house despite the long commute into the city, despite the mosquitoes and despite the upkeep. Back then Olinda was the place where the artists and squatters and anarchists lived. It was where they had gone for subversive meetings during the dictatorship and now that that time was over forever they regarded it fondly. All up the steep slope of the hill houses stood, big and small and old and with their walls against the street and their shutters open to the street, a quilted rainbow chaos, only bright colours and on every corner colonial churches heavy with gold plundered from other parts of the continent and contorted into the shapes of angel heads and wings. A horizon of palm trees and cactus fingers, Juliet balconies and Iberian, North African-looking spires. No, this was not São Paulo.

The house was part of history. The whole street was part of history, the whole of the hill was a World Heritage Site, protected by none other than UNESCO. That hill was said to be the best carnival in the whole of Brazil – the least gentrified, the least policed carnival that lasted for months, full of street art and artisans and Bohemians and queers smoking mellow homegrown marijuana.

This is how the story goes –

Oh! Linda! A beautiful place to build a town! the Portuguese colonialist Duarte Coelho said of the hill from his ship in the sea, calling with his words the settlement into being.

It is a myth, Sônia would say if you asked her, It is a retroactive projection of love and the subjective perception of the beauty of Olinda by the Olindenses of today who romanticise where they are from.

(This is the story)

Catarina and Larissa play cards on the 31st of December 2002, the night before the inauguration of the new president from the Workers' Party. They are thirteen and fifteen. They've been playing cards for days, adding new packs so that the canasta game doesn't end and the runs of cards hardly fit on the table. They say to the adults that they will keep playing until the new year strikes at midnight. To Catarina the idea of the moment of year change staggering across the planet is like science fiction. Catarina gets up only for mealtimes and to jump into the plastic pool when she is too hot. Catarina has never spent so many days without her mother. It is only allowed because she is with Tia Lamis and Vovó Olga and Tia Lygia, who drove them all there. She has spoken to her mother on the phone every morning and every night before returning to the white table to play canasta with Larissa. The sítio extends below them, matted and dry.

Sônia and Miguel have been in the city all week but are now getting in the car ready to drive four hours across the sugar cane fields to the sítio. Tia Lygia, who only has sons, indulges her nieces' anti-social card playing. Catarina is such clever girl and so polite and so pretty, and it is so nice to see her playing with her cousin Larissa when she is so shy. Tia Lamis thinks they should play with their other cousins who are staying in the house next door but Catarina calls Larissa back when she leaves the card table. How will we get everything ready in time? Tia Lúcia says, cuticles in her mouth, and Tia Lamis shrugs, lighting a cigarette. That is a terrible habit, Lygia says.

Your turn.
Your turn.

From their card table, which they have positioned under the lychee tree at the back of the concrete house, Catarina and Larissa listen for the sound of dry city tyres on the dirt road. The first car arrives at 1pm. Tia Lygia's grown up son. And at 2.30pm Tio Zeca's grown up grand-children Júlio and Janice. They slam their car doors and shout their greetings. Let us play music! Let us play music! Janice says.

Battered and new cars fill the drive through the afternoon. They come from the airport and from the city. Some go to the house on the lot next door which their cousins own. Catarina and Larissa watch as each boot is unloaded, as their cousins and tias and tios stretch their legs, greet the groundskeeper Wagner, greet each other – Catarina and Larissa rising for hugs and kisses – lock their cars, and disappear into the house for beers or to unpack or to change their clothes.

The house fills.

It is like a *Home Alone* film or a Gabriel García Márquez novel. Quintessentially, continentally American. Forty of fifty of them traipse and run across the sítio in and out of the house and the lot next door and the open gate, chasing children and guiding parking cars. The men are either topless or wearing button up shirts with combed hair. A child runs between the houses holding a bucket of shrimps. Everyone is there: Biso, Tio Zeca and his children – the senator will be in Brasilia of course – Tia Lygia's son's latest baby. Someone's wife is breastfeeding while talking on the house phone. Tia Lúcia's sons play dominó around a white plastic table. Small children run through low branches and into the undergrowth. Hats and bikinis and bottles of mosquito repellent appear on every surface. Poema Sujo, German poetry, the plays of Agosto Boal appear on every surface. The TV is on. The inside is buzzing and outside is buzzing with the sound of electric lights, the sound of the kitchen plates, the sound of insects in the trees that touch the ground. It is about to get dark.

Your teeth will fall out, someone's husband says.
If you eat this much sugar

When their cousin Oskar asks if he can join Catarina tells him no because he always cheats. When little Vitória asks if she can join Larissa says no, because she is too young, but she can watch. Vitória sits on Larissa's lap. They keep eating sweets. The adults fill the room around the television holding beers and babies. Somewhere a dog is barking. Tia Lúcia runs between the rooms and chairs and tables in her silver dress and lipstick. The night comes.

Larissa nudges her cousin, You are getting chocolate on the cards.

Catarina licks the back of the queen of spades, accidentally revealing its face to Larissa.

Larissa squints at it in the darklight.

Catarina says – So are you.

Larissa licks her fingers. She places a six in the middle of the table.

What time does it start?

The inauguration does not happen until tomorrow.

They are going to get really drunk

Larissa nods. Really drunk.

They keep playing. The adults have not noticed that they are not dressed. Catarina and Larissa sit in silence playing cards. Eventually Sônia and Miguel's car arrives. The adults open more beer, the first champagne, brought by Janice who was in Europe recently. Tia Lygia protests, No not yet! You are not all dressed yet! but they open it anyway. Tia Lamis moves through the house, holding a cigarette, to the kitchen, where her speech becomes audible again from their card table under the lychee tree. They hear her offer Wagner champagne, A glass? they hear her say, And what about your wife? Take the bottle? Because it is today, because it is this great occasion –

On the veranda Wagner's wife Carolina brings out the cakes and pudims and fruit. Back in the kitchen she wipes her hands on a cloth and drinks the champagne from a crystal glass. After all is this great victory not hers also? (This Brazil will be a new Brazil)

Lúcia's husband Nelson walks out of the light towards the card table. He drinks from a can of beer; he is not dressed yet. He slams the wet beer can and then two hands on the green tablecloth, disorganising the neat fanning cards which they have been arranging for days. He speaks too loudly –

So here you are
Meninas –

Let me tell you a story
Let me Let me tell you

Ei – (clap clap clapclapclap)

Lúcia approaches the card table and the dominó table and grabs a child from the floor –

You are none of you dressed! She is in a silver dress, plum lipstick on. She claps, two adults turn from the television to look at her. She turns to them –

It is 11pm already! And I have made this whole feast for you and you are not dressed. Tá na hora Tá na hora!

Suddenly – the adults disperse. Small children are brought in from the branches of trees. Larissa puts on mascara. Catarina locks the bathroom door and looks in the mirror, pulls a little moisturiser through her moving hair. How many minutes how many minutes until midnight, Oskar is asking. Little Vitória is redressed in a white dress. Catarina watches Miguel run a comb through his hair. She watches Sônia put on perfume. Someone is shouting – I can't find my bracelets. Vovó Olga and her brother Tio Sílvio sit on the sofa, legs crossed. They have been dressed for hours, since the daylight. Tio Sílvio holds a crystal glass.

At 11.50pm Larissa and Catarina sit to resume their game of canasta on the plastic table under the lychee tree behind the house. Something is making a static buzzing sound – cicadas or electricity touching water. They're wearing white dresses. Larissa is covered in mosquito repellent and a single spritz of Tia Lamis' perfume. Catarina looks at her cousin in her white dress with her combed brown hair. She looks at the adults who are moving, chaotic and loud. A child comes to sit in Catarina's lap. She lifts them up and between her crossed legs. She picks up her cards.

It is your turn Larissa.

Two minutes!

Everyone is there. The adults push against each other, all the doors are open, children cover every surface. Tio Sílvio stands but there is no hallowed silence for him – they are too noisy, too jubilant, too dancing (they must be 200 kilometres from the sea) – they clink their glasses and the fireworks of other families with other early watches begin to crack outside, the trees heave to touch the ground, it is hot and windless and dark except under the lights where their bodies move the air. Everyone is wearing white.

One minute!

How many years have we waited for this?
Crash clink Crash. They are in the new millennium, ten years after the fall of the Berlin wall (there will be no future wars no future war) –

Fireworks crack and crack and crack across the neighbourhood, car horns beep dogs barking

Miguel is shouting – Brazil! This will be a new anew
Somebody calls out for LAURA and the name rings out long and round –
Everyone is here. Everyone is wearing white.

Democracia
Have you ever seen such a wonderful thing

1988

On the night that Brazil redemocratised Sônia's eldest sister Laura got in her car, foot on the pedal, and drove off a bridge into the sea in the middle of the night.

(splash)

Catarina puts down her cards.

Under the white green midnight lamplight she watches Sônia take a drag from Tia Lamis' cigarette and turn to kiss her husband on the mouth full tongue night breath between them, leaning him back, and – they stagger there – the thick new hum of that inland night, the dry earth, the damp air, the treeleaves, the equatorial line, the hot hump of that country, a continent, five hundred years, behind them.

Vem filha! Sônia drops onto her knees. Wet face, she calls to her – Vem abraçar!

But Catarina, the baby born thirteen months after Laura died, was never allowed out after dark. Sônia still didn't let Catarina get in cars driven by anyone other than Miguel, or her big sister Lygia when Lygia was in town. The roads are too dangerous, she said. We have the highest rate of road accidents in the world, she said. Did you hear about what happened to Dona Flor's brother in law? So tragic. Tia Lygia is a very sensible person, like your father, who drives like a tortoise who is concentrating. Despite living in Olinda, over an hour from the university campus and over an hour from a school she deemed good enough for her daughter, Sônia herself drove only when Miguel was away for work and it could not be helped.

It is not sane, Tia Lamis had said, shaking her head.

When Catarina was thirteen Sônia came back from an academic conference in Europe with two mobile phones: one for her and Miguel to share, and one for Catarina. At first she couldn't find the phones, so she unzipped her suitcase in the middle of the living room, blouses and underwear spilling onto the tiles. Catarina waited. Sônia was beaming. She said to her daughter –

This will make everything easier. You will be able to text me where you are and I won't have to worry. Can you imagine? Mamãe not worrying! And you can text your friends! My colleagues in Europe say their children are always on their mobile phones sending text messages to their friends. You will be the coolest kid at school.

Catarina held the phone in her hands. She opened it and, using the adapter that Sônia had thrown onto the sofa, she put it to charge. Catarina entered Tia Lamis and Larissa's home phone into the contacts section and saved it. She entered her own phone number and saved it. If Dona Flor got a mobile phone she would add her number too. She held the phone between her palms. She looked up at her mother.

They had moved her from the friendly hippy private school where she could ask any question of any of the teachers at any time, the school that didn't do exams, to the best high school in the city with all the preppy kids who lived in Recife and already knew each other and went to each others' houses at the weekends to get drunk on their parents' alcohol and there was no way Catarina could do that with them, even if she hadn't lived so far away, even if she had wanted to.

Thirteen-year-old Catarina read long fantasy books in English and watched documentaries on YouTube late into the night on her mother's PC. She read Wikipedia pages sometimes for two or three hours a night on topics like World War One and Greenhouse Gas Emissions, leading her to become a vegetarian. Sometimes she stayed up until it got light reading a book that her mother had left on her desk from front cover to back or downloading and watching videos online. Even books in English because by the time she was fourteen, Catarina's English was so good she had got into the habit of correcting her mother's pronunciation in front of her work colleagues and students. She read *Daniel Deronda, Iracema, Pamela, A Moreninha*, the longer the better. She did not think the old English books were so different to the old Brazilian ones. She had filled her old English vocabulary books years and years ago and now she kept new exercise books full of words she found notable or weird, arranged by prefix. She made lists of them

behove
betoken
belabour
behold
belove
bely
bewitch
bequest
behest
beknow
besmirch
befuddle
beget
befall

benight
bejewel
bedazzle
betell
bestow
bedeck
befriend
begrudge

Catarina sat at the kitchen table while Dona Flor cooked. She was taller than Dona Flor. Catarina wore her white school uniform polo shirt and grey jeans. Dona Flor wore cut off jean shorts and a T-shirt that said Believe in Love on it. She had little blue sunglasses on that cut into her sea waves of white and grey hair and white and grey eyebrows. That day she was wearing earrings in the shape of fuchsias. Catarina spread her homework out on the table. Evangelical music played on the radio by the stove.

Another song about our saviour Jesus Christ Dona Flor

Yes, it is.

Catarina pressed her lips together. She put her pencil down.

What do you believe happened again, that he died and came alive again, like a zombie or something

I believe that he died for our sins

Catarina spoke to the back of Dona Flor's head.

You know I believe Jesus was a historical figure; I agree he was real

Dona Flor flipped over a pork chop for dinner in the pan. Catarina continued.

But it's not *rational* to believe he had died for our sins – and that he came alive again after that

Dona Flor shook her head, putting a new piece of meat in the pan. She smiled.

Catarina looked back at her books. After thirty seconds she spoke again –

How can you cook that?

What do you mean young lady? I season it then fry it with oil and onions

No – I mean – how do you know that animals don't have feelings like us?

Dona Flor turned from the pan.

I do not know if animals have feelings but that is not a reason not to eat them. She leant against the kitchen counter. We all die don't we?

When you die would you like to be eaten Dona Flor?

Dona Flor began to laugh. Absolutely not! My dear.

Catarina held her pencil in the air. I think I would like to be eaten.

Dona Flor transferred the brown and oily chop to a plate.

In that case, will you eat this pork I have prepared? Word has it that this pig wanted to be eaten too.

She threw a new raw chop into the pan.

Catarina frowned. She wrinkled her nose, pausing. No, because I still object to the conditions the pig was raised in.

Outside a dog barked.

Fifteen-year-old Catarina sat at the corner of her mother's desk at the university. She moved her legs and bum against the hard plastic chair that was a little too low. She knelt on the plastic chair, her cotton school trousers soft between her knees and the plastic. She listened to her mother's fingers hitting the keyboard. Plec plec plecplecplecplec. Sônia squinted into the glass of the square computer monitor.

The office was a mess. The desk was as wide as the room and dusty and covered in end of term papers, each a crinkled set of that student's handwriting and over the top her mother's red comments. Library books and private books were stacked on their sides on the shelves on the wall and the desk and the floor without order. On the floor were printouts of journal articles and chapter drafts, stapled and unstapled, flapping and floating with the rotation of the face of the electric fan around the room. Stuck to the side of the monitor were the posters and leaflets of student campaigns and protests and theatre shows from as far back as 1993. Sônia did not like to throw anything out.

Catarina shifted on her seat and cleared a small space at the corner of the desk. She opened her backpack and began to unpack it.

Catarina watched the university students pass by in the corridors. She wanted so badly to be them, to be an adult. To walk around the campus and not look like a child. Catarina knew, from what Larissa had said her older friends had said, what university students did. They debated important subjects together. They read big books in many languages. Some lived away from their parents in repúblicas. There were all communists apart from the ones who weren't. They went to motels to have sex. They used condoms and sometimes took the morning after pill. When she passed students and professors in the corridor with her mother she hoped that they might think she was also a student.

But everyone had seen the photographs of her on her mother's desk. Students and professors treated her like a special and familiar person because Sônia was always writing someone a reference or helping a student or calling in a favour for a colleague, and Sônia was always talking about her daughter, the child. Sônia's colleagues brought Catarina chocolates and presents from their conferences and trips. They had heard so much about her and there she was in her school uniform, exercise books in her arms, ponytail, braces, Sônia's precocious vegetarian daughter.

Catarina put her geography textbook and her exercise book on the desk. She began to copy from one to the other. The fan spun and the papers floated. Plec plec plec. Her mother typed. Catarina put her pencil down.

The expensive after school English classes were held in an air-conditioned room in Casa Forte in Recife. Catarina was wearing her school polo shirt, jeans and trainers, her hair out. She looked around the room. The students were arranged in a semi-circle, her chair at the far edge. She recognised two or three people from school, the rest she didn't know. Someone she didn't know sitting in the middle of the room put his hand up. He lisped a little. He had braces.

He put his hand up again. And then again. Every time Catarina raised her hand, his was already in the air, bobbing. Like her, he was a nerd. Unlike her, Pedro's speech seemed free-flowing, easy. He talked too much. In answer to the teacher's question, What would you like to study at university? he said –

I am a vegetarian and I have one older sister; I have a YouTube channel where I review manga cartoons and that's how my English got so good. (Shrug.) My mum is a teacher the school I go to and my dad works in IT and my afro is a political statement, because I am proud to be a Brazilian of African descent, in fact the language that my ancestors would have spoken is Yoruba—

At this point the teacher said, Thank you Pedro that is very interesting but could he answer the question, to which he said –

Yes Yes I have been getting there – I want to study law because equal access to the law means equal access to justice. Pedro cleared his throat, smiling.

Catarina spent all afternoon listening to and looking at him from the edge of the semi-circle where he did not see her because he was looking at the front of the room. When she asked a question, and he turned to face her, she forgot whole syllables of words.

After class, before her dad picked her up Catarina approached Pedro's desk. He had just told the instructor that the instructor should also be a vegetarian. He was still packing up, had just finished writing.

I am also a vegetarian, Catarina said, blinking.

Oh yes?

Pedro reached to high five her and she clapped back, thrilling and dizzy under her forehead. She could not form the words that she had planned.

She stood there. Pedro zipped up his bag, still sitting. She vomited a series of sounds at the top of his head –

Areyouvegetarianforenvironmentaloranimalrightsreasons?

Pedro frowned and then he smiled at her.

I believe in both. You?

Catarina swallowed. Same.

She thought of what he must see when he looked at her; it was true that she was obviously also a nerd, despite all the things Larissa promised would happen if she waxed her eyebrows and cut her hair and stopped wearing Green Day T-shirts.

But she did not need to stop wearing Green Day T-shirts. At their next English class it was Pedro who approached her.

What school do you go to?

She said the name.

The fancy one in Madalena

She nodded.

And where do you live?

Olinda

And you travel in for English lessons?

Yes. My dad drives me everywhere.

And how many siblings do you have?

She shook her head.

It is just me.

Pedro nodded again.

She lets her voice fill the quiet. Where do you live?

Torre

You have a sister, I heard you say

Yes.

And, she swallowed, And you want to study law? I heard you say

Yes.

That's impressive

I might have to sit the vestibular twice, law is very hard to get into at the federal university.

I think you can do it.
Really?
Catarina nodded and nodded again.

Pedro looked at her.
What do you want to study?
História
História? You won't get a job with that
Catarina shrugged.
You want to teach?
I don't know
He looked at her.
And what do you think of the quotas?
Racial quotas for university? She blinked. I think they are good. Claro. She blinked again. My mother says the students who come in on quotas are the smartest ones.
Pedro nodded then smiled at her. Your mum teaches at the federal university?
Uh huh.
Pedro nodded.

Pedro and Catarina became friends. The other kids on the course were too sporty or too girly or not curious and clever enough. They were like Larissa or like Pedro's sister – content and without dreams of living in Europe or Japan, or travelling the world or even Brazil. They started getting ice cream or a juice or smoothie together from the stall outside the building where they had their English lessons. One Saturday they went to a mall. They got fries and soft drinks from McDonalds and ate them from trays in the food hall.
Have you ever gone abroad?
Yes. I've been to London and also Argentina and Paris and New York.
On holiday?
Argentina and Paris were on holiday. London my mum went for a conference.

A conference?

Uh huh.

Cool.

What about you?

My sister has been to Miami on holiday. But not me.

Pedro looked at her.

I wish I had been to New York.

New York is really cool. It's like being in a TV show.

Yeah? He drank a milkshake through the straw. He thought for a moment and then said – How rich is too rich?

What do you mean?

How rich do you think is too rich?

Catarina frowned. I think it is good to have enough to have a car, a house, not be hungry and to have some nice things – but not like designer clothes. She touches her fingers together. And some holidays. What do you think?

I think enough not to be hungry or to not have shoes. Not to give up things. Enough to go to the beach but not enough to own a beach house.

Catarina nodded.

Do you have a beach house?

Catarina paused. No –

Pedro narrowed his eyes at her and she could not stop herself from smiling.

No – we have a sítio in the interior. It is very far from the beach.

For the full thirty minutes of their conversation, Catarina did not check her phone.

The first time Pedro came over she met him at the bus stop by the sea and they walked across the square, dodging kittens and trash and shards of glass, then went up the hill over the cobbles. Pedro's hand held almost on her back. He could feel the damp beneath her T-shirt. An older-looking man without shoes stepped in front of them and asked them for money. He held out his hands. Catarina gave him three two real coins and called him senhor. She looked at the man then she looked at the pavement. They turned up the hill. They turned onto Rua do Bomfim and Catarina looked for the blue wall with the pink and white flowers falling over it. Pedro was talking about geometry. She reached for her keys to open the white gate. She breathed and waited for him to realise that this was where she lived. They spoke at the same time.

It is a very beautiful house –

This is my house –

The ferns lolled over the veranda. Catarina called for her parents and Dona Flor stepped into the garden, speaking, putting her hands around Catarina, kissing her –

And are you the young man who is also a vegetarian? This is not a problem I have been cooking for this young vegetarian for years she does not eat Fish she does not eat Chicken she does not even eat *lobster*. And she has threatened to stop eating eggs or butter can you believe it? Deus me livre

Catarina looked at Pedro from under Dona Flor's armpit. Pedro was laughing with Dona Flor, he put his arm around her.

But I know what I will make you queridos, I will make a banana da terra stew, God knows I would rather have it with fish or prawns but you will have what you want I will not stop you from

Pedro closed his eyes and opened them. He was easy with her. You are too kind Dona Flor, it will be delicious Dona Flor, it is your recipe Dona Flor perhaps you can share it with me? I love to cook. And your earrings, what are they tiny hibiscus flowers?

They stepped onto the veranda and they walked through the house together. Pedro looked at the abstract paintings and the oil paintings and the big smooth and modern vases. He looked at the boxes of papers everywhere on the floor and the bookcases and English and French book titles and CDs. Pedro turned his head.

Water?

Yes

Coffee

Yes

Wait. Sit here. Catarina inhaled. My father says we should work here, Catarina said without looking at Pedro, My father says there isn't space on the desk in my room.

Quietly, Pedro unpacked.

They ate dinner hours later, when it was dark, after Dona Flor had got the bus home, on the glass table on the veranda. Tia Lamis was there. Ferns swayed in the night at the height of their heads. The sound of drums came from beyond the walls of the house. Sônia and Catarina and Tia Lamis set the table, fetching plates and knives and forks from the kitchen. Pedro stood to help them.

Sônia waved a hand at him. Senta-se Senta!

Sit with me, Miguel said.

Pedro sat.

Beer?

No thank you.

The bottle top popped as Miguel lifted the bottle opener.

A bird made a sound.

You would like to study law?

Yes.

Sônia's family are all lawyers

Yes – I have heard of them.

Yes, great man Lipo.

Did you know him?

We used to sit on this veranda together.

Pedro held on to the wicker under his hands.

My parents love him. They say he understood truly working people in Brazil

Miguel nodded.

Yes he understood that class is the great problem facing Brazilian society. There is much talk about race, with quotas and –

Catarina stepped onto the veranda, ready to interrupt – Pai

Pedro spoke – There is no class without race in Brazil

Miguel drank from his beer, he looked at Pedro and spoke gently – Yes exactly this. Race is just class

Pai –

In that moment, voices interrupted them. Tia Lamis and Sônia came up the stairs and onto the veranda, disagreeing, about the news, or the traffic or the tablecloth –

Não é–

É sim –

Não é –

Tia Lamis set a dish down on the table.

Sônia looked at Pedro and Catarina. She put her hands on her hips and sighed.

Banana da terra for the two vegetarians (scoop scoop) Miguel can you serve the rice –

After dinner Tia Lamis lit a cigarette.

That is a terrible habit

Tia Lamis waved a hand. She started to laugh, she took a drag and blew it away behind her into the night.

I know I know sister.

Catarina smiled at Pedro. Under the table, she touched her fingers on his fingers.

He drove her to the Motel Desejo at night, in his sister's car. It was full of her car debris, wrappers in seat crevices, empty bottles, crumbs. They had the windows down because it wasn't hot: it had been raining and the air was cool and still. They let in the sounds of the traffic, and the sounds of the pavement and sounds of people arguing and laughing and selling snacks to passersby. The road out of the city was slick and grey black wet and full of puddles over potholes. Pedro drove carefully. She watched his hands on the wheel. It was a Friday. He had said to his parents that he was going to a friend's house for the night and she had said to her parents that she was going to a friend's house for the night. When her mother called her on the phone, she said calmly they were just settling down to watch a movie, not to worry. Her cousin Larissa had said go to the Motel Desejo and Pedro's sister Patricia had said take my car, take these condoms. They were both eighteen years old.

The words shone with neon possibility at the side of the road

Motel

Desejo

purple then pink.

It was not exactly something that was not allowed. But something they had waited for, anticipated, chosen, suggested decided planned. And she knew herself. Had made herself come by herself by then, and by pressing her clit against the firm heel of his palm under a canga on the beach. She knew with her hands the outline of his body, his thighs; she knew the taste. She was so sure. He was so hers.

They picked up the motel key card at the drive-thru window. She held it.

And so

In a wide bed with the satin motel sheets and the outside sound of the once rainforest rain on the road. In a bed with the new white motel sheets, in the midnight darkness, in a bedroom filled with the tack slush tack of the rain, pink neon lit with the light from the road

He touched her hair, her neck, he put his hands on her back, her shoulders

Like this

Like this

And the rain tack tack slushed outside of the window onto the midnight road and the air conditioning unit strummed above them and the pink light spilled under them

Later that night she would pull the cover over their heads and hold his face between her hands in the darkness and kiss him again and again on the mouth and the nose and the cheek and the mouth and forehead, the cheek bone and cheek meat, on the eyebrow, brow, upper lip tongue, hairline, his ears, his eyes his mouth, his shoulder

VANISHES HEAVILY

On the night in 1988 that Laura drove off a bridge into a river, the phone had rung at 2am. Sônia and her mother and her sisters knew these madrugada phone calls. They had not got one in years. And, as if transported back in time, Vovó Olga's hand closed in a fist around the landline receiver. Sônia stood in the darkness of the corridor of the house and looking at mother's silhouette, the details of her visible only in outline, except her mouth, which the light from the street covered in grey and white. Vovó Olga's legs were shaking, her nightie was shaking. She brought the receiver to her mouth, speaking calmly and without pause –

Shame on you senhor, there has been a legal amnesty, law number 6.683 of the 28th of August 1979 forgives all militants, including my eldest daughter, Laura. But do not think I have forgotten your crimes senhor. No. You will not continue to torture my family, não senhor, my daughter is a free woman, safe in her bed, you cannot hurt her now. You cannot hurt her now.

Vovó Olga took a breath and the voice on the other end of the phone spoke.

Sônia watched her mother's shadow still itself.

On the morning of the next day, they identified the body. On the morning after that, the news was in the papers.

Even on her worst days, even on the days where she had been nasty to her husband and short with Dona Flor and too controlling of her daughter – always seeing a child where there was more and more a woman – even on those days, when Professor Sônia gave lectures she became like the sea. Vast. The swell of her voice like the crashing of the sea into the crust of the earth. You have to see it, her colleagues with glasses and beards would say to Catarina when they saw her sitting in Professora Sônia's office. In her best years it was a thing to behold, Professora Sônia, the daughter of the great governor of the state, sister of the infamous revolutionary, giving a lecture. Back when her hair was still black with the grey at the front.

Sônia would come dressed in long light clothes. Sleeves that she could hold up and out and would hang to her hips. Long necklaces made of red seeds.

And she would speak –

It was the year that Shakespeare wrote *Romeo and Juliet,* the year he wrote his sonnets, and the year Shakespeare returned to London after he had fled the plague which killed over 20,000 people. It was the year that an English sailor called James Lancaster left the court of Queen Elizabeth of England not knowing he would return a year later, sunburnt and seaworn and bringing with him the richest, largest haul Queen Elizabeth of England would ever see. Gold and rubber and rubies and wood. Billions in today's money. Taken from a port on the northeast coast of a Portuguese colony in the new world. A port called Recife adjacent to a bustling and wealthy settlement called Olinda.

Turn to page 10.

(She stood at the back of the large cool room in the belly of a concrete building. The lecture theatre was modern, cool, dark as a bowel.)

Shakespeare was writing in the time of empire and theft and genocide and slavery and this was when the world we know was built – and therefore you must understand its machinations and its magic.

257

(She made them read *Pericles* and *Othello* and *The Tempest* and told them these sea-faring war-making texts were about the making of Latin America as much as they were about Europe. She told them about Edward Said and *Orientalism* so that they would know that *here* tells stories about *there* in order to have a story about itself. And, insofar as *here* and *there* are real, they cannot not be separated. Think, she said, this is true of the Northeast and Southeast of Brazil, even.)

Ahem

and let me ask you this – in 1976 a revolutionary theatre group put on a performance of *Coriolanus*, a play about a corrupt king who is deposed and killed by the people. They chose this play believing that Shakespeare would not be censored by the military dictatorship; they were right. But not only this, nobody who saw it understood their revolutionary message. It was a European play, it had not been censored; those things foreclosed the possibilities of the text. The signifier obscuring the signified. So let me ask you this, can such a text ever *speak?* Can it be living in *our* hands? Can it be *ours?*

Look then at page 203. *The Tempest.* Look at the moment that the masque collapses around Prospero. What is Prospero if not a Latin American dictator? Ein? He conjures the masque, the spirits, in performative ritual around him; a military parade; their spectacle endows his authority and his authority creates their spectacle; is this not the divine right of kings and generals? Please. Read aloud to me the stage direction, as the magic collapses, remember, close your eyes, imagine we are in a theatre, imagine, yes you read it please, louder –

Vanishes heavily

What is this? How can they *vanish* – it means to disappear, from the Latin *evanescere* – in such a way that is *heavy?* Pesado. A disappearance, a murder, the tumult of regime change – of system change, of the killing of kings – is not a quiet thing. No, it is not a quiet thing. But it can be made so – or, attempts can be made to make it so. Yes. Shakespeare says to us – Look at this concealment. There is all this making of this authority. An art, a magic. As there is of any authority – now, then and since. You must know this. Shakespeare says – Look at the magic, look at the making of it. Look – and see: if it was made, it can be collapsed.

If you ask Lúcia she will say she believes Laura drove off a bridge because she was drunk

If you ask Lygia she will say she believes Laura drove off a bridge because she was driving recklessly

If you ask Lamis she will say she believes Laura drove off a bridge because she had, as a result of torture, sustained long-term PTSD and injuries to the brain, both of which can lead to parasuicidal and impulsive behaviour

If you ask Sônia she will say she believes Laura drove off a bridge because Laura wanted to kill herself

If you ask Vovó Olga she will say she believes Laura was murdered by the police

65.

Small girl – no – young woman –

it is 1981

Young woman, Sônia sits by the sofa, waiting for Laura her sister to wake up. Laura her sister is asleep. The sun is bright white outside; the shutters are closed but somehow inside the house is bright too, white floors, white walls, thin white dust in the air.

Sônia waits. Bare feet on the sofa. Bare hands on the sofa. A closed book on her legs. She opens the book. Looks at it. Closes it.

Breathe

The post is on the table. A pile of letters. She touches their thick paper edges with restless hands. She begins to shuffle the envelopes. Her mother's name, her father's name, her father's name. She does this idly, anxiously, to pass time. She stands. She listens for the sounds of the house. She looks at the envelope at the top of the pile. She reads in clear and unknown handwriting, her sister's name –

LAURA

She stares at it. She touches the edges of the envelope with the edges of her fingers. She turns it over in her hand, looks at the front and back. The envelope is thin and light blue. It's been addressed in big and easy letters, as if the loop of her sister's name came easily to those fingers. It looks – intimate. Important. She thinks, with pride, that she will give it to her sister as soon as she wakes up. She tucks it between the back pages of her book.

Half an hour passes. The sun gets brighter and in the places where its rays fall through the gaps between the shutters it is impossible to see. The road outside is loud; cars and motorcycles honking. She waits on the sofa, eyes on the inside of her book. She turns the pages without reading; she does this idly, anxiously, to pass time. The dog climbs onto her lap and with her right hand she touches his ears. She talks to him. You're getting old, she says to the dog, You're going grey. The old dog yawns. Sônia lies back on the sofa; Sônia stares at the ceiling. Sônia hears her name spoken from a back room of the house and, jumping up, she stands, leaving, with her left hand, the book on the bookshelf. Her left hand tucks it in, between two other volumes.

Her sister's waking living voice calls out to her –

Sônia?

They will eat together. A breakfast of fruit and couscous and coffee. Laura her sister will be wearing soft indoor clothes, pyjamas, Sônia will look like a young woman in smart trousers, smart grown up shoes.

66.

Sônia there are things I regret, that I think about at night. Can I tell you? Yes? We were at a congress, in the South at a university in the Southeast. There were three hundred or four hundred of us there. It was right before the amnesty, right when we were thinking Meu Deus we have finally done it. We are this close to democracy. I was just out of – prison. The dictatorship is this close to finished – and we have finished it. We were asking for amnesty. You know the slogan. We were asking for amnesty. Ampla. Geral. Irrestrita. We were asking for amnesty. Recíproca. We were discussing this three hundred or four hundred of us at the meeting. Many students and I was there because I had been in the South during that time, it was before the amnesty before I came home to you Sônia. And there was one man who made a presentation. He was so anxious to speak in front of us you could see it in his hands. He had to wait several hours because the meeting was all day and for hours he was there he was so anxious to speak in front of us. He had dark skin. He was older, he was shaking in his hands as he waited to speak. He wore a brown suit, a white shirt although no one else was wearing smart clothes. And then he said to us, I am from the movement of people in prison. Not political prisoners. Common prisoners. They torture us there too, they beat us, they abuse us, they starve us, they make us work, they kill us in there too. There are thousands of us. I speak on behalf of the common prisoners to ask that we are included also in the amnesty. That was what he said. That was what he asked of us. And Sônia we voted no. We voted no because common prisoners were in prison for common reasons, not political reasons, and this was a political amnesty, that would complicate things and we wanted to keep things simple because we were this close to democracy and oh his hands were shaking when he spoke

Sônia there are things I regret

In late 2009 Sônia woke from a nap at her desk in a panic. She could hear cars on the street and people shouting. She didn't know what time it was. She called for her daughter. Got up, couldn't find her daughter not in her room not in the house, couldn't see anyone not Dona Flor, she called her daughter's phone, no answer. Called her again. Called her again. She pressed her hands against her chest and the terror moved from her fingertips into her heart. She started shouting, where was her child where was her child – Dona Flor said Calma

Sônia started shouting, Where is Catarina She is not answering her phone

Screaming

It is okay Doutora. She will be at her university, at her lectures.

Screaming under her forehead

Sônia picked up the house phone dialled. No answer. Sônia picked up the house phone dialled. No answer. Sônia picked up the house phone dialled. No answer. Sônia picked up the house phone dialled. No answer. Sônia picked up the house phone dialled. No answer. Sônia picked up the house phone dialled. No answer.

She got in the car and drove. She didn't like to drive alone or for long distances like all the way across Zona Norte across the mangroves to the city. She drove down the cobbles by the sea by the bus stop and the kittens and the trash she drove across the bridge over the river through the city in the traffic to inland to the university through the campus and when she found her daughter walking out of a lecture, she started shouting. She said you're coming with me why didn't you answer my calls. She took her phone from Catarina's hand and threw it into the road. Catarina looked up at her mother's face. Pedro, standing next to her, looked at her too.

There had been another suicide. Two days before. A woman, eighteen years old. From the fourteenth floor in the middle of the night. Professora Sônia, by now a senior member of faculty, her hair totally grey at the roots, shouted at her colleagues in the faculty meeting –

Availability of methods impacts the suicide rate!
It is not the case that these students cannot be stopped
The building is a desgraça – for shame!
The suicide is our shame also

Put the fucking puta wire fencing up
Clear every knife from the food hall
Sell no more paracetamol in the pharmacies

Her colleague then had said quietly, Ahem yes it is true there are studies that show this. The Golden Gate Bridge for example, gas ovens.

She had gone back to her office and stared at her computer screen. Legs tense. Had images of a woman who looked like Virginia Woolf and Sylvia Plath or Clarice Lispector, head in a black box, and of the girl at the end of *The Bell Jar*, swinging, her sister's face

That year, 2009, two years after Catarina had begun studying in the fifteen-floor social sciences building, they put up the wire fencing, over all the balconies of all the floors.

Moqueca de Banana da Terra

Ingredientes

    4 colheres de azeite

    1 cebola picada

    3 dentes de alho picados

    1 pimentão verde picado

    1 pimentão amarelo picado

    1 pimentão vermelho picado

    3 colheres de dendê

    3 tomates picados

    1 banana da terra em rodelas

    200ml de leite de coco

    Coentro

    Sal

Preparação

Numa frigideira refogue a cebola picada, os pimentões picados com o alho em azeite por 10 minutos.

Acresente a banana da terra e cozinhe por 5 minutos

Acresente os tomates

Acresente o dendê e leite de coco

Cozinhe por 15 minutos.

Acresente sal a gosto e coentro.

Catarina added four words she already knew to the end of her list of F words.

foresee
foreknow
forebear
foreplay
forename
forehead

forgive
foretell
forget
forsake

In another window, she began to populate a spreadsheet with funding opportunities and deadlines for her and for Pedro. She thought of the quiet of the airplane carriage over the sea.

They landed in Heathrow on 15th September 2014. Here was the ever-grey metropolis; London.

MILE END III

(2016)

Pedro's first love was the Quetzalcoatlus, Pedro's mother had said to Catarina, raising her eyebrows.

It is a flying dinosaur, he was crazy for it.

Pedro had itched as she spoke. He had elaborated, moving his hands.

It's a kind of Pterosaur. *Ptero* meaning with wings and *sauros* meaning lizard. They were the first vertebrate animal to evolve to fly. They are very interesting actually, I still think so! The first Pterosaurs were alive 233 million years ago and the last Pterosaur died 66 million years ago. That's longer than humans have existed. The biggest Pterosaur is the Quetzalcoatlus, it is the biggest animal ever to fly.

The year that Pedro turned ten his father retrained in IT and started working for the Recife branch of a Brazilian telecoms company. They got a new car and moved apartment. His mother, who had taken a job at a private school so that Pedro and Patricia would be given free places, used to come home with new shoes on. Don't tell your father, she would say.

Back when it was 2.5 reais to the dollar, Pedro's sister Patricia used to take him to the new Imperatiz bookshop at the Plaza at the weekends. They always ended up at the bookshop. He had read and picked out his birthday present six months in advance. His aunt Paula turned the bookshop in the big mall in Casa Forte inside out upside down looking for another dinosaur book; his cousins in Rio sent one that he did not own although he had already borrowed it and read it from the school library. For his tenth birthday Pedro got dinosaur bedsheets and plastic dinosaur toys and blew out the candles on a dinosaur birthday cake in the shape of dinosaur that was flying, a dinosaur the size of a house. When his sister Patricia had argued with their evangelical uncle André about the creation of the universe, she had called Pedro over to tell him about the Quetzalcoatlus.

When Pedro turned fourteen Patricia showed him a programme called Google Earth on the new computer in their mother's office. It loaded slowly. Our house isn't on there yet, she said. But you can zoom in on New York, São Paulo, Hong Kong. Pedro clicked and clicked and clicked, watching the squares blur and then each time magically sharpen until they became treetops and rooftops and swimming pools. They found their cousins' cousins' house in Florida. Pedro zoomed into the sea until it was two squares the colour blue.

To Pedro – a child who had once thought in terms of 66 million years and of how, 66 million years ago, the South American continent was attached to the African continent and the Atlantic Ocean did not exist – change was an imaginable, inevitable, righteous thing.

Originally, Pedro's plan had been to be a palaeontologist. Then he had wanted to be a zoologist or a botanist. But everything was being destroyed too fast for him to study it. So Pedro made a new plan. His plan was to be a lawyer and to use the law and courts to protect the land and its peoples and its forest and rivers. And then he met Catarina and Catarina had said come to Europe with me and he had made a sub-plan to go to the place where the first companies had come from who had first sought the frontier.

Pedro could be a lawyer and do what he wanted to do in three places: at the frontier, where the government and the companies met the forest; in Brasilia, where the federal law met the government and the companies; or in São Paulo, the financial centre, where the companies lived and made their deals.

By August 2015, he hadn't made up his mind on which. Pedro had sat the exams to be a public defender for the state of São Paulo (population: 44.04 million), for the Federal District of Brasilia (population: 4.73 million) and for the state of Roraima (population: 496,936).

Pedro's apartment in São Paulo had a small living room with a sofa and a television, and beyond that a balcony, where he arranged a small collection of cactuses (barrel, prickly pear, cabega, calico). The balcony of Pedro's apartment faced the unwindowed, concrete side of the building opposite. At the top the concrete was still white, becoming more and more grey and city stained as it continued towards the street. This concrete wall occupied the entire view from the balcony, apart from when Pedro stood in the left corner of the balcony and looked south, around the corner of his own apartment block. When he did this Pedro could see, within the oblong strip between the buildings, a great grey and blue grey and pink expanse: block after block after block of city. Twenty million people. Apartment blocks rising out of the pollution air as if out of clouds. And at their feet, like flowers, the rainforest canopies of trees.

To Pedro, São Paulo was a Quetzalcoatlus. A miracle of heaven and earth, 66 million years in the making.

Unimaginable, and yet

Every day he took the elevator to the ground floor and walked out of the gates into the street with the crumbling kerb and the tipuana tree roots touching the handlebars of the parked motorcycles of delivery boys. The Japanese supermarket was opening and a man put fruit out. There were bin bags of trash on the islands between lanes of traffic between mid-century concrete blocks painted pink and red and yellow and white, all stained with pollution. He walked to the sound of the six-lane intracity motorway two blocks to the east until the road widened into the old centre of the city. The cathedral rose in gothic horror, as jagged and distorted as the ones he had seen in Europe but this cathedral was in too good, too recent health, only seventy years old its walls were too bright in the sunlight. He gave one of the homeless women who lived there R$20. He approached the Courts of Justice of the State of São Paulo, hard shoes on stone steps.

Back in London, in the flat in Mile End, Catarina was looking at the moving image of Pedro's face on the screen. His eyelashes were wet. He rubbed his face with the bottom of his T-shirt.

Remember the day we arrived in London?

I remember

It was like 7am and our phones with the English SIMs my mum gave us weren't working. And we had come via New York and we were so tired. And for some crazy reason we decided to get the tube to Westminster. We took pictures outside Big Ben and sent them to your mum. Do you remember? And we sat in the Pret there for hours using the wifi and charging our stuff. For hours

I remember.

Remember when we drove to the motel, for the first time

Motel Desejo

Motel Desejo.

You spoiled me Pedro

He looked up at her on the screen.

What do we do now?

There were two ways for Catarina to stay in England: to prove to the Portuguese government that she was the grandchild of a Portuguese citizen, and apply for Portuguese citizenship, giving her the right to live and work anywhere in the European Union, or to get a job that would sponsor her visa – for example, an academic job. Otherwise she would be asked to leave the UK six months after finishing her PhD, when her student visa expired.

In the morning after the night she had spent on Skype to Pedro, Catarina sat at the table in the kitchen / living room with a mug of coffee and wrote an email to her mother and father. She listed the documents that she needed: her original birth certificate signed by a registrar; a photocopy of her birth certificate made within the last year signed by a registrar; her father's birth certificate signed by a registrar; a photocopy of her father's birth certificate made within the last year signed by a registrar; her original high school diploma; a document issued by the Brazilian Federal Police showing she did not have a criminal record, or a copy of her government ID card signed by a registrar, or, if this has not been issued recently, a copy of her passport signed by a registrar. They must either send the birth certificate of her father's mother, Vovó Alícia, or instead should provide: the place of her birth, the date of her birth, and, if known, the civil registry office in Portugal where her birth certificate could be found, and its name and number. The cost was €175, which Catarina knew her parents would insist on paying, along with postage and everything else.

She imagined her father and her mother reading the email and finding the documents in the bottom drawer of her mother's desk in the study and taking the documents to the mayor's office for the registrar to sign, understanding, while doing so, that their only child was trying her hardest not to come home.

She opened a new window in her browser. She made a list of every academic job at every history department in the UK, which was five in total. She emailed her supervisor Professor Henrietta saying that she did intend to stay and she would be pleased to go for coffee with her colleague at the History Department in Bristol. She made a separate list of every academic job at every history department in Europe and then in North America. She made a list of Australian jobs and jobs in China and India and Latin American universities everywhere except for Brazil.

Catarina boiled the kettle to make more coffee. She watered the monstera plant by the window, which was uncurling a new leaf. The plant pressed itself against the glass. She misted it with the little green spray bottle that Melissa had bought. She took care to wet the bottom of the leaves as well as the top.

Her father replied immediately to her email asking to speak to her. He said they were with Larissa and Tia Lamis, and that they had good news to share, could she speak now?

She looked at their pixelated faces. They moved in front of the bright light of a window.

Can you move so the light's not behind you?

The what –

The light

The what –

Mãe, the sunlight

For a moment they pointed the camera at the tiled floor, and then at the veranda and the ferns. It was so bright. Catarina closed and opened her eyes.

Mãe

They directed the camera at their foreheads.

Can you sit back a bit

They readjusted the camera angle. They were both in short sleeves and both wearing reading glasses. Their hair was so grey. Her mother was wearing big green slab earrings. Larissa and Tia Lamis entered the frame on either side of them

Querida!

Tia

We have something very exciting to tell you –

So exciting

I'm pregnant!

Larissa is pregnant!

Larissa is having a baby!

Catarina's hand moved to her face.

Shit – that's

It's maravilhoso

I am so happy Catarina

It's amazing. Parabéns

Tia Lamis pushed into the middle of the screen – And me? Imagine! I am in *heaven*. I have already invited her boyfriend to move into the apartment with us, we can turn the spare room into a nursery

Larissa was laughing

Boyfriend or no boyfriend it doesn't matter –

Catarina was nodding. That's amazing

Her mother spoke. It is good to have some good news in these times. God knows. We need this good news in these times.

Her father nodded.

Her mother nodded.

She looked at their faces on the screen.

Is it cold there? Querida? Is it raining? We miss you so much. And Pedro is he coming to visit you soon? Tell us

This time they lit the tiny candles outside the embassy without a problem because there was no wind. It was too hot for early June. Sweat ran down the inside of Melissa's arms into her palms as she crouched in the afterwork sun. She had told Marc that she had a gym class and couldn't stay for a drink. She could smell the moisturiser rising wet and salty on the skin around her mouth.

There were more of them than last time, perhaps twenty-five people. Meena and some others were there. Two people from the nightclub were there and had brought a small speaker system on a supermarket trolley. The megaphone was connected to the speaker system. There weren't enough of them to block the road and on the road the cars were loud, backfiring, revving, breaking, stinking. The pavement was thin and tourists pushed in waves around them, looking for Trafalgar Square or Buckingham Palace. Someone was handing out fliers with the word 'Maricumbia' on them and the date 29th August 2016 next to a papaya. Catarina thought she recognised the tall South Asian girl and her white friend with the nose stud from her Modern Latin American History class. Two solemn-looking white guys with glasses and backpacks stood next to their dark-haired girlfriends.

At 6.45 they began. Melissa held her placard up. A person they had met at the protest at King's Cross unrolled a banner. Catarina spoke into the megaphone, and Melissa repeated her words in English afterwards. She heard her voice big and loud through the speakers. Through the glass of the embassy a woman in a skirt suit looked at them. An older woman spoke on the megaphone. Two women from the university cleaners' union spoke, first in Spanish and then in English, and asked for solidarity with their upcoming strike.

Melissa held up her placard. It said in all bright colours (pink, yellow, blue, green)

NÃO AO GOLPE

While she spoke into the microphone reading in English what Catarina had said, Melissa had wiped her brow with her wrist, smudging the sweat around. The pavement was thin, the cars drove close to them.

A car started to beep, honking and slowing. Melissa kept talking. Around her placards stood high and still in the air. A person carrying flowers and tangerines. The car honked and a man's face appeared at the lowered window, angry and ready to scream. He looked Melissa in the eye –

Vagabunda!

He turned his head back to the road and accelerated. Melissa kept speaking, the crowd in front of her tensed but did not turn. Apart from the tallest person, Femi, who shouted loudly above their heads, one finger in the air

Fuck off

They took photographs, packing themselves in together to make the crowd look bigger. The speaker played a song by Chico Buarque and then a song by MC Carol. When a policeman arrived, somebody said in a cut-glass English voice, We are just moving on, sir.

On the Central line home they hunched into a carriage of commuters by the inner door that connected the carriages. Dirty warm wind blew through the open window into their faces. Catarina's back pressed against the back of another person. She scrolled through Twitter.

There have been other protests. New York, Bueno Aires, Dublin, Madrid.

Melissa nodded.

It is an important thing, to show the world is watching, especially you know powerful countries

Melissa leant over Catarina's shoulder at the pictures.

And in two years there will be the election.

Yes.

Melissa turned her head. Next to them a woman leant into a man's neck. At Liverpool Street Melissa refreshed her phone.

Julieta's messaged me. She says that she has blocked the sink. And that she's moving out of the flat this month. Melissa pressed her hand against her forehead.

Fuck For fuck's sake

Matt had seen her before she had seen him, hurrying towards her in the middle of the little road off Gower St. Afternoon pubgoers scattered off the pavement into the road beneath the shade of huge plane trees. He held up his hands. When he began to speak he grimaced –

Can you believe it?

I know!

I can't believe it! I've been so upset all day.

I know, it was very unexpected.

Yeah –

They stood by an open window. Catarina leant against the window ledge. Matt took off his jacket

This round's on me

No no

Yes

I will get the next –

Matt nodded.

Catarina looked into the window and around the pub, which was full. She looked at the people drinking and she looked at the television in the corner of the room showing the news. Matt came back holding two pints.

Fuck. He drank. How are you? How is writing

Good, yes I am nearly finished with my chapter on the marriage plot and bourgeois family relations but – she looked at the street – But today of course it was difficult to concentrate

Of course

Everyone in the department was in chaos today, just walking around so tired and they couldn't stop talking about it and some people were crying

Yeah?

Yeah two other researchers, they're from Italy, were very upset.

He put his hands on his head. I was crying this morning.

You cried?

Yeah

Did you stay up all night?

I stayed up until one, when the first results started coming in. Then I slept but I woke up at five . . . that was when I cried.

She took a drink.

I think I'm going to apply for Irish citizenship

Irish?

Yeah, my dad's family is Irish.

Right.

I got the paperwork today.

Okay.

They looked at each other.

Why?

I just –

Is it a European identity thing?

No, it is a pragmatic thing but – he was thoughtful – But also I don't feel like I want to be English right now.

Well. Catarina laughed. We are not all so lucky. I have just asked my parents for the documents I need to apply for Portuguese citizenship.

Matt was quiet.

She held up her drink.

He held up his drink, and they toasted. After they put their glasses down there was a silence. The pub was filling and a man bumped into Matt, swearing as he passed. Matt cleared his throat.

You know what this feels like? she said

What

It feels like that football match during the World Cup, you know the 7–1 match?

He looked at her like he didn't know if she was joking.

No of course I realise that was just a football match but it was also a revolution in expectations and also our sense of who we were and what we did and there were people crying in the streets

I wouldn't want to be out on the street if that happened in England

No?

No ... in England people would have been fighting on the street

Well in Brazil people were crying and the same people were laughing about it

Right

It felt like nothing like that had ever happened before

Right and I guess it hadn't

No but also – she shrugged – So what?

This year on the other hand –

Right with all the

This year has been unbelievable. But we have seen it before

Right because of how

We have a history of coups and instability in Brazil

Yes of course

In Latin America

Yes yes of course

Whereas this – she touched the windowsill near his hand – This is the first in a long time that you in England have felt of true political instability

Yes

And I don't think you understand it at all

He looked at her without speaking.

The pub lights started coming on. She felt embarrassed. She had pushed the conversation too hard. She felt flush with alcohol. She put her jacket on. The bartender was shouting that it was time to leave.

Matt held his hand out, as if to touch her.

I do understand – he paused to breathe – I think there have been times like that here. And not so long ago – under Thatcher. The Troubles, for example, Northern Ireland was a warzone. The miners' strikes, deindustrialisation, the north of England was falling apart, and it has never recovered.

Catarina looked at him.

Two streets away, Marc was in uproar. He'd come into the office at lunch-time saying he'd slept three hours. He couldn't believe it. Thank God he hadn't put on a referendum party for the clients like he'd been thinking of doing. He put his hands in the air, drank more coffee, zipped and unzipped his fleece. He could not believe it. He had come in at lunch-time and then he had been on the phone nonstop, refreshing the news on his laptop. At 4pm he said let's get a fucking drink. He got them pints Estrella Guinness and finished his in five minutes. His friend Alasdair the ex-BBC producer had arrived. And his friend Peter from the think tank. They stood on the pavement outside the pub in the small street. Femi leant in, speaking to them. Melissa listened, back against the pub wall, rolling a cigarette. The weather was mild, the sky too bright.

Marc was shaking his head. He stepped off the pavement kerb and then back onto it.

It is incredible what is happening to this country

Alasdair nodded solemnly.

It is just unbelievable.

Everything has changed since we were in power. So much. People voting against their own interests.

You look at Cornwall, for example, totally reliant on subsidies

And Wales – my whole family voted for this thing – recipients of huge EU subsidies, grants for farming, schools, infrastructure –

And yet

And yet.

Peter leant in to Melissa, You wouldn't happen to have a spare one of those, and you couldn't roll it for me too, could you?

Marc held his hands out, pint in the air.

This generation of politicians is something else—

Unscrupulous—

They will lie to the nation without blinking. I've never seen anything like it—

Absolutely—

Could not have happened in our day—
Absolutely not—
The most fatuous, baldfaced—
The NHS will not benefit—
Not a fucking penny!
And the economy will suffer.
God.
Sterling is already tanking

Marc was bouncing from one foot to the other on the pavement kerb. Alasdair held his hands together. Peter threw the cigarette butt into the street. Melissa looked at them.

Turkey was never going to join the EU—
Never—
But some people actually believed that. Some people actually believed that and that's the thing isn't it—

Melissa looked across at Femi.

Femi opened his mouth – it takes real British exceptionalism, doesn't it, to think this would be a good idea? An imperialist delusion, a racism

There was a pause.

Oh yes
Vile racism
Yes.
Severing all our connections to our neighbours—
What will happen to the Europeans who live here? Deportation?
It's inhumane

Marc moved his hands together and then apart. He shook his head.

You know what I think it is? We need much better regulation of social media—
Not only that Marc, our side needs to learn to use data—

Better messaging, storytelling, clearly something didn't *click* with the average voter—

Let me tell you, I think we need an investigation—

How can they just lie and lie and get away with it, that is what kills me, it is not democratic—

It certainly isn't—

No – but perhaps it can be revoked—

Yes—

Yes – absolutely no chance it'll actually happen if you ask me

Mmhm.

Melissa looked at her phone. Peter turned to them.

What do you young people think? You're the ones getting fucked

Melissa pressed her lips together. She shrugged.

Femi shook his head. He breathed in.

Well I—

Marc began again –

It is the Labour leadership's fault if you ask me.

Femi looked at Melissa, he opened his mouth to speak. A woman walked past them on the pavement in a T-shirt that read

Wednesday
Thursday
Friday

The next day Melissa went to the supermarket after work and spent £12 on sink unblocker. She had tried putting her fingertips under the sink water to pick out the smushed onions and coffee granules and yoghurt that she had felt there but still the water wouldn't drain. She poured the sink unblocker into the sink. She hoovered the corridors with the hoover which did not have good suction and then the stairs and then the kitchen / living room. She cleaned the brown stains on the wall above the bin and wiped all the surfaces including the crumbs, including the tomato sauce stains on the hob. She mopped the strip of lino in front of the kitchen units and tidied the shoes in the hallway.

When Catarina came in she said, You're doing the bath including the toilet and Julieta's room. Looks like she didn't hoover the whole three years she lived here.

Catarina nodded.

Melissa had called Femi and said why won't you come live here and Femi had said I need to look after my mum and keep saving, I'm not going to work for Marc forever am I, and she had said Aren't you? So she called Ivy and said, Ivy can't you leave Will and come live with us or bring Will with you, and Ivy had said that it would be so fun to live with them, but no it would be too crowded with Will and anyway they were settled now in Camberwell. Melissa had said, I wish we could live next door to each other and not forty-five minutes away and Ivy had said me too Mel I wish that too. Melissa used the pictures of the rooms she'd used in the last ad, the one that Catarina had seen, and posted them on the spare room site. Julieta had said, You have two weeks to find someone because I'm not paying rent next month.

The first person arrived at 7pm. Catarina opened the door. A small woman introduced herself with an Australian accent. She said –

This is the living room? And it's £550 for the bedroom? Is that including bills? Can I see it? Can I check the water pressure in the shower? Who else lives here

It's me and Melissa – who was in the living room – and Olivia, she works nights which is why she isn't here.

What do you do?

I'm a student, Melissa's a developer and Olivia is a journalist.

The small woman stood in the corridor. How much is council tax?

£65 a month each.

Thank you I'll think about it.

When could you move in? they said.

The second person didn't turn up.

The third person arrived at 7.45pm. Melissa opened the door. They introduced themselves in an Eastern European sounding accent.

I'm twenty-one, they said. I'm a student.

Melissa and Catarina looked at each other.

I like to go out a lot

Melissa nodded.

When could you move in? they said.

The fourth person arrived at 8.10pm, a man wearing a vest.

I work in recruitment, he said. And I'm trying to get into wrestling

Melissa nodded.

Where are you from? You don't look

She's from London

And where are *you* from?

When could you move in? they said.

The fifth person came at 8.45pm. The person Olivia knew from work. A woman with a drawling voice.

Is this the living room?

Yes

And the kitchen

As you can see

And Mile End is the closest tube?

Yes

And I was wondering, do you have any trouble around here? Walking home at night I've heard it's a bit rough around here and this being an estate too. Is it safe?

When could you move in? they said.

The sixth person arrived at 9pm. She was tall and had dyed pink hair.

I came because I saw on your ad that one of you is a vegan? And I was wondering is it a queer-friendly household?

Yes

And yes, yes.

Catarina and Melissa looked at each other.

The fifth person stood in the kitchen / living room.

The only thing is I need you to know I am a very messy person to live with. I'm not so good with tidying up and cleaning rotas. Always leaving apples cores and biscuits and finding them under sofa cushions two weeks later.

Melissa closed her eyes.

When could you move in? they said.

They lay slumped on the sofa. Melissa stood to make tea. She began to write a message to Olivia and then stopped.

The guy has messaged me to say he wants the room.

Catarina didn't say anything.

I don't want to live with him.

She put a vegan pizza in the oven.

They ate the vegan pizza sitting on the balcony. Melissa was sat next to a mini palm she'd bought in Sainsbury's. She rolled a cigarette, sprinkling a little hash into it. Catarina sat behind her, her legs flat, her back almost against the wall. Behind them was a wall of plastic bottles that Olivia had cut in half and filled with soil and hung up in April. The plastic cast a foggy green onto the balcony. Lettuce seedlings poked out of them. Melissa put the hash cigarette in her mouth and lit it. Their spiderwort plant and all its spiderwort children hung around them.

Catarina closed her eyes. She listened to the sounds of the street and the street behind that and the street behind that. Catarina thought of a tiny lizard climbing up the wall of a white house with a white veranda. She spoke –

I have been thinking

Yeah

I'm not going to cling onto Pedro

Melissa nodded. Fair enough.

My mother always clings to everything – or she used to –

Catarina frowned.

Pedro can be my best friend instead

An upgrade

Yeah

Melissa leant her head against the brick

Catarina held her hand out. Melissa passed her the spliff. Catarina inhaled, looking at the street.

I am wondering Melissa

Yeah

Do you think you can have really good sex with someone you're not in love with

Melissa paused. Yeah. It can be really exciting

Catarina nodded.

It's different good isn't it.

Catarina was silent.

Melissa spoke

I guess it's harder to feel comfortable straight away. Melissa tilted her head. Depends on each person's mood. How wanted they feel.

Yeah

There will always be nerves and stuff

Melissa shifted where she sat.

I – I spent so long trying to work out how to feel comfortable myself

Catarina nodded.

How to feel control and surrender at the same time

That is what I had with Pedro
Always?
Always.

The building opposite and the street and the sky changed colours.
Melissa shrugged her body.

I had this girlfriend once

Yeah?

Yeah at school. We were friends from when we were really young,
like ten years old.

Catarina listened.

She arrived in the middle of the year and no one wanted to be her
friend.

Catarina nodded.

I got stuck with her on a school trip to the London Aquarium. There
used to be a sting ray tank where you could lean over and touch the
sting rays. The whole class was there and no one was really touching
them. But she wanted to touch the sting rays. She was holding my hand
and she pulled us right up to the glass and she leant over trying to reach
them but they kept swimming away and she kept leaning and leaning
until she fell in. Still holding my hand. She just looked at me. From
inside the tank. That's what she was like. For her art GCSE she painted
a huge picture of me using a lot of glossy dark colours and bits of cloth
and sequins and all kinds of shiny things. Photographs of the galaxy
and other planets. She made my hair 3D like it fell out of the canvas.
They hung it in the school dining room, everybody saw it, all the other
kids and teachers. It was the worst thing. And the best thing

Catarina tilted her head

What happened

Melissa shook her head. She breathed out. We stopped talking. We
were really different

Catarina opened her mouth to ask a question

But I guess most of all I needed to reject her before she could reject me. For a long time I was really angry at her. And then – And then when my mum died she never called me

Catarina said nothing. A motorbike revved and slowed. Melissa looked out at the street and the building opposite. The sky was lilac and then orange and then blue.

She was your first love

Melissa nodded.

Pedro had always said that life in London would be like the film *Notting Hill*. Sedate and quiet and unperturbed by politics. And she had said, And then you meet a famous actress, fall in love with her. And he had squeezed her hand and said, Or you will be awkwardly seduced by an English gentleman who owns a bookshop?

They had gone to Notting Hill, in the end. The weather had been shit that day but they were determined to go – not only because of the film but because of the line from the song. They had begun at the very top of Portobello Road where the rickety stalls sold antiques and the shops were filled with ball gowns and expensive vintage clothing. They walked down the hill past the houses that were painted pastel colours like in Olinda. Pink, yellow, green, blue. The road narrowed and the stalls started selling cannabis paraphernalia and tourist tat that said I Heart London and The Beatles. Someone was playing Bob Marley and selling pictures of Carnival. They had walked down a side street into a crescent road where every house was at least five Georgian floors of smooth white wall like giant hanging bedsheets. They passed a roundabout with a fanning palm tree. As they walked back past the Electric Cinema, Pedro looked at her. They walked past the vegetable market and the Starbucks and the stall selling gourmet mashed potato to the market by the huge underpass. Pedro tried on a leather jacket that cost £200 and Catarina put on a pair of knee-high boots. Tourists moved around them. They didn't buy anything.

So this is where Caetano Veloso and Gilberto Gil lived

Pedro half-hummed, emphasising the plosives, saying something about a policeman, something so pleased to please them.

Catarina looked at her phone. Apparently David Cameron has a house around here now.

Pedro looked around.

He had hummed the song, and she had sung it, before turning down between the tower blocks to Ladbroke Grove tube station. He had said, Portobello Road, Electric Cinema – you remember the song, about the sound of reggae –

And she had looked at him, *I'm alive*

It was August in London. The trees were full and heavy with leaves, and the city moved slow in the heat. Carnival weekend was grey and they stayed at home. On the evening of 29th August 2016 they sat on the L-shaped sofa. Pedro was on speakerphone. Five thousand miles away in the upper chamber of a country a vote would be held.

The buildings were modernist, concrete made into the shape of an upturned bowl and a downturned bowl, around them the land was flat with grass. The buildings in that city were 500km from the sea and had been planned in straight roads and right angles up to its edges where it became unplanned. Airplanes flew into the city. Outside the building was hot, 25C. Inside the building people wore suits in air-conditioned rooms and sweated with emotion. Airplanes flew out of the city. On the grass people gathered and shouted and waved placards and banners, standing in two groups.

One group shouted –
Democracia

One group shouted –
Tchau querida

In the upturned bowl men with mostly white colour skin stood in suits and some women with mostly white colour skin stood in suits; their bodies lunged and sweated in their suits. Green and yellow placards, and red and white placards. Their voices rang –

Democracia
Tchau querida

An older-looking woman approached the podium in the middle of the chamber. The chamber was round. The chamber rose around her. She wore red lipstick and had an overbite. She wore heavy eyeliner. Her suit was black with flowers on it like a curtain. Her hair rose in a quiff. When she spoke, she was slow and not so charismatic. She was a little stout. While she watched her Melissa felt a weird pull in her chest. Something like patriotism, something like history inside of her body. This woman looked her mother's age if her mother had got older

The woman began to speak

You can understand what she is saying? Catarina said.
Melissa watched the woman adjust her jacket.
Sort of
I will say it in English

They leant forwards on the sofa. Melissa moved her hands together then apart. She felt cold under her clothes. She looked at Catarina, who was staring at the screen.

Catarina whispered in English –

Twice I have seen the face of death close. When I was tortured for days and days, submitted to acts that make us doubt in humanity and the very meaning of life, and when a serious and extremely painful illness could have shortened my life.

Catarina breathed

From that time, apart from the painful scars of torture, a record has survived, in one photo, of my presence in front of my executioners, in a moment when I looked up with my head held high while they hid their faces from fear that they would be recognised and judged by history. Today four decades later there is no illegal prison there is no torture.

Pedro's whisper came through on the speakerphone – Incorrect
Catarina shook her head through her fingers – Pedro
Melissa breathed in. She listened to the woman with the overbite on the screen speak in Portuguese.

Não tenho dúvida que
também desta vez
todos nós seremos julgados pela história.

                                    I have no doubt that
                                    this time also
                        we will all be judged by history.

The senators voted.

Catarina was shaking

Wine?

No

Vodka?

Vodka.

Okay

I'll go to the shop now – Catarina, you come with me

Okay

We'll drink it with coke or soda

Okay. And you Mel smoke as many cigarettes as you want

Yes

Let's go out

Yes

Olivia you're here, you're coming out.

What

I'm going to get vodka now. Olivia are you working

In the morning

Okay well have a drink with us

Now?

Have you seen the news Olivia

No?

The president of Brazil's been fucking impeached

Dilma?

Yeah

Oh fuck

I have 489 unread messages on my family whatsapp group

We'll see you in five minutes.

On the way to the shop Catarina ran through the estates down Hamlet's Way across the road across the nighttime park until she stood, panting, in front of the satin black canal. She reached into her pocket and threw her phone into the canal water while Melissa watched. It plopped into the water, screen still bright, then sank.

Music on loud. Nothing old. Synthetic sounds and cigarettes on the balcony. Nothing sad. No happy music. Olivia eating beans out of the tin.

I'm calling a cab

Olivia you call Ivy and tell her she's coming out, I'm calling Femi

In the uber the driver said – Where you from? Brazil? This one, she looks more Brazilian but she says she is from London, You you look like European like me I'm from Hungary

Anyone can look Brazilian

You could be Brazilian, Dilma's family was from Bulgaria, Clarice Lispector was originally Ukrainian

Dilma. She is the president right?

There were no doors just plastic sheets like at a butcher's at the place that the fliers with the papaya and the guava directed them to. It was August and the night was too hot too humid. The plastic sheets hung from a doorway on a side street off Bethnal Green Road. A tall person with a blue wig and stripper heels sat with their legs crossed at the door beside a sign that said –

Solidarity - £8
Waged - £5
Unwaged - £3

They paid £15 and stepped into the plastic sheets. The dancefloor was concrete. There were no doors. The outdoors was inside. The room was not big; it had a raised part and a bar and DJ booth and all over the room was bedecked with fairy lights and plastic fruit and flowers. Tiny watermelon halves. A disco ball. Plastic monstera leaves and ivy. The space was not yet full. Reggaeton. They stumbled.

People speaking Spanish and some people speaking Portuguese. People wearing wigs and crop tops and big heels and skirts with leg hair and armpit hair and moustaches and people wearing trainers and people wearing big flowing skirts and people wearing latex and people wearing leather. Feminine-looking people dancing with feminine-looking people. Men dancing with men. Men wearing lipstick that was silver. Catarina's body started to move. Ivy and her boyfriend, Will, arrived.

A voice rang out in that accent that struck and bent Melissa's bones. A woman wearing rings and a sheepskin coat who she had seen before, her hair in curls, greeted her with arms outstretched –

Te vi em King's Cross!
At the protest –
Hi
E sua amiga –
Yes this is Catarina
Yes
The woman wiped her eyes with her hand
Eu não acredito
Eu não acredito
Eu não acredito

They held each other. Catarina's fingers in the sheepskin coat. The woman's rings around her shoulders. Catarina reached for Melissa's hand.

This is Olivia
This my friend Maria
Marissa
Zé
Melissa
Catarina
Olivia
Ivy
Fala sério minha família também mora em Olinda

Someone beckoned to her and Catarina felt her body begin to move. Oh. Someone beckoned to her. She imagined Pedro. Where was Melissa. Olivia pulled her into a toilet with graffiti all over it (ACAB / i love pussy / ACAB) pulling a baggie and a key out of her jacket pocket.

Catarina was drunk   Yeah sure

It hit the back of her nose like ice and she felt the inside of the back of her neck and her mouth and her teeth.

It won't kick in now
Ok
Let's dance

The room was dark and the plastic fruits shook and all their bodies shook moving in time. Melissa danced with a person who looked like a woman with forest brown armpit hair and Catarina was almost staring. She had never been to a nightclub in London but   the music was music she had not danced to at home but heard playing over walls and in the street. Music like the music Pedro played at home. Her shoulders moved good movements. She would have to contact Pedro. Her mother. She put her hand in her pocket for her phone and it was not there but Catarina was not worried about it because by that time she had forgotten what her hand was in her pocket for. Olivia danced around her, Ivy grinding on her boyfriend, Femi danced around her, shirt undone, like she had never seen him

The lights came on. It's all we have a licence for 2am   She couldn't see Melissa   couldn't see Olivia. But Melissa knew exactly where they were going grabbed her in a swoop came from nowhere,

We're going to Tottenham
What

There's a party there, Jenny invited me the other day in Clapton, Femi's here did you see Femi just arrived.

In the uber Catarina put her forehead against the glass   she was un peeling

It was that kind of N22, N16, N17 terraced Victorian house with four bedrooms and coving above the small bay windows that Melissa knew. It had new cheaper floors, lino in the kitchen and old beige carpet in the living room. The furniture had been taken out apart from two sofas

302

in the living room. Cigarettes indoors. Spliffs. Everything smelt like smoke and outdoors, the front door opening and people coming in, pushing past each other shouting and greeting each other. Shorts and jeans and shoes for dancing in; music so loud the house shook. The best parties were always in August. White girls with shaved heads kissing each other. Olivia dancing with someone. Black girls wining on each other. Catarina lost her thinking self. She was suddenly so fucking good at dancing. She moved all of her, each bone in sequence like the keys of a piano. Every song was The Song was The Song. Time passed around. She smoked four or five or six cigarettes in a row. She remembered everyone's names. Melissa disappeared talking to someone and someone saying something to her something like Oh you went to school with Ruthie Curtis Femi in the corner of the room kissing another person who looked like a man Big speakers Catarina un peeling like a bana na

On the sofa in the living room the sun still wasn't rising. Someone called Hasan was passing a zoot around they said I felt so much more at home back home even though I was born here, I think it was the sun I think I need the sun

And Catarina said, There's no such thing as home but here it is too cold

They lost Ivy entirely

She overheard someone say

Oh you went to school with Ruth Curtis

Ruthie

Senhoras e Senhores

Women and

men

Senadores

Senators –

Catarina had followed Melissa through this bit of the curve of the earth from east to north, sliding spilling frictionless across this bit of the curve of the earth this nighttime city like kids in tights gliding on their knees across parquet floors, their bodies as tall as all the buildings

Nothing ever happened in August

pedaço de mim
(1969–74)

1.

A woman at the side of the road with no bag on her back. Tall. Her skin is light brown, young. Chin high.

A woman in a blue beetle car with dark hair around her face and her foot on the pedal. Her skin is worn out white.

The nighttime is purple.

> Get in
> You will drive?
>
> I will drive.
> How far?
> 200 kilometres, 300 tomorrow
> To where
> A safe house
> Where
> West of here, no interior de Pernambuco
>
> You have said goodbye to – everyone?
> I have.

The woman in the driver's seat starts the engine. She says
> What should I call you?

> *Clytemnestra*
> What? Cli-tem que? I cannot call you that, it is not even Brazilian,
what is
> It is an ancient name, from Greece
> Greece? No you cannot –
> Why not

You know why not.

You must have a name that disappears, just as you must disappear. A name that dissolves into the air after it is spoken – Maria or Ana – if you want you may make it diminutive, like Aninha

If the great communist leader Carlos Marighella can be *Professor Menezes* why can I not be—
Carlos Marighella was killed
What –
It happened yesterday
No – it is a lie, it is always a lie, to demoralise us –
Open the glove compartment. That is today's newspaper

MORTO O CHEFE TERRORISTA MARIGHELLA

There is a picture of his body inside

You will have to be Maria or Ana

Silence. Inside the car is dark. The woman in the driver's seat turns the steering wheel.

I carry his writings with me everywhere
Marighella?
Yes.

Clitemnestra wipes her face with the back of her hand.

Why did you want this name, Clitemnestra?
She was a warrior, killer of kings
You want to kill kings
I believe in revolution

The woman with her hands on the steering wheel looks at her

> I can call you Clitemnestra but only when we are alone
> Clitemnestra looks at her.
> But you must respond to Maria in public.
> Clitemnestra nods.
> The other woman smiles.
> Clitemnestra, killer of kings

They hit a bridge. The traffic around them slows.

On the other side is a military blockade. A young man with close-cropped hair, military police, holds a gun the length of his torso. He looks ahead at them and they look at him through the windows of the car. Black boots.

Clitemnestra killer of kings says
> Merda Merda
> Do not worry. They will not stop us –

> Isha
> Do not worry
> It's the police, their boots
> Don't worry, breathe

They pass through the blockade. Glide. Into the outskirts of the city. Bad housing.

The woman in the driver's seat sits back. She pulls the wig of black hair from her head, revealing short brown hair underneath. For the first time, Clitemnestra killer of kings sees her properly, her mouth and eyes and nose illuminated and then dark, illuminated and then dark again in the headlights of passing cars.

And Clitemnestra killer of kings says
   Menina

And Clitemnestra killer of kings is speaking, turning her body in her seat, her hands on the dashboard, Carlos Marighella's dead body on the newspaper sheets falling to the floor of the car.

You are the governor's daughter! You are the famous revolutionary! I did not recognise you in your black wig but it is you—
   I—
Is it true what the newspapers said? That you killed one of the military police? Right in the centre of the forehead. Bang. Is this why you are running? I know your name, I've read it in the newspaper – How is your father? He is a good man. I know your name –

And Clitemnestra killer of kings is saying the other woman's name. She shouts it.

LAURA

Laura the famous revolutionary exhales. Foot on the pedal. She looks at the young woman to her right.

2.

The little beetle car moves west, inland, through black hills that roll like giants' shoulders. Sugar cane grows blue on the fields. No moon.

Clitemnestra killer of kings turns to her companion. She speaks quickly –

Are you a Marxist-Leninst or Maoist or a Trotskyist? Are you aligned with the urban or rural fight? Ideologically, that is to say? And what about tactically? What about the electoral path, such as the Brazilian Communist Party and the Communist Party of Indonesia have chosen? What is your view on violent resistance? I myself believe that unjust violence will be met by just violence, that we must follow the path that is left to us with revolutionary love –

Laura the famous revolutionary looks at the road

Did you train in Cuba? Or China? Or kidnap any ambassadors? Or, you must have robbed a bank, I think at least one or two for revolutionary funds

Laura the famous revolutionary frowns. She says –

Então. You know who I am.

Clitemnestra killer of kings looks at her.

Yes.

You have read in the newspapers about my father

Yes, he is in exile in Paris

You know my mother, my sisters

I do not know your sisters? How many do you have?

Laura the famous revolutionary looks at the road.

I have four sisters. The youngest will be eleven years old in March. She is a baby

Ten years old is not a baby

When they saw us together people used to think she was my daughter, because of the age difference.

313

What is her name?

Sonita, Sônia

Would you like a daughter?

That is a strange question

Laura the famous revolutionary looks at Clitemnestra killer of kings in the dark.

You do not have sisters?

No

Brothers?

Yes.

(breathe)

Clitemnestra killer of kings looks at her. But I should not say anymore. It is better not to compromise my identity. She looks away from Laura the famous revolutionary. You should not know who I am. That it is what I was told.

Laura the famous revolutionary looks back at the road. There are no other cars. They sit in silence.

The sun rises around them, turning the sugar cane from blue to green.

3.

They arrive in the early hours. A man stands at the side of the road outside a village. Laura the famous revolutionary stops the car next to him and he gets into the back seat. He leans forwards, tells Laura the famous revolutionary there is a shack where she can leave the car so that it is hidden. They walk through matted undergrowth parallel to the road over dry palm leaves. A goat eats caju fruits from the ground. Laura the famous revolutionary pulls a mango from a tree. They reach a shack with one room or two rooms. He takes them inside. There are two chairs and a concrete floor. An older-looking woman sleeps on a mattress under a sheet. Behind a door, there is another mattress and sheet.

Thank you, Laura the famous revolutionary says.

Wooden shutters block the sunlight. When Laura the famous revolutionary closes her eyes the outside sounds get louder, closer. A car changes gear. A boot steps onto the dry palm undergrowth. She hears a thud, heavy like a shot.

4.

Clitemnestra killer of kings wakes. She needs to find a toilet. By the
stove, an older woman makes coffee. Laura the famous revolutionary is
already sitting at the table. Laura and the older woman talk as if they
have known each other for a long time. On the table is a paper bag
of caju fruits. A vessel of coffee. The room is empty, except for some
things, a statue of the Virgin Mary, some pans. The concrete walls have
been painted pastel green. At some point, the older woman leaves.

You know them?

I have known Wagner and his mother for many years. Laura the
famous revolutionary's gaze moves sideways. I have family connections
here.

What's his name? Wagi-nar? It is not a subtle codinome either.

It is just his name

Clitemnestra killer of kings fills her mouth and throat with coffee.

So we leave tonight?

Yes

Laura the famous revolutionary cuts a caju fruit in half with her
knife. She pours herself more coffee, adds sugar.

But there is somewhere I would like to go to first.

5.

They walk along a small footpath away from the village for thirty minutes. It is almost like the desert. Like a Lampião fairy tale. Clitemnestra killer of kings imagines that they are cowboys, cangaceiros riding horses, wielding guns to protect the Northeast from the government, stealing from the rich and shooting them on the spot as they beg for mercy. Mosquitoes bite Clitemnestra killer of kings. A cactus blinks. The sun is low in the sky at the end of the dirt path. At the end of the dirt path there is a river. As the path veers to the left Clitemnestra killer of kings sees that plants and the leaves of trees hang and slip into the river. Big monstera leaves, drooping jaca fruit on drooping branches. There are boulders in the river and the water pools and crashes between them. There are frogs and fish and snakes in the calm parts of the river. The riverbed is like sand.

At the riverbank Clitemnestra killer of kings watches Laura the famous revolutionary undress herself of Laura. She disappears, dissolves. Small woman. Thick thighs and back. Sun worn. Hair stuck against her ears.

Laura the famous revolutionary steps into the water.

Clitemnestra killer of kings says
    What if someone sees us?

Laura washes herself.
    They will not know us

Clitemnestra steps into the water. She folds her body under the cold river. Her hair rises in a pillar over her head.

6.

They leave at dusk. We must drive by the cover of the night until we leave the state, Laura the famous revolutionary says. The beetle car moves west under the pink and setting sun.

Clitemnestra killer of kings speaks
You could be in exile in Uruguay or Paris or Algeria, instead of running here
It is expensive for the movement to send people abroad
(Pause)
But you have the money – your family –

Laura the famous revolutionary moves her hands on the steering wheel.

If it was me I would go to Cuba, or to Vietnam where I am needed in the fight
You would go so far?
She shrugs
I have already left where I am from
You are young.
I am not so young.
Laura the famous revolutionary looks at the road.

The duty of the revolutionary is to make revolution. I cannot leave Brazil
Clitemnestra killer of kings holds up the newspaper – The revolution is everywhere. It is in Liberia, Mozambique, Indonesia, Ireland, the coal mines of England, Spain, Vietnam –

Laura the famous revolutionary moves her head to the side, a nod not nod. They move through the sugar cane. Foot on the pedal.

7.

The nun meets them before the sunrise, while the land is still blue and silver. Her habit is long and grey not black. She has furry eyebrows. Olá irmã, she says, smiling. Laura the famous revolutionary leaves the car under a sheet under a tree in the garden of a house. She puts her black wig on. They walk down a dirt road and then a dirt alley into a church. Inside the church is painted white with gold. The nun takes them to a small room with a mattress and a sheet. Candles and bibles pile up on the floor of the room. The Virgin Mary looks at them. The Virgin Mary looks at her baby. The nun whispers to Laura the famous revolutionary for some time and Laura the famous revolutionary listens. The nun hands them a jug of water. The nun makes the sign of the cross.

Laura the famous revolutionary listens as the town outside makes its waking sounds. Her companion closes her eyes, closes her body, around the bedsheet. Laura the famous revolutionary does not sleep. She thinks of her youngest sister.

To Laura the famous revolutionary, Clitemnestra killer of kings looks like a teenager, seventeen or eighteen. She wonders what she has left behind.

8.

One woman makes a sound. The other woman hears her, half awake.
The woman shakes.

She murmurs to her
    Can you hear your body breathing
    Yes
    Can you hear your body breathing?
    Yes
    Again, and again?
    Yes
    Again and again
    Yes
    Again and again
    Yes
    Can you count the breaths
    Yes
    Can you count the breaths?
    Yes
    Tell me when you get to two hundred.

    Keep counting

In the morning, they sit in silence as the people of the town sing in
chorus on the other side of the wall.

9.

The new motorway will be the new the great Brazil. No part unknown, unreached, indomitable. From Acre to Belém; from the Federal District to Imperatiz. No dark heart in this country the size of a continent. Two, three, four day journeys into the forest will become one-hour drives. The end of the land found, located, mapped, to be had and known by a narrow strip of hot black tarmac called the Transamazônica. Government posters announce:

VOCÊ CONSTROI O BRASIL

And the newspapers declare an economic miracle and the economic miracle means more motorways, more mines, more factories, more dams, more of this great country Brasil.

10.

They drive once in the daytime. West. Their car wheels spin against the tarmac, which the sun appears to melt in the distance. They see, ahead of them, something blocking the road. Laura the famous revolutionary thinks she should turn the car around.

It is just an overturned truck –

Laura the famous revolutionary squints.

Laura the famous revolutionary slows and veers around the steel which spills out of the truck in logs. Clitemnestra killer of kings leans her hand and head out of the window. Steam rises from the belly of the truck. Two men stand beside it smoking cigarettes.

Two hundred metres ahead an older-looking man is grilling chicken and beef on skewers over charcoal. The smoke and the smell move into the car.

Please –

Laura the famous revolutionary slows the car.

Clitemnestra killer of kings jumps out of the car and buys two skewers of meat.

Laura the famous revolutionary looks sideways.

Clitemnestra killer of kings sits on a rock under the sun next to Laura the famous revolutionary's car door. She bites into the meat and it is wet and hot.

Come on, sit outside.

Laura the famous revolutionary inhales.

They will not know you

Laura the famous revolutionary looks at Clitemnestra killer of kings, the sun on her head. She takes one skewer of meat from Clitemnestra.

Clitemnestra killer of kings closes her eyes. She pulls a piece of chicken off the wooden stick into her mouth and chews.

I have been wondering, do you have a husband?
Would I be here, if I had a husband?

Clitemnestra killer of kings frowns
  You might be running from him.

Laura the famous revolutionary looks at Clitemnestra killer of kings.

  How old are you?
  Nineteen

Laura the famous revolutionary wonders how many years she is adding.

  How old are you? Thirty? Thirty-two?
  Twenty-nine.
  Twenty-nine! See you are not so old yourself
  What were you doing – before
  I was going to study, at university

Laura the famous revolutionary nods

Laura the famous revolutionary looks behind them. Two truckers approach them, smoking cigarettes. One of them is holding a magazine. He buys a skewer of meat. He looks at the blue beetle car. He has light eyes. He puts down the magazine.

  I'm going to talk to him
  No –
  Clitemnestra killer of kings stands. Laura the famous revolutionary wants to stop her. But she cannot bring herself to step out of the car into the light.

Clitemnestra killer of kings walks up to the truckers. She is as tall as both of them. She points to the magazine. Laura the famous revolutionary wants to grab her.

Have you finished reading it? Can I take this?

He looks at her, throws his cigarette on the floor. Nods.

11.

In the car Laura the famous revolutionary thinks that they should not travel in the daytime again. She checks the mirror.

She keeps driving. They could have been police. The sun lowers in the sky. Clitemnestra killer of kings reads the magazine.

Clitemnestra killer of kings says –
    Look at this look
    What?
    Stop the car and look
    What? I cannot
    Clitemnestra killer of kings opens the magazine to the centrefold. Laura the famous revolutionary turns her head to her.
    What – What is it? Do not poke me!
    Look
    Laura the famous revolutionary looks at the photograph in the magazine.
    The bottom third of the photograph, the close foreground, is grey and filled with light. Above the grey foreground is blue almost black, an infinite background. Something is suspended in the infinite blue almost black. A half orb. It shimmers as if covered with cobwebs.
    It is from Apollo 8
    What is that?
    A spaceship, a rocket
    The North Americans have gone into the heavens
    Yes.
    Laura the famous revolutionary inhales.

We are there, under the clouds. This photograph is Earth.

Stop the car, there is nobody here. Look at it properly.

12.

All around them they hear the sound of crickets and insects in the undergrowth. Fireflies over water somewhere. In the leaves of the canopies of trees, treebirds make speaking sounds. Mosquitoes bite their hands and necks and ankles. Laura the famous revolutionary makes a small fire. She places four cobs of corn on it still in their husks. They rub salt under the husks before they eat them and the salt melts. They hang their hammocks on adjacent trees. Clitemnestra killer of kings shits in a hole in the earth that she digs with a spoon. She uses the spoon to cover the hole with earth again. As she crouches she looks up at the stars and the sky. Everything is indigo.

One woman puts her hands behind her head.
 I feel free
 The other woman exhales.
 I feel free too tonight
 Something in her unbinds.

When they meet strangers they call themselves Maria and Ana. Laura the famous revolutionary does not know if there is anywhere that Clitemnestra killer of kings can return to. In the states that they drive through, there are posters of terrorists but none of Laura the famous revolutionary's face.

VOCÊ CONSTROI O BRASIL

This is the first year. Waiting.

13.

Brazil wins the 1970 World Cup. And Maria and Ana dos Santos watch it in colour on a television in a bar in a small town in the middle of the country. Maria's boyfriend Jorge has his arm around her. Everyone in the small town is in the bar because of the colour television. Children, old men, old women, dogs, everyone is in the bar. Watching the colour television makes their eyes big. No one is in the street. Everyone is sweating, singing, hoping. When the whistle blows it is the best day of Ana's life and Maria's life and Ana throws her beer in the air, she hugs the person next to her, an older lady with a walking stick. Maria throws her beer in the air. Jorge kisses her. He's crying. Fireworks go off like guns. Dogs run down the street and then cats run down the street. Maria and Ana dance for hours. They wrap themselves in the flag. Green and Yellow. Green and Yellow. Green for the forest and Yellow for the sun and for the beaches. Blue and White. For the sky and for the sea and the sea foam and the stars.

14.

Maria is eighteen and Ana is twenty-five. Maria has black hair to her shoulders and Ana has black hair to her shoulders. Ana has lighter skin than Maria. They are sisters who have come south to the town by the mine in the middle of the country from another city looking for work just like everyone else who moved south to the town by the mine in the middle of the country has come there from another city looking for work. Maria and Ana go to church. In church they make the sign of the cross over their bodies. They live in a two-roomed house in the outskirts of the town by the mine where they sleep under a sheet on a mattress they share. When they arrived they painted the inside lilac and the outside blue. A house as blue as the sky, Ana said. There is a cat with a tear in his left ear who they name cãozinho and they feed every night. They are friends with their neighbour Diana, who is a teacher. They are friends with their neighbour Edivânia who works at the mine and used to be a union leader. They are friends with their other neighbours. They know a couple of people in the town next door. Their family is from the Northeast they say. They go to work every day in the factory. They drink beer in the bar that plays football and cheer for Pelé when he scores against England. They dance to Chico Buarque songs until those songs are banned. They try to sing along to Construção but it is hard to learn the lyrics. Maria has a boyfriend called Jorge who is known locally for his very hairy chest.

15.

Maria and Ana go to the meeting where Edivânia who used to be a union leader speaks about conditions at the iron ore mine where they work and then they go to another meeting about conditions at the factory that processes the iron where Jorge works. They print pamphlets for the meetings on a mimeograph at night in the local school which Diana who is a teacher gives them access to. The pamphlet has a list of the names of the workers who have died at the factory and the names of the workers who have died in the mine. It is also true that wages have not increased in six years while profit and productivity have doubled though they do not write this. It is also true that there are military police on the factory floor and even a room where they take people. They do not write this either. Maria knows how to work a mimeograph. Maria and Ana sit in the school together at night. They hope there are no boots outside, no knock on the door. The mimeograph makes this sound: plec plec plec. They hold a meeting in the room of their house. Edivânia who used to be a union leader is speaking. Dust in the air. Sweat on their foreheads. When the police come the first time Maria and Ana say they do not know what the police are talking about. It was a birthday party, see here are the leftover brigadeiros, would you like one senhor? When the police come the second time, they are gone and so is Edivânia and so is the blue beetle car.

16.

The mimeograph works like this: you put a sheet of paper into the mouth of the tray and you put your stencil over the paper full of ink, and then you turn the handle. This sucks in the sheet of paper and the stencil over it. Make sure they are the right way around! Then you put your papers in the lower tray. Then you turn the handle again. Then the copies come. The mimeograph makes this sound: plec plec plecplec.

17.

They drive 700 kilometres until they get to the sea. They lie on the sand. They drink beers. Sand pushes through their hair to the backs of their heads. The sun is not too bright yet. The sea pushes against their feet.

A child kicks a ball at them. They kick it back.

When this is over I will have a child
You are too young
No of course I am not
A child?
A daughter

With Jorge?
With anyone
Perhaps you are pregnant now and we will bring the baby up together

On the road
Yes
In the car
Yes, we will show her the whole country

Then we will keep driving! Up the spine of Latin America to Cuba to liberation!

Laura the famous revolutionary closes her eyes.

The sun starts to glare.

They drink beer until they cannot see.

18.

The sea is on its back. They dive into it: hands elbows shoulders body

Clitemnestra killer of kings explains the rules of canasta to Laura the famous revolutionary, and they play cards in the heat of the day under an umbrella.

When Laura the famous revolutionary cannot sleep Clitemnestra killer of kings asks her if she can hear her body breathing.

They meet a comrade and the comrade gives them a large box, which is heavy, and a set of instructions.

Clitemnestra killer of kings suspects the box is full of paper and ink; Laura the famous revolutionary assumes it contains ammunition.

19.

They drive 1000 kilometres until they reach the place where the tarmac ends. Construction abandoned to the rain. They drive along a dirt road to a shack surrounded by the forest at the side of a river. Rainwater cuts and runs through the orange earth till it gets to the river. They can go no further by car. They take a heavy box out of the car. A man will take them across the river in his canoe. The river laps against the earth where it has been eroded into the roots of trees and mangrove lip. They lift the heavy box into the boat. The man crouches in the boat. He steadies it with his feet as they step onto it.

Paulistas, he says, smiling.

The river is soft for them and it carries the boat. All they can hear is mosquitoes and water flowing. An older man and a woman greet them holding pistols. The woman has a rifle on her back. When she sees Laura the famous revolutionary's face, she smiles.

Their house is made of straw. Inside, the woman, who is a nurse, who had the rifle on her back, makes them coffee. Laura unloads the box.

20.

That night there will be a party in the forest. In a clearing not too far and not too close to the road, not too far and not too close to the village. Three local families will dance with twenty communists from the forest. Children will run into the clearing in the forest and they will be given hot chocolate in metal cups. A woman will follow them, bringing three trays of soft doce de castanha. Two men will bring a deer from the forest. A woman will bring a jacu which is the supplest forest bird and a jabuti from the forest. A villager will bring a pig. And the children will carry sweetcorn in husks and when they drop the corn their older brothers will shout after them. They will pick yellow mangos from the trees.

21.

A communist from the forest will play a wooden flute and a man from the village will hit a drum with the palm and then the back of his hand Tec Tectec Tec by light of the fire against the dark of the forest and the dark of the sky, women from the village will lift their skirts in dance, toe heel, toe heel toe heel and hips Tec Tectec Tec as people clap around them children will displace them in the centre of the circle demanding praise and sweets even the old commander the one with the two grandchildren in Salvador will move his commander hips and so will the commander with the darkest skin who is 2 metres tall who trained in China and has a degree from the university of Prague and so will all the young communists the one who is an engineer and the one who is a nurse and who opened the pharmacy they will shake in their canvas trousers and their hard hands will turn soft Tec Tectec Tec and the woman who teaches the children to read in the school will turn her body inside the arms of the children and their bare feet will move on the earth, bodies over the earth, and their hair will rise dark brown skin, light brown skin, burnt white skin Tec Tectec Tec and the two women who crossed the river to the forest the day before will turn and slow and spin a hand in a hand step and stepstep step and stepstep the fire on one side of their bodies someone will play the guitar and they will sing the Romance of the Liberation of the People and they will sing Apesar de Você by Chico Buarque and they will sing The International and they will read the pamphlets they printed with the mimeograph in the forest and the communists from the forest will listen to a terecô priest from the village who will repeat the words *meus guerrilheiros quero ver estremecer* and they will play a recording from Radio Tirana that tells the world of the communists in the forest who are fighting with the people against the big capitalists and landowners and police who are in their pockets and who will despoil the Amazon for the profits of the North American imperialists and Radio Tirana will send to the communists in the forest the solidarity of the Albanian people

And they will salute their socialist comrades in Albania for their solidarity

And they will point their rifles into the sky

And they will salute to the liberation of the poor

And they will salute to the liberation of the Indigenous

And their shots will ring into the indigo night

22.

A communist who arrived recently to the forest says to Clitemnestra killer of kings –

The truth is that everyone is gone. All of our comrades are in prison or exile or dead. When I joined the revolution there were a hundred of us in a room and now there are ten. The new leader is a twenty-three-year-old boy who cannot grow a moustache. Young, like you. No one else is left. Even before Marighella died. The urban guerrilla is tired. In prison or the torturer's basement. In the cities they are disarming. The unions are dead. The fight is here. Without the support of the masses there will never be liberation or a liberated zone. And the fight of Brazil has always been the fight of the masses against the powerful in Canudos, in Contestado, of the slaves against slave masters to create quilombos

(breathe)

I have not seen Laura the famous revolutionary's photograph in the paper for a year. I know some students in the South if you need somewhere safe to go

They wake to the sound of helicopters.

23.

They sit in the blue beetle car. They drive south waiting for the police.

What will you do after the revolution
Play cards in the evening
What else
Plant a small garden, some fruit, some vegetables, some flowers. I will take Sônia to eat ice cream, and while we eat she can tell me what she has learnt at school. I will see my mother. And you
I want to become a doctor like Che Guevara, I will have my own house and a daughter
Oh yeah? You would be a good doctor I think
You think?
I do
I will finish university and be a doctor
You were at university?
Yes, I left though.

What do you think your sisters are doing now?
Right now? Sônia will be at school. Or at a friend's house. She must be looking like a young woman now. Lygia, I don't know I think she will be working, maybe as a lawyer? Lúcia too?
Perhaps they will be married. Or have children.

What about your family?
The movement is my family. You are my family.
You are not tired?

24.

They see the big city. The biggest city. They buy city clothes and they dye their hair – Clitemnestra killer of kings goes brown and short and Laura the famous revolutionary goes black and stays long. They dump their blue beetle car at the outskirts of the city and get in the revolutionary student's car and he takes them into the centre.

He tells them his codinome
    They nod.
    I am Maria.
    I am Ana.
    The revolutionary student nods.

The revolutionary student drives them into the part of the city that is beautiful. Where the houses have marble floors and chandeliers and guards. They hide in the back seat under a blanket as he talks to the porter of an apartment block. The smell of an underground garage. He takes them up the service lift. A woman in a maid's outfit gets in. She stares at the floor.

25.

Inside the apartment the revolutionary student makes them coffee and pours it into three small cups. Sugar? he asks. He slices up a mango. Would you like some? His parents own the apartment. It has a colour television. Out of the window Clitemnestra killer of kings sees more concrete than she had ever thought existed. It climbs into the sky, touches the cloud and blue.

The revolutionary student has a study and in the study there are books from floor to ceiling. There is a bedroom for each of them. And in the back, in the servants' quarters, next to a disused maid's apron and hat, there is a mimeograph.

We can help with that.

You know how to use it?

Clitemnestra killer of kings nods.

26.

Laura the famous revolutionary and Clitemnestra killer of kings disappear, dissolve. They are Maria and Ana again. If the revolutionary student knows who Laura the famous revolutionary is he does not say. They say they are sisters and he never disagrees. They sleep in the same bed. The revolutionary student studies at the university. He is young. He is from a rich family but he believes in the redistribution of capital amongst the masses. The apartment is paid for by his father but he uses it as a safe house for revolutionaries. His parents live in Germany. The revolutionary student is out most of the daytime. Most nights he is at his friend Antônio's house. The revolutionary student has a tiny moustache and large brown eyes. He is about Laura the famous revolutionary's height. He is studying medicine. His flat is tidy and the only rule is that they must close all of the windows because he is anxious the cat may jump out of a window. It is his mother's cat. He has been to Europe. He shares his lecture notes with Clitemnestra killer of kings because she tells him she wants to be a doctor. He successfully bribes 4/5 of the apartment porters not to snitch. Clitemnestra killer of kings leaves with him sometimes in the car. She goes to the university campus, and brings back textbooks. The revolutionary student calls at 18.00 every evening to let them know if he is coming home, and to check that they are okay. I will always call you; it is both for safety and for courtesy; I do not want to disturb you, the revolutionary student says.

27.

They stay up printing subversive material that the revolutionary student and his comrades will distribute at the university. Sometimes the materials say things like

ABAIXO A DITADURA. POVO NO PODER.

And sometimes they say things like

FIM ÀS PRISÕES, TORTURAS E ASSASSINATOS

They do this in the evenings and at night. At 18.00 the revolutionary student calls them to tell them that he is coming home.

28.

The mimeograph says

    plec plec plecplec
    plec plec plecplec
    plec plec plecplec
    plec plec plecplec
    plec plec plecplec
    plec plec plecplec

29.

The revolutionary student throws a party. He asks their permission first, would they mind if he had a party? That evening the apartment is full of young people, smoking marijuana and cigarettes and drinking beer and cachaça and talking about Algeria and Ireland and Vietnam and Patrice Lumumba and Gilberto Gil and Chairman Mao and Clarice Lispector. And a young man in glasses says to Maria, did you hear what happened to Commander Lamarca he lived in the forest for three weeks and then assaulted a police car and then dressed in the military police uniform and then drove to the Marginal Tietê where he abandoned the car and went to watch the football at his favourite lanchonete with a pineapple juice. And, she says, what is your opinion of Albanian socialism and the political direction of the USSR? And someone says to Ana, Did you hear about the Japanese consul who was kidnapped and stayed up all night discussing Political Economy with the kidnappers? He never gave their names to the police. And someone says to the revolutionary student, Did you hear about the communists in the forest? And the daughter of the exiled governor of Pernambuco who shot a policeman in the forehead?

Maria feels drunk. She imagines a new life in the city. She looks out over the balcony edge and sees so many lights.

30.

The revolutionary student says that if they want to leave Brazil he could arrange this. He says Argentina isn't safe anymore and nor is Uruguay. London, he says, is very nice, very cultural. Caetano was there. Cold though.

31.

One night Maria and Ana are playing cards sitting on the kitchen floor eating cheese from the supermarket and watching TV while printing subversive material for the revolutionary student. It is 19.00.

He hasn't called, Maria says

32.

plec plec plecplec
plec plec plecplec
plec plec plecplec
plec plec plecplec
plec plec plecplec
plec plec plecplec
plec plec plecplec

33.

plec plec plecplec
plec plec plecplec
plec plec plecplec
plec plec plecplec
plec plec plecplec
plec plec plecplec
plec plec plecplec
plec plec plecplec
plec plec plecplec
plec plec plecplec

34.

At 22.00, Maria says
    He has not called

35.

plec plec plecplec
plec plec plecplec
plec plec plecplec
plec plec plecplec
plec plec plecplec
plec plec plecplec
plec plec plecplec
plec plec plecplec
plec plec plecplec
plec plec plecplec

36.

At 23.00 Ana says

What will you do when this is over?
I will be a doctor like Che Guevara, then I will travel the world

I will be an old lady with many pets and plants, I would like two cats at least one called Elefante and the other called Tartaruga, I will find my sister Sônia and make her tell me what happened each day that I was gone, and we will play cards and we will eat ice cream

37.

What do you think your daughter will say of us
I think she will imagine –
When she talks about us
What will you tell her?
My daughter?
Yes
Well I will say
I think she will imagine that we are fighters, heroes
Martyrs
No, I think she will imagine that we are set in our ways, conservative and too stubborn
They will think we are not beautiful with our wrinkles and our white hair
Yes she will, she will think that we are beautiful
Beauty will not matter
Yes it will
She will think that we did not do enough
She will continue our fight
She will write and speak about us
No
Yes
Or tell reshapen stories

38.

plec plec plecplec
plec plec plecplec
plec plec plecplec
plec plec plecplec

39.

Is that the sound of –

It is the sound of the mimeograph

40.

Read me a poem
From the book on the shelf
Yes

41.

                    voais comigo
                    sobre continentes e mares
E também rastejais comigo
                    pelos túneis das noites clandestinas
                    sob o céu constelado do país
                    entre fulgor e lepra
debaixo de lençóis de lama e de terror
                    Vos esgueirais comigo, mesas velhas,
armários obsoletos gavetas perfurmadas de passado,
                    dobrais comigo as esquinas do susto
                    e esperais esperais
que o dia venha
                    E depois de tanto
                    que importa um nome?

42.

                                              fly with me
                                  over continents and tides
                        And also crawl with me
                    through the tunnels of the clandestine nights
                        under the constellated sky of this country
                              between fulgor and impurity
        beneath bedsheets of mud and terror
                              You leave quietly with me, old tables,
        obsolete wardrobes, drawers perfumed with past,
                              turn corners of sudden fear with me
                                      and hope hope
                        that the day comes

                                      And after all
                                  what's in a name?

43.

plec plec plec plec
plec plec plec plec
plec plec plec plec
plec plec plec plec
plec plec plec plec
plec plec plec plec
plec plec plec plec
plec plec plec plec

44.

Read me a book from the shelf
This is Shakespeare
Read it

45.

Read me from a book on the shelf
It is Marx
Read it

46.

Read me a book from the shelf
It is empty
Read it

47.

And the terecô priest sings
Meus guerrilheiros quero ver estremecer
enfrenta esta batalha que é para a canalha ver
soldado véio, amarelo e encapuçado
dá um tiro no danado
que ele vem amedrontado
Minha irmandade, vamos se arreunir
vamos compactuar que é para a coisa ringir
vou trabalhar, trabalhar para vencer
estando no campo da luta perde o medo de morrer

48.

plec plec plec plec
plec plec plec plec
plec plec plec plec
plec plec plec plec
plec plec plec plec
plec plec plec plec
plec plec plec plec
plec plec plec plec

49.

My guerrilheiros I want to see you shiver
Face this battle for the people to see
the soldiers spent, yellow and hooded
Shoot the coward
he comes filled with fear
My sisterhood, let us be together
let us make a pact because this thing must ECHO
I will work, work to win
on the battlefield you lose the fear of death

50.

Let the ruling classes *tremble* – at the communist revolution!

Workers of the world unite!
You have nothing to lose but your chains!

51.

plec plec plecplec
plec plec plecplec
plec plec plecplec
plec plec plecplec
plec plec plecplec

52.

THERE ARE MORE THINGS IN HEAVEN AND EARTH

53.

Where is that from? Who said *there are more things in heaven and earth*

It is from the Shakespeare, Hamlet is speaking to his friend Horatio

Horatio is worried that Hamlet will kill himself

And Hamlet says No, he will not kill himself, because there is everything to live for because so much more is possible than what they have imagined yet, because there are more things in heaven and on earth

54.

Is that the sound

of boots?

55.

Clitemnestra killer of kings I must tell you now why I am running. Something happened to me, it was two months before we met. For years I had been in the same working cell in Recife. With my friend Paulinho, he was also younger than me. We were working together since the beginning. Sixty-four to sixty-nine. When we started we thought that it might all be over soon and by the end we thought these are the worst years the heaviest years, years like hands and feet of lead. I had just finished studying at the university, I was studying history but by that time I did not care about the diploma. Even before the coup I did not care about the diploma; I was a communist, a revolutionary, I thought my father was a liberal for believing that elections could change anything, I believed that the duty of every good revolutionary was to make revolution. The library was for revolution and revolutionary knowledge. The classroom was for revolutionary teaching! The campus was for revolutionary organising! I was not a big reader but my mother had said to me, Read Marx, read José Martí, Rosa Luxembourg, and so I did read, because it was a revolutionary thing, do you understand? It must have happened to you when you were recruited – you had to read the books. So I read the books. I had been reading them already, books from all over, books from Europe, novels from Russia. My mother was from a Jewish family from Eastern Europe, and she knew of a whole other world of persecution but another intellectual world also – Hegel and Shakespeare and Tolstoy. She brought books to our house from book fairs and libraries. She was friends with the family who set up the original Livraria Imperatiz, went to their house for Friday night dinners. She had small round glasses. She taught us to love Brazil because it was the place that had wanted us – green for the forest and blue for the sea and yellow for the beaches and the sun – and loving Brazil meant fighting for the people as if they were also our sisters. They had my sister Sônia by accident when I was eighteen. When my father became the governor my mother did not want to live in the governor's palace.

The coup changed them, changed everything because of my father. The men came to our house and it was my mother who shouted at them, they had come in their black boots with guns. And we were all there that night apart from my father: all my sisters Lygia, Lúcia, Lamis and Sonita. My mother told me afterwards she was scared that they would rape us. It did not occur to me. So many women in one house and what could we have done if they had. Spat in their faces, bitten off their cocks. Every day my sisters went to university and to school and I went in sometimes, but by that time I did not care about the diploma, what good would a diploma do after the revolution. In the mornings I looked after Sônia read to her played with her in the garden. In the afternoons I went to do my revolutionary work at the other end of the city. Me and my cellmate, Paulinho, we went every day to educate and agitate the people. We worked in a church with an old man Dominican priest. He used to make us laugh. He used to say to us well you may not believe in God but you are good Christians. And we used to say to him you do not believe in Marx but you are a good communist. And so on. And so on. The work we did sometimes was talking about the means of production, sometimes it was reading classes. There were these three old women who used to come, always, I forget their names, I forget, who used to come with cakes and coconut sweets for the discussion always and one young woman, so smart and so angry, we recruited her brought her in, she has been a militant for many years now in Jaboatão you might know it as Moscouzinho, because it was really a little tropical Moscow and this is what it was, me and Paulinho, organising, agitating and moving on when we were no longer needed. Because truly we were often not needed Paulinho was so nice so bookish. But me and Paulinho stayed in one area too long, you might know the area, it is near the textile factories. This is what they said was the problem at first. They said why do you stay in this area when they do not need you anymore, and Paulinho didn't tell them, no, it was one of the higher ups, the other men who sometimes would give us instructions. He found out somehow what I had done. And what I had done was not acceptable he said. He said it put the whole movement at risk and undermined our credibility with

the people. The People. The People. The People could not find out.
He told me remember o peso dos companheiros mortos. Remember.
And I said, But it is a soft thing, a sweet thing, I have fallen in love
that is all, these are just quiet nights spent at her house with the
light low and he said, No there will be rumours and remember your
father's sacrifices, remember all our comrades who have died and
been tortured in the basements of the military regime? Can you feel
the weight of them on your shoulder? Oh! Will you risk all of this?
For what? The truth was she had a child, I used to go round and we
would continue our discussions together and eat together a little rice
or beans and farofa just simple food, and yes, people saw me there but
they did not mind. We just were. Once we drove to the beach, me
and her and her daughter and Sonita and we swam in the sea. I never
told my mother. But, he said, This is an Order you must leave now.
He wanted me to leave the movement, he threatened me. But I said
please no, and instead he separated me from Paulinho. Punished him
too for protecting me. So this was how it happened that in sixty-eight
I was in the cell that shot the policeman during an action, yes, I was
there when the violence broke out and the policeman was shot. I do
not know how it happened exactly. I am sorry he is dead. Or perhaps
I am not sorry. But I did not shoot him, I did not have a gun. I was
driving, that was my task. But the newspapers found my name, and
this is why. The newspapers called me a terrorist. I think only to dis-
credit my father, my family, to threaten us. My mother was so anxious
every day that I would be killed. She was sure. I don't know what she
thinks now. I told her I would be back. I will go back. I think of her
every day. Yes, I am an adult woman but to my mother I am her child,
in danger always in danger. I do not know if this explains everything
Clitemnestra, querida, killer of kings, I know I am not the revolutionary that you thought although yes, it is true I trained not in Cuba but
in the South, I was taught to shoot a gun, to rob a bank to kidnap
foreign dignitaries but in the end that is not the work that I did. No.
I didn't kill anyone. I do not know if this makes me a coward. When
you met me and I drove us west in the night I was broken hearted,
lost. That is that is what happened.

56.

plec plec plecplec
plec plec plecplec
plec plec plecplec
plec plec plecplec
plec plec plecplec
plec plec plecplec
plec plec plecplec
plec plec plecplec
plec plec plecplec
plec plec plecplec
plec plec plecplec

57.

So let me tell you, Laura the famous revolutionary. I was always a child who dreamed of somewhere else. Somewhere else from my father's house. Somewhere else from the town I grew up in, some other country, some other earth, some other planet. I had a boyfriend. I had two boyfriends actually. My friends they used to say to me, you have boyfriends like buses they take you where you want to go. The first one, he was the one who got me out of my father's house I was fifteen and he was eighteen and he worked in the factory and I went to live with him. He was the one who helped me escape my father and for that I will always be grateful. He was my real love. He showed me – everything – reading, politics, communism. He gave me books that were not allowed. He was a good man. So gentle. I loved him so much, I told people I was his wife and he laughed at this. Together we read Marx and Engels and Lenin and the *Minimanual for the Urban Guerrilla* by Carlos Marighella and I wanted so much to move to the city and to be an Urban Guerrilla. I went one time to a meeting in Olinda and I had this feeling this feeling like, Oh this is my real life, I have found it, suddenly here, I wonder if you were there, I wonder if you were there, and my husband, I used to call him my husband, when I told him he said to me, he said my name, you should go to university, you should leave this town and study. He used to play the harmonica. I lived with him in the town I grew up in didn't look my brothers in the eye when I saw them in the street. It was a small town run by crooks who were also the police. For example when I was a child I took in a little grey kitten from the street and fed him and picked off his fleas and cleaned the cuts on his paws and fed him till he got soft and fat and healthy and he slept on my belly and I put him in my pocket but my brothers said they had not given me permission to have a pet, and I held my kitten and the oldest brother he took my kitten crushed his head under his boot. I hated my brothers so much, they were like scum to me, I used to spit in the street at the thought of them. My brothers did not dream of leaving and neither did my father although maybe my mother did. We used to go to meetings in the small town and everybody knew I was the policeman's daughter with the policemen brothers and so I had to be twice as militant twice as always ready to show them that I was a revolutionary. So I read all the books. I said train me, give me a gun, I'll do anything. I was afraid of nothing but also I was always afraid of my father and my brothers and sometimes I could not sleep in the nights (I still do not sleep always in the nights). When I left I wrote my family a letter saying forget my name, do not look for me, I have no regrets, and this is the life that I have chosen because I believe that the people should own the fruits of their labour, that the factory worker should not toil for the capitalist to profit, that the Brazilian gold and iron and coffee and sugar and wood from the forest and oil must not be extracted for the profit of the North American imperialists and the landowners in their pockets when there are children without shoes without food or art or books, I believe that no one should be poor, I believe that no one should be unfree or unloved or shackled, I believe you know I believe in the armed struggle. If they are armed then are we to lie on the floor? Like kittens. Let ourselves be shot in the face. I hated my father so much, mean hands mean way of looking at me as soon as I got my periods, he was descended from a Portuguese man who raped a Tuxá woman and he used to tell us this, speak of my own foremother like this, in my memory he has red pupils as well as blood shot through the white parts of his eyes. My mother my mother oh my mother, she stops my heart even now my mother when I was growing up I used to hate her too. Why did she let him hit her shout at her bully her? Why did she let her sons bully her? Why was she so weak? Why did she not protect me? Why had she not educated herself so that she could leave him? But now But now I see that I see that if she had fought him then he would have killed her. He had no respect for her. He ran that town. He thought she was trash because she had dark skin and she had given him children with dark skin. Ugly, he used to call her. I don't know why she married him, her family were from another town, her mother's mother's mother had moved there seeking

375

land for herself to live on and work off after slavery was abolished. When I left I wrote her a letter and I read her the letter and then I burned it. I kissed her and she held me and I stood in her embrace and then she released me. She was waiting for the day that he would be killed in a fight. I think sometimes I became a militant because I was hoping they would ask me to shoot him. In between the eyes. But they didn't. They told me to help with the newspaper for the alcohol factory workers. They said education comes first and now I know they were right. I used to write articles and I used to help print them at night while studying the entrance exam for medical school. Always at night. Only now I see what a dangerous job it was. Like this I used to sit in a small room in the school at night and the mimeograph would move and talk like plec plec plec plec plec and I would wait for my father to walk into the room plec plec plec plec plec plec so that I could hit him over the head and kill him but he never did plec plec plec plec no he never walked in plec plecplec. So that is why I had to run from my town, why I asked for work outside of my town, why I left my husband although I was ready to leave him, why I never sat the medical school exam because there would be time for that. My father and my brothers are police. I am a revolutionary. I was always a different child black sheep only girl we lived in a small town and I always dreamed of leaving. I used to stare at the mountains in the distance, at the sky, at the city on the television and dream of leaving. I wanted so much to find another place, another way of living. My father's family had used to work in the alcohol factory and when there were strikes he was there in his uniform holding his gun. He would threaten his own brothers, he would beat his friends. His policeman job made him big. His uniform. His boots He used to beat my brothers and he used to beat my mother and he used to beat me His father had been violent to him and before him. He knew no other way And my mother's mother was born of rape and so was her mother and this is what this country the size of a continent is you know

I was a child who dreamed of somewhere else

58.

Na praia, na beira do mar, sentada na areia

Ela disse assim

Aqui, com você, é como se não tivesse ditadura

Como se não existisse e nunca tivesse existido ditadura, nem torturador, nem conquistador, nem explorador, nema minas, nem corporações mineiras, nem imperialistas, nem espiões estadunidenses, nem portugueses, nem língua portuguesa, nem Portugal, nem Brasil, nem branco, nem escravidão, nem casa grande, nem senzala, nem varíola, nem rei, nem princesa ou imperador

What will our daughters say of us

61.

Remember? You know what happened next. When the boots came at the door, Laura the famous revolutionary said, Go and I will meet you downstairs. And Clitemnestra killer of kings ran past, through the servants' quarters past the mimeograph towards the service stairs and she took the maid's uniform apron and hat from the back of the door and she swapped her boots for the maid shoes by the door, and she snatched a carrier bag with the supermarket logo on it from the kitchen cupboard. And she walked down the stairs in her maid's uniform and at the gate she nodded at the military police with their guns the length of their bodies and she bowed her head to them and they looked at her in her brown and white maid's uniform and her brown skin and downcast eyes and supermarket bags and did not see her. Then she was in the street. Her heart beating in her mouth. She couldn't breathe because her beating bleeding heart was in her mouth. And she waited around the corner. Hot night. The city traffic was so loud. She held her face under the water from a public water fountain. And the city traffic was so loud. And she waited for hours and she bought a hot dog and she ate it and the night got darker, lilac black to black. And Laura the famous revolutionary didn't come. And so Clitemnestra killer of kings ran.

62.

Remember? You know what happens next. You've heard the story. In September 1974, Laura the famous revolutionary the infamous eldest daughter of the exiled governor of Pernambuco State, was taken into police custody to a building in the Zona Sul de São Paulo where she was tortured until she could not speak. The revolutionary student with the small moustache was disappeared by the military police and they never found his body despite the solidarity campaigns in London and in Berlin. There would be no more strikes or meetings and the union leaders were killed in so-called suicides or arrested and tortured or like Edivânia they were put on blacklists so that they had to move from state to state to find work taking new names everywhere they went not underground but alone so that they would not go hungry. And the communists in the forest were killed by government soldiers. The commander told them to fight. Every single one but the six who were imprisoned and the two who escaped 1000 kilometres through the forest. The commander with the grandsons in Salvador was killed and his son was killed. The commander who was 2m tall and had studied in Prague and whose parents had been born enslaved was killed and his body was hung from a helicopter and flown over the forest. And the woman who had opened the pharmacy and the man who was an engineer were killed. And the teacher was killed. And the man who had caught the jabuti and had danced by the fire was killed and the local women who had danced with their skirts raised to show how their toe and heels and toe and heels moved were killed and if they were not killed they were tortured. And the man with the canoe was killed. And all the other people who lived by the forest who had migrated there for cheap land in the decades after slavery was abolished were killed by government soldiers, and if they were not killed they were tortured, or their sons or daughters were tortured or killed and their stocks of rice and flour and corn were burned. The soldiers cut down their fruit trees. When the great tarmac road advanced to forest by the soft river the soldiers had stationed themselves in every town around the forest by the soft river and when the local people tried to blow up the new tarmac bridge over the soft river the bridge had not exploded. The soldiers tortured the priests who had said prayers for the communists in the forest to gods that were not the Christian god. And soldiers landed in an airplane in the Aikewara village in the north of the forest by the river, and the airplane blew the straw roofs off the houses, scaring their children who ran into the forest because they had never seen an airplane. The soldiers pushed rifles into the backs of the Aikewara adults. The soldiers said take us to the communists in the forest and burned their stocks of corn and pushed rifles into their backs. The soldiers starved them for three days as they walked through the forest.

Those were the darkest years, heavy like lead. The movement disarmed. The demands changed; amnesty, elections, democracy. And five years later, in 1979, the amnesty came, and the torturers were forgiven and all the people who had been communists were forgiven. And Laura the famous revolutionary went home, back to Recife, back to Sônia and Olga and Lúcia and Lamis and Lygia and the rest of her life. And she did not know if Clitemnestra killer of kings had been killed or disappeared or if she was alive. And she did not know how to find her because she did not know her real name. And it was a grief the size of the earth, as big as a life.

63.

After the Amnesty in 1979 Clitemnestra killer of kings wrote a letter. In it she wrote everything that had happened to her in the last five years. She had found out the address. Had written the name of the road and the name of the city and the state and five letters LAURA and put it in a blue envelope. She put the seal to her mouth, ran her tongue along it.

64.

Minha querida LAURA –

Eu acabei de fazer vinte e nove anos, a idade que você tinha quando nós nos conhecemos aquela noite no nosso carro azul na periferia do Recife. Aos vinte e nove anos, eu não sou médica, nem Che Guevara, como disse que eu seria. Sou estudante de enfermagem no interior do Rio de Janeiro. Tenho uma vida boa e simples aqui. Acordo todos os dias numa cama que é minha. Meus lençóis. Tem uma mesa do lado da minha cama onde eu boto os meus livros. Tomo café na cozinha. Me sinto livre.

Aquela noite eu usei o dinheiro que tinha nos bolsos para ligar para uma pessoa que eu lebrava das festas no apartamento. Eu não lembrava o nome inteiro dele e as moedas quase acabaram antes do operador me falar o telefone da casa certa. Ele me ajudou a fugir. Eu me escondi durante anos.

Eu li sobre a sua família no jornal. Sei que seu pai voltou depois da anistia e que você está em casa. Sei que sua mãe ficou doente. Das suas irmãs eu não li notícias. Eu sei que a sua irmã Lygia mora aqui e eu quase que liguei para ela. Eu achei o endereço dela e quando estive na cidade eu fui ao prédio onde ela mora. Fiquei parada lá. Se eu tentasse explicar ela não me acreditaria. Voltei para casa. Foi dois anos atrás.

Eu penso em você. A Sônia deve ser adulta agora. Espero que vocês comam sorvete toda noite. Flocos, Manga, Chocolate.

Laura. Esta carta foi a primeira vez que escrevo teu nome mas pensei em te escrever tantas vezes.

Sei que você foi torturada. Todo dia eu penso nisso. Todo dia eu me arrependo de ter te deixado. Eu te esperei por horas aquela noite. Penso em você todos os dias. Procuro notícias de você em todo lugar. Sonho com você. Continuo te esperando.

Nunca me senti tão livre do que quando estava com você.

Ainda não tenho uma filha, mas continuou querendo ter uma, um dia. Continuou tendo namorados, eles vêm e eles vão. Cada um me leva para onde eu preciso ir.

Ainda penso em ir a Londres. Vem comigo.

Com saudade, amor
e solidariedade infinita,

C

67.

Clitemnestra waited for a reply to her letter. She waited for Laura. Laura to appear on her doorstep, Laura at the airport, Laura getting off the bus, Laura's voice on the telephone, Laura behind the wheel of a blue beetle car.

Until one day she read in the newspaper that Laura, the infamous revolutionary, the guerrilheira daughter of the exiled governor of Pernambuco, had driven off a bridge in the middle of the night and died.

68.

But here is the thing

Laura had found the letter, tucked into the end of a book on a bookshelf, waiting for her in a volume of poetry. She opened it with trembling fingers on a hot and starless night –

69.

And here is the thing

The driving had not been a suicide. Not a death knelling. It was a certainty that had come over Laura, the famous revolutionary, clear and as calm as the light of the moon on the sea. She was driving to Clitemnestra, killer of kings. As fast as she could, in the old blue beetle car. Foot on the pedal! Letter open on the front seat. She had a tank full of petrol and she would have crossed the whole country, the continent to her; crossed the rainforests and the rivers and the cities and the swamps and the hills and the savannahs and the sea; she would have searched every tower block of every city and every governor's palace, every church, every shack made of straw, every forest, every river, every torturer's basement. Clarity like fireworks! Like the infinite flat of the sea. A bridge over a river 2km from her family house.

Foot on the pedal!

That is That is what happened.

My dearest LAURA –

I have just turned twenty-nine, the age you were when we met that night in the outskirts of Recife in our blue car. At twenty-nine, I am not a doctor, not Che Guevara either, like I said I would be. I'm a student nurse in the interior of Rio de Janeiro. I wake up every day in a bed that is mine. My sheets. I have a bedside table where I put my books. I drink coffee in the mornings. I am free.

That night I used the money I had in my pockets to call someone that I remembered from the parties in the apartment. I could not remember his full name and I almost ran out of coins before getting the operator to tell me the phone number of the right house. He helped me escape. I hid for years.

I read about your family in the paper. I know your father came back after the amnesty and that you are at home. I know that your mother has been ill. Of your sisters I haven't read any news. I know that your sister Lygia lives here in Rio and you won't believe it but I almost called her. I found her address and when I was in the city I went to the building. I stood outside it and I froze. If I had tried to explain she would not have believed me. I went home. It was two years ago.

I think of you. Sônia must be an adult now. I hope you eat ice cream every night. Mango, chocolate, vanilla with crunchy bits.

Laura. This letter is the first time I have written your name but I have thought of writing to you so many times —

I know you were tortured. Every day I think about it. Every day I regret leaving you. I waited for you that night. I think about you every day. I seek news of you everywhere I can. I dream about you. I am waiting for you, still.

I never felt as free as when I was with you.

I do not have a daughter yet, but I still want to have one, one day. I still have boyfriends; they come and go. Each one takes me where I need to be.

I still think of London. Come with me.

With saudade, love
And infinite solidarity
C

MILE END IV
(2017)

The early morning radio played the sound of a meadow. Lavender attracts more bumblebees than honeybees because of their longer tongues, a zoologist who had never expected to speak on the radio said. The presenter laughed in their older person, educated person, Radio 4 way. The zoologist corrected the presenter. The presenter said that the weather that day would be crisp and fair, an English word meaning both light haired, light skinned, just and reasonable and moderate, and the experience of clement weather without rain or cloud or unbearable heat. Across the small island, and across one part of the other smaller island, people woke up, got dressed, showered, drank coffee, fed their children, overslept, got on trains and buses and started their cars; they walked into school halls, churches and community centres and voted.

Melissa woke with the sunlight. She lay in bed. She pulled back the curtain. The window in her bedroom, in the room that had once been the kitchen, looked onto the outdoor walkway of the building. She put on her glasses and checked her phone in bed. She played the radio on her phone and remembered that political news was banned until the polls closed at 10pm. Femi was taking the day off to get out the vote in Tooting. The rumours were, he said, that the Labour Party was going to lose its majority of 2,800 there. In other words, the gentrifiers are going to show up and they're going to fuck us, Femi had said.

Melissa showered and she brushed her teeth. She moisturised her face and applied eyeliner. She got dressed in jeans and a black T-shirt. She did her hair quickly in the mirror. Put on her black boots. She made coffee in the kitchen and drank it on the balcony. She looked at the leaves of the hanging spiderwort plants and decided not to water them. Outside, a child in school uniform ran along the first-floor walkway of the building across the road, hitting a bookbag against the railings. Tec tec tectectec. A woman in a hijab shouted at him to stop. Melissa read the news on her phone. It was 8am. She buttered a slice of toast and left the flat, descending the stairs two at a time.

She walked down the edge of the park past the vegetable shop and past the Algerian shop with the good olive oil almost to Lidl and then she turned back into the estates, away from the park. The words POLLING STATION and a black arrow had been printed onto white A4 piece of paper and sellotaped to the black iron gates of a primary school. Melissa did as the arrow instructed.

The building was late Victorian. She looked up at it. She knew it already: three floors of brown and yellow bricks, one stone entrance labelled BOYS, one stone entranced labelled GIRLS, an assembly hall with parquet floors, and above that another assembly hall with parquet floors and wooden benches for sitting and somewhere a library. When she breathed in she felt the building stick to the inside of her ribs.

She moved the weight of her body onto her toes.

The hall was like every other hall. She had run around a hall just like this hall in her pants and a vest for dance and PE, they'd put mats on the floor for gymnastics and sat on them cross-legged for assembly and sung in her loudest singing voice *we all live in a yellow submarine, yellow submarine, yellow submarine.* Shanice. Jamal. Travis with the runny nose. Anna who had left in the middle of term. Ruthie holding a child-sized tennis racket her child-sized hands.

The poll worker said, Do you have your polling card?

Melissa shook her head, her hands in her pockets.

Name and address then.

48 Bevan House, Joseph Street

Right.

The poll worker scanned the lists of names in front of her, flipping through her list. She found Melissa, crossed off her name, and handed her a ballot paper.

Melissa stood in the booth in the assembly hall and held a small pencil in her hand. One year, when she was little, the year they had just got their passports, her mother had taken her into the booth and let her write the X, small pencil in her smaller fingers. Melissa looked at her ballot paper. In her constituency the Labour Party majority was over 20,000. Her vote would count for nothing. She breathed in.

It was the year that a twenty-year-old boy called Syed Jamanoor Islam was stabbed on the street in Mile End. It was the year of the most recorded murders in Brazil since records began, the year that Catarina reminded Melissa that she must get her mother's documents from the basement of Femi's parents' house and go to the consulate to register herself as a Brazilian citizen so that she could vote the next year, when the time to vote came. It was the year of the snap general election in the UK, and the unexpectedly good general election result, which had brought with it the mildest weather.

No one slept. They stayed up all night. Melissa and Catarina watched the results come in at Ivy's flat in Stockwell. They were drinking beers and gin and wine and eating pizzas. When the exit poll came they started to shout and grab each other. Femi called Melissa at 1am.

We kept Tooting. By over 15,000 votes. We took Battersea too.

She could hear him crying.

I didn't think it was possible, he said.

Four days after the election, they descended on a courtyard between two buildings in Hackney from all directions. As if from nowhere, at 7.55pm the space filled with the slush and buzz of voices and feet and bikes. People were shouting and embracing. Catarina and Melissa ran down the street towards the sound, Melissa checking the location on her phone.

The meeting had been called urgently in the days that followed and because there was no rain, and if the days were fair they met outdoors. They sat in a circle. The sun was at the height of the treetops although it was the evening time. Two people clapped their hands. They passed a phone around. Each voice rang and echoed as it hit and hit against the concrete. When the chorus rang in the night, people leant out of their windows to hear it –

We are women and gender non-conforming people

fighting for liberation and planetary justice

For centuries
hetero patriarchal capitalist imperialists have ruled over the people

using violence to dominate, exploit, and extract from the people and
*   the land*

But
we are many

We fight together: alongside our sisters, our siblings

alongside our ancestors

by any means necessary

Because none of us

Black
brown
poor
disabled

migrant
woman
non-binary
gender non-confirming
trans
queer

are free
until all of us are free

A tall woman with waving hair to the bend of her back stood in the middle of the circle. She shouted –

ABUNDANCE

And the people gathered there spoke back to her, words echoing from every direction, forming, somehow a chorus –

> *abundant JOY*
> *abundant JUSTICE*
> *abundant CARE*
> *abundant LOVE*
> *abundant DANCING*
> *abundant LAUGHTER*
> *abundant REVOLUTION*

There was a shifting. Two hundred eyes moved from the two people leading the meeting to whoever was speaking. The sunlight fell in lilac shafts between the buildings and the trees. Bikes were scattered across the courtyard. A person with long hair to their bum said they thought it was time to decentralise and organise across the country. Another person believed they weren't yet strong enough and that would make their influence too diffuse. Another person said that now in this historical moment they should be organising within the Labour Party and the person who spoke next said that the Labour Party were snakes that they were and had always been racists, the party of the Iraq War and Controls on Immigration and more police on the streets. A woman who almost never spoke said that she thought now was the time to capitalise on the national tumult with direct action; a woman who always spoke said that what they needed to be doing was large scale accessible political education.

Catarina put her hand up. She spoke loudly to project her voice.

Melissa watched as Catarina spoke, she heard the curves and corners of her accent. Catarina gesticulated. Behind Catarina's hands and the profile of her face, the buildings turned blue under the lilac sky.

The blue buildings and the lilac sky filled her. She felt something like sureness in her body. Sureness that came from the words that Catarina spoke and the one hundred people listening with intention, who would discuss and think together into the night. They could make anything, unmake anything; the world stretched itself for them, as expansive as time, open and opening, mid pirouette

Melissa closed her eyes. She let herself fold into the night. She felt herself un bind.

Five days after the election Melissa sat down at the kitchen table, saying
    Catarina I've met the most beautiful woman Oh my god

Catarina looked at her friend.
    Tell me
    It was like the best kiss of my life
    Catarina laughed.

Catarina put her hand on Melissa's hand on the table. Melissa held it.

    One of the other PhD students from Italy thinks that an EU pass-
port won't even be enough, she says she is thinking of leaving
    You don't know
    No.

Catarina leant her forehead on Melissa's hand.

    We could go anywhere, anywhere you get a job —
    You would wrench yourself from this city?

They were quiet.
    Yeah. Yeah I would

Catarina lifted her head.
    Show me a picture of her then.
    Yeah?
    Yes.

They had met at a quiet bar in Holborn. Outside was light and they sat at a table half in shadow. They were both wearing all black, sat next to each other on stools. Melanie had her hair in a ponytail, pulled back tight and smooth and shining. She was wearing thin golden hoops in each ear. She had a sleek looking dress on and was drinking white wine. She worked in something to do with music. She'd lived in three different countries. Melissa leant an elbow on the bar. Melanie had said –

You can call me Mel

But I'm Mel

Melanie smiled. Are you?

Yes – not to everyone. At school all my friends called me Mel. My best mate, my flatmate, she calls me Melí sometimes

Mel-ee?

But just – but just call me Mel

But I'm Mel!

Melissa then.

Alright. And you call me Melanie, just like my mum and all my teachers

Melanie.

What's your favourite tube line?

Victoria, the Ferrari of tube lines. Why is that making you smile

Cos you're right, obviously, it's the only right answer

Where did you grow up?

Tooting. Do you know it?

Yes

And you?

East End, near Bow

Really? That's where I live?

Yeah? Where

Joseph Street

I used to live by the cemetery

No

Yeah!

I grew up in a big family with lots of cousins
How many
Twenty-seven
No
Yes!

What about your family

It was me and my mum, but then my mum died.
I'm sorry
It's okay

No really it really is okay. I was really lucky to have my mum.
What was she like?
I guess – she was quite anxious, and she was sometimes kind of reserved, tired. She worked a lot. But she also was the opposite of that, like, always singing and dancing in the house, sitting in the living rooms of her friends who lived on our road. Always hugging me and everyone else. Do you know *West Side Story*? Yeah she really loved that film. Especially the song that goes Maria, Maria. Especially the part where they just sing her name over and over like twenty times in a row. I dunno why. Her best friends were these three grannies who lived on our road, Jean Janine and Jasmine, and they became like my grandmothers. Jasmine had come from India after partition and Janine had come from Trinidad in the fifties and Jean had come from Ireland and they had all been nurses at St George's like my mum. They used to look after me, I'd go round to their houses for tea after school when my mum was at work. They used to slam back gin and tonics like nobody's business and chat shit and talk politics all night. All their husbands were dead and they never talked about them apart from Jean whose husband was alive but he just watched telly all day and she really never talked about him either. We all had those white net curtains in the windows. Do you know the ones?
Yeah I do. We had them too actually.

Yeah?
Yeah.

That was our family. Us and Jean and Janine and Jasmine.

What was your mother's name?
Glória

Melanie looked at her.
Melissa finished her wine. Melissa looked back.

They walked to Euston in silence. Melissa didn't look at Melanie. As they turned away from the big street, she felt Melanie's body move beside her body in the dark. Melissa didn't say anything. She lit a cigarette. They walked along the small patch of grass in front of Euston station, where the buses stop. They walked on the east side next to the railings. Melanie spoke –
I like you
It was not a busy street, and it was badly, romantically lit – at this time of year the evenings were dark but the trees still had their thickest leaves, obscuring the light of the lamps.
It was badly, romantically lit.
Euston station was in front of them down an alley, separated from them by other buildings. And it was dark already, late summer. There were people around them, but no one passing close.
Melissa had a cigarette in her hand. Melanie stopped walking and faced her.
Melissa kissed her without thinking – she felt Melanie's hip catch just below her own. She felt the flat of Melanie's hand against her stomach. Melanie pushed into her and her back pushed into the iron railing.
They kissed for sixty-seven perfect seconds.
After that neither of them spoke. Melanie looked her in the eyes then turned and caught her train. Melissa stood in the street. Her cigarette still lit in her hand.

As she walked down the street she found herself humming the *West Side Story* soundtrack. The words came to her like water

Maria

Maria
Maria Maria
Maria Maria
Maria Maria Maria

Seven days after the election Melissa sat in the kitchen / living room in the early morning. Her laptop was open in front of her.

She watched the shaky footage taken on a mobile phone in the early morning on a street between Ladbroke Grove and Notting Hill. She watched the fire burn and spread across the face and body of Grenfell Tower. She watched, live on the BBC, as the smoke, still thick and living, pushed into the sky from a hundred bedroom windows.

A news presenter with a certain kind of voice asked a man with a certain other kind of voice how he had escaped the building with his family. A news presenter spoke to someone who had been woken up by the screams although she lived three streets away. A news presenter spoke to a man in a salwar kameez from the local mosque who was giving out meals and blankets. A news presenter spoke to a man in glasses from the residents' fire safety committee who said they had told the council it was unsafe many times. A news presenter spoke to a man who said there were still people inside. A news presenter spoke to a local celebrity who had come from the tall white houses to say Where is the government? How did this happen? A news presenter spoke to someone from the London Fire Brigade who said that the building was 67m high but they could only reach as high as 32m with the hose and the platform that they had. A news presenter said that the Stay Put policy meant official advice had been for residents not to leave their flats in the case of a fire. Official advice had been wait to be saved. Behind him the building was still burning. The list of the missing was long, and of the names that were known most were not English.

Catarina's relatives kept messaging her to ask if she was OK. At work Melissa couldn't concentrate. It hurt her in the west part of her body. Marc wouldn't stop talking. Femi sat with his long legs bent, his knees against his chest.

Catarina submitted her thesis in August. She sat at her desk in the History Department office with all her notes beside her open folders, library books piled around her on the desk, read and shut. She closed her eyes. No one else was there. She rubbed her hands against her eyelids and her forehead. She organised the library books into a pile. Threw the empty tortilla chip packets and cereal bar wrappers in the bin and took the empty mugs with dried out teabags to the sink. She put them in the dishwasher. Turned her laptop all the way off. She threw a pile of seminar handouts from a year ago into the recycling bin, revealing a large book opened flat against the desk. *Daniel Deronda*. She must have put it there before the seminar. When she picked up the book in her hands it re-flattened itself, opening at the same page towards the end. She reread it. Gwendolen Harleth emerged from the sea, saying

I saw my wish outside myself

Outside, the streets were dark and hot and overspilling. It was so hot she could have been in Olinda. A smell sweet like bin bags rose around her. All around her European tourists in wet T-shirts shouted at English women tripping over their New Look heels. It was a Saturday night. She walked down Tottenham Court Road and listened to the hum of the city. Rickshaws with flashing lights drove up Charing Cross Road. A busker played George Michael on the xylophone. She stood in the street and listened to the sound.

Her train moved in the opposite direction to the revellers – apart from the ones who had gone too hard too early – away from the West End, SOUTHBOUND down the Northern line. Catarina sat next to an older-looking Black guy playing backgammon on his phone. She watched over his shoulder as he moved his pieces around. She got off at Kennington.

Melissa had said to her, It's my old friend's party. Come and we will celebrate.

It had been a coincidence. Anastasia had messaged Melissa on Facebook. They hadn't spoken since the funeral. She had said –

Hey mel, how are you doing these days? haven't seen you in so long xx

She arrived early for Anastasia's birthday. Melissa looked around. The pub was full of people she didn't recognise. Australians from Clapham. She looked at her phone and checked the address on the event. She checked the address of the pub she was in on Google. If she left now no one would know that she had been there. She could tell Catarina not to come. She did not know who would be there. She did not know if Anastasia and Ruth still spoke. She reread Anastasia's message. She went to the bar and ordered a drink.

Excuse me, do you know where Anastasia's birthday party is?

The bartender pointed at the back of the pub.

Okay. Melissa drank. Thank you.

At the back of the pub was a garden. Bulbs on strings had been arranged around the edges of the space. Anastasia was standing at the table in the middle of the garden. She had dyed her hair. She had blond highlights now and her eyebrows were bushier. Still short. Melissa knew her without a second glance. Anastasia called her name —

Hey

Anastasia held her.

Melissa.

Happy birthday!

Thank you

How are you?

I'm good. Fuck it's good to see you

You too

This is my boyfriend, Ben

Hi Ben

This is Melissa, we've known each other for what? Ten twelve thirteen years?

Yeah, I think

I'm an accountant now

That's great

What about you

I'm a software developer

No fucking way

Yeah

That's amazing. That's amazing

Anastasia

Are you here alone, is your friend coming, let me introduce you to

She's coming, she's a bit late

This is Fiona

Hi

And Emma

Hi

And Jonny

You alright

And Mel are you seeing anyone? Any boyfriends

No

No boyfriend?

No

No – I was actually seeing this woman

Oh?

I met this woman

A woman?

Yeah a woman

Oh

Yeah

Oh cool

Yep

So

I mean I don't know really what's going on there

Oh

But she

But she is – she's cool

Aw

Yeah.

Aw well hopefully it'll work out

Yeah –

You just wait. Anastasia winked at her.

Let me get you a drink. Happy Birthday!

Catarina arrived. Tired-looking. Melissa put her arm around her. She turned to the people next to them –

Catarina's just handed in her PhD

Two people from Anastasia's work nodded

Melissa repeated – A whole fucking PhD literally just now

Two other people from Anastasia's work exclaimed

Wow

Congratulations!

Oh yes

She's going to be a doctor – Doctor Catarina

Doutora

Not a medical doctor

No I know like Ross Geller

But not yet I have to defend—

Doctor Doctor – I think I'm a pair of curtains

Catarina looked non-plussed

Pull yourself together woman!

Pull yourself *together*

Meena arrived because she had stayed in touch with Anastasia and when she arrived Melissa told her that Catarina had just handed in her PhD and Meena pulled her into a hug. Max was there but he didn't look tall anymore and he had long hair. That skinny boy who was now really fit was there. Catarina danced with him. Anastasia had her arm around her new boyfriend who wasn't even that new anymore. Melissa looked around but no one new arrived. Melissa looked around, because the night tube meant that anyone could arrive at any time, but no one else arrived.

They danced to old eighties and nighties ballads that Anastasia liked. Catarina had drunk at least four drinks and was singing out loud. Whitney Houston was playing. Tina Turner. Melissa wondered, for as long as it took to smoke a cigarette, where Ruth was. What side of the city

When Catarina found her smoking she said, That is a terrible habit

Lionel Richie sang – *Life is good, wild and sweet*

Catarina danced, her body moving more slowly than the music.

On the night tube home, Catarina asked Melissa a question.

What's happening with Melanie

What about Melanie

You know

I don't know

What's happening with Pedro

Catarina frowned. I don't know, we live on different continents.

Melissa sat with her chin on her hand. Opposite them a woman in hightops slid across a pile of sick. She clung onto the yellow railing. To their left a woman ate a McChicken sandwich, mayonnaise gloop getting onto her dress. Without thinking, Melissa handed her a tissue.

When I was seeing that therapist she said that I should let the other in

Catarina nodded

She said What about opening up to difference, to another person, it is a sign of healing

The train paused and the door opened and then closed.

But you do do that

Melissa looked up.

With me. With Femi with Ivy with Olivia.

Melissa didn't say anything

The night tube rattled around them.

the night was
arroxeado

Seven years and five hundred years and 66 million more

(show us)

At work Melissa watched six episodes of *Desperate Housewives* in a row. She put her head in her hands. She thought of Catarina, handing in her thesis. Marc was out at meetings. At 5pm Femi came in holding two beers.

I've been offered a job
What –
In an MP's office
Fucking hell Femi.
She grabbed him round the shoulders.
I'm so fucking proud of you
Femi looked at the floor. He made eye contact.

She's one of your lot, believes what you believe
Marc won't like that
No.
So like what's next
I think I'll start by becoming Home Secretary
First act – abolish the Home Office
Then I'll become Chancellor
Then backstab your way to Prime Minister
Exactly.

She looked at her old friend, who was so tall and handsome and had grey hairs by his temples
Femi I need to get that box from your basement
Next weekend?
Yeah.
Great, my parents would love to see you
Wait no that's Carnival
Oh yeah
I'll get it after
Whenever

Melissa and Ivy sat on a patch of lawn in front of a skyscraper in Canary Wharf. The sunlight turned the glass buildings white. Ivy was wearing a pencil skirt. They were eating handmade sushi that Melissa had bought from the Waitrose in the shopping centre.

This skirt is making my butt sweat

It's hot today

Yeah

Yeah

Melissa rolled over on the grass.

I decided to get my Brazilian citizenship sorted

You don't have it already?

My passport and loads of other shit is expired and Catarina convinced me to get it in order to vote in the election next year

That's cool

Yeah. So I'm gonna get all those documents of my mum's that are at Femi's house, that we left in his basement

Ivy looked at her. Want me to come with you?

No it's okay.

There was a lot of stuff in that box

Yeah. But I just need a couple of things.

Ivy nodded. She squinted in the sun.

How's your mum Ivy

She's a lot. Always surprise visiting us. The other day I had to distract her at the door while Will hid ten litres of bottled water that she'd given us under the bed because I didn't want her to see we hadn't drunk it. She doesn't trust the tap water

Melissa laughed.

Ivy shook her head. She looked at her phone and then held it up to show ten unread messages from her mother.

She shook her head.

Melissa laughed.

Melissa lay with her back against the grass. She closed her eyes.

You still shoplifting

Ivy waved at the shopping centre complex. Sometimes yeah sometimes. Not here. Westfield and Duty Free and shit. I just walk out
holding stuff and no one says anything. I'd never steal from like an off
licence or family-owned shop

Obviously. What does Will think

Ivy shrugged.

Melissa looked behind Ivy. She held her hand up above her eyes. Men
in suits walked by them.

Do you think it's weird my mum never took me back

Ivy looked at her.

To Brazil?

Yeah

Maybe.

Hm

Ivy paused

I don't know. Did you ever ask?

She just said, There is no going back

Right

I used to think she meant in time

I don't know anything about her life there

Ivy blinked. She looked at the grass and then at her friend.

My mum never talks about Vietnam. She mentions it, obviously, but
she never really *talks* about it. I don't know why exactly she left or why
the rest of my family left. I learnt about the war off fucking Netflix and
Wikipedia.

Mel looked at the grass

What about your uncles and stuff?

They just ask me how my job's going and if I'm getting married.

Melissa looked at her friend.

Melissa had always lived in London. I live in East London but I'm from *South London*; wherever she was it was impossible for her not to explain herself. East London was for start up pricks. North London was like going on holiday to a Zadie Smith book and what was Hampstead Heath and how had it got so big. West London? She almost never thought about it. Apart from in August. She had always been at home in August, never on holiday, and she had always ended up there with whoever was about: Shanice, Anastasia, Lucas, Ruthie. People always said, you're Brazilian course you love Carnival and she'd say, Yeah yeah yeah. Carnival's in my blood.

In Olinda they were proud of their Carnaval, which was the best in Brazil and therefore the world. The pre-Carnaval began as early September and drums and tambourines and practice continued throughout January and by February or March every house on every street of the old town was full with the people who lived in there or rented and all the roads were blocked off and everyone in the whole country even in São Paulo knew what was coming. Even Tio Chris who was a neurologist in Amsterdã came for Carnaval and he would wear shorts and eyeliner and a T-shirt of sequins and shimmy his shoulders. Carnaval was when Tia Lamis would smoke without apology and wear tiny denim shorts with a bikini top and occasionally make out with somebody's dad's brother's slightly younger friend who was in town for the weekend, she would always say to her sister, Sônia why don't you and Miguel have a party here, and everyone could flow in and out when the blocos come up the ladeiras and we could watch from the veranda fanning ourselves and drinking cold beers from the fridge, and Sônia said no no no I could not no, and so Miguel brought a couple of friends from the office over and they drank his expensive cachaça before smoking a little spliff and wandering into the street in their T-shirts and rainbow hats to dance behind brass bands and effigies of politicians and people wearing jester hats and cowboy hats and pink wigs and blue wigs and sailor hats and nuns' habits and priest's robes. And Sônia was in the house and she listened to the TecTec Tectec of the maracatú moving up the hill of the city and Tia Lamis said to her

Pelo Amor De Deus don't be so miserable Sonita. Drink this Sonita. Take my hand Sonita. Such a big house and so empty today. You are so silly. Come walk with me, dance with me Sonita, yes we can bring Catarina. I don't know where Larissa is she is with her friends. Nothing will happen to Catarina, she knows her way around, and she can come back to the house anytime. Everyone is so Happy, look at all this all this alegria Look Look out at the city Can you hear the music? Can you hear the drums and the singing and all of these colours. Red and green and dark blue and light blue and orange and yellow and green and gold and white and silver and light green and turquoise and pink and white. Look Sonita at all the people in their hats and crowns and visors and look at their cleavage and their shoulders and their bellies and look at the old women watching from the balcony, look at the man in the tutu holding the dildo and the children on the shoulders of adults dressed like pirates holding tambourines, have you ever seen so many tubas or people singing together all dancing frevo together Sonita? Look at the gringos nodding their heads and the men running up the hill and the women holding a banner that says PAZ and look how bright the sun is sister And now look out at the sea, Sing with me Sonita, sister, move your feet, Sônia Sônia Dance with me sister

Ivy got to the flat early. They had brought gin and tonic in tins and cigarettes. Olivia was up and smoking a spliff indoors with the balcony door open wearing silver leggings and a pink bum bag. Will closed his eyes and sat patiently as Ivy smeared glitter over his cheeks. Music was playing.

He's never been to Carnival

Shut up!

No I haven't

What

What about Catarina

Don't be stupid Catarina is from Brazil she knows all about Carnival

Catarina came into the kitchen. Yes, I've been to Notting Hill Carnival. It was founded in 1959 by the communist activist Claudia Jones after the Notting Hill Race Riots of 1958. It is different to Brazil of course. Many more police, now, and it is in the Caribbean tradition, although there are some things in common it's true. I went once with Pedro.

Melissa poured her coffee

Catarina has handed in her thesis this week
They cheered and clapped and whooped
You're done! you're done!
I'm exhausted. I will meet you there –
We'll never find each other
Go – Femi will be waiting at Tottenham Court Road
I'll text you the name of the road and then we will not move
If you stay in the same place then I will find you.
Okay
Okay –

The door slammed shut.

Catarina sat with her head in her hands. It was still daylight. She pushed and pulled her body into the bathroom and sat on the floor. She slouched out of her clothes. She sat on the floor. She turned on the taps and sat in the bath as it filled. She turned on the shower and sat under the shower water like hot rain.

When the hot water ran out she got out of the bath. She had forgotten a towel. In her room she got a towel out of the dirty laundry basket and dried her body. She lay in the duvet. She wanted to text Pedro. She put on a pair of pants. The sun outside was bright. She put on a T-shirt. She put on a pair of jeans.

Go to the Carnival! Pedro had said. Send me a picture, Pedro had said.

She grabbed her keys and her debit card and her phone and slammed the door behind her.

When she got on the Central line at Mile End it started off like any other tube journey any other day but by the time she passed Oxford Circus it started being the Carnival tube full of people with bejewelled bedecked nails holding beers wearing tiny shorts, groups of Black teen-agers dancing together like the tube was all theirs all of the year.

She didn't have any ID. The cashier at Sainsbury's in Notting Hill said, Sorry I can't serve you. She looked around her, people were dancing in the aisles. But I'm twenty-seven –

Sorry

I can't just bring my passport out because it has my visa in it, and if I lose that

Sorry ma'am

Catarina left the shop. The street around her was so full and people were shouting for their friends. She turned into a side road of big white mansions with boarded up front gardens and huge trees and balconies. She stepped and unstepped between revellers towards the square in Ladbroke Grove where Ivy and Melissa and Olivia would be. Behind her a teenager was sick onto a Porsche. The sun beat down on the crowd. Women dressed in dresses with puffy gold sleeves and women dressed in red bikinis and women in white and green T-shirts that said Justice for Grenfell.

She pushed with the crowd against the police line. Her cheek in the light brown hair of a white woman in front of her. The woman smelled like cloves. Someone pushed Catarina forwards. The woman turned, apologising to Catarina, I'm so sorry.

Catarina shrugged

She moved through the crowd. She had missed the parades and the floats and the minute's silence. Carnival was not subdued, people wearing green and white danced and sang. A group of Black women dressed in purple samba clothing passed her. They spoke in Portuguese. Catarina listened to them speak and walk away from her. She tripped forwards.

Somebody grabbed her and she turned.

Matt

Hey

I heard you submitted

Yes

Congratulations

Thank you

The sound system next to them started to play. He handed her a beer.

Do you want to dance Cat?

I have to meet my friends

Oh

But I can dance for now. I can dance for now.

Good

And he moved in his English man way wearing his English man shorts, his friends around him, and she danced with her hips and shoulders and feet over the tarmac. A woman on a balcony wearing sunglasses nodded her head at them and another woman peed on the street. Kids ran towards them down the street holding big plastic cups.

Oh shit Matt

What

It's a group of history undergrads – I took them for the Latin American history module

Catarina crouched by a car wheel.

Hide!

Matt could not stop laughing.

She found Ivy and Melissa and Olivia and Femi by a square with a low brick wall. Dancehall. Come here, they said. Come here.

She let her body move between them. The sun was hot and the sky was blue and bright. She danced in their embrace

In her drunk mind Melissa thought about Melanie. Whether Melanie was at Carnival. Whether she was dancing. Probably yes in some friend's house around here maybe with a sturdy wide white patrician ledge that she could hook a leg over, drinking expensive gin displaying tasteful cleavage and her hair straightened shaking down her back. She thought about Tara the year 7-11 teacher. She thought about Daisy with the red cheeks in the morning. She thought about Eleni and her vibrators and Ruth and everyone else who there had been. In her drunk and dancing mind she felt, for the first time in years, she felt sure she would see Ruth right around the corner, she remembered Ruth dancing in somebody's living room in the best hours of a party, off rhythm off rhythm, her mouse brown hair like a mushroom cut her closed eyes

Olivia danced between two lanky men

Ivy moved surely, instructing Will, taking his body slowly, laughing encouraging instructing

Femi had wandered off down a side street with a group dressed in green who had been dancers in the parade

The day had been hotter than Melissa had imagined. It would be one of the last hot days of the year. She moved her body, the streets were not as full as they had been the day before, Black teenagers danced as if they owned the streets; it would be one of the last hot days

She thought – for a small moment – of her mother's feet in the narrow kitchen, stepping round and round and round

wearing slippers

Melissa looked at her friends. Together they danced in the square

in the heat and noise and the shade of the city

they turned and turned and turned

I want

I want

I want

I want

I want

I want

I want

I want

I want

I want

I love

I love

I love

I love

I love

I love

I love

I love

I love

Melissa did not want Catarina to leave. Where Catarina was was home.

It's the wood, it's the stone

It's the end of the way

It's the stump of a tree

It's just a bit lone-ly

It's a shard of glass

It's life it's the sun

It's the night, it's the death

It's a bow it's a hook

These are the waters of March
closing the summer

This is the promise of life
in my coração

it's the mud
it's the mud

it's the mud

it's the mud

Epilogue

I

But

this is the version of the archives (the scraps of paper, the lists of births and deaths, the history books and silence), that is a novel.

And so

(let me tell you)

Having taken a new name, living in the south of a continent spanning half the side of the planet Clitemnestra marries a man who will take her to England.

For ten years she had been living, repairing, getting older. Before that – those had been the freest days. Before. Where nobody knew her. Where she could spend a day kneeling in the earth, with purpose, hitting the road again life on her back like a cowboy.

And she might have stayed living that way. But she was lonely and on some nights she had bad dreams and on some nights she couldn't sleep and on some nights she made herself come quiet and almost without moving in her bed just to get herself to stop thinking words. On some nights she felt that her heart was rotting, unsolid, its muscle unfleshing unpeeling. She felt a nothingness ahead of her like a road, this grief the size of a life. She writes a letter and for years she waits for a response.

She meets him in a bar on the corner of a big city. One of the biggest cities the ones with buildings the size of rainforest trees with boulevards the size of ocean valleys, more lights more people more concrete than nature ever imagined (and yet) –

He talks to her with a leer without blinking, smells like chest hair, a hearth, and makes her remember what it is to feel small and held like a woman again.

He is, like so many men like maybe the meaning of the word man, built from the domination of her. He calls this love. And, maybe, this is what the word means to most of the world, and therefore this is its practised meaning. (Like Clitemnestra the real meaning of this word love is in hiding.)

She thinks of her past self – the one who would have carried a gun – she imagines that self would have told him to go to hell vai se fuder without a second glance, the wind rising in her wake.

It's 1988 and the country is free. Across the country a woman dies in an instant or possibly slowly, desperately over hours. She reads about it in the paper – a car over a bridge in the middle of the night.

He says to her, let's get married. Let's go to Europe. Let's make a life, start a life, have a child.

(this is a story of this is the story)

And so

A woman, with a new name, a visa, a new life, Clitemnestra boards a plane to London. She is not yet pregnant but she would like a child, a child would be a beginning, a person she could be herself with, share the meaning of love with. Not hiding but a newness. Not a person to own but a person to make free.

She says a name to herself and repeats the name to herself

LAURA

She kneels in the new cold England earth and prays for a way to be free.

II

THERE ARE MORE THINGS IN HEAVEN AND EARTH
THERE ARE MORE THINGS IN HEAVEN AND EARTH
THERE ARE MORE THINGS IN HEAVEN AND EARTH
THERE ARE MORE THINGS IN HEAVEN AND EARTH
THERE ARE MORE THINGS IN HEAVEN AND EARTH
THERE ARE MORE THINGS IN HEAVEN AND EARTH
THERE ARE MORE THINGS IN HEAVEN AND EARTH
THERE ARE MORE THINGS IN HEAVEN AND EARTH
THERE ARE MORE THINGS IN HEAVEN AND EARTH
THERE ARE MORE THINGS IN HEAVEN AND EARTH
THERE ARE MORE THINGS IN HEAVEN AND EARTH
THERE ARE MORE THINGS IN HEAVEN AND EARTH
THERE ARE MORE THINGS IN HEAVEN AND EARTH
THERE ARE MORE THINGS IN HEAVEN AND EARTH
THERE ARE MORE THINGS IN HEAVEN AND EARTH
THERE ARE MORE THINGS IN HEAVEN AND EARTH
THERE ARE MORE THINGS IN HEAVEN AND EARTH
THERE ARE MORE THINGS IN HEAVEN AND EARTH
THERE ARE MORE THINGS IN HEAVEN AND EARTH
THERE ARE MORE THINGS IN HEAVEN AND EARTH
THERE ARE MORE THINGS IN HEAVEN AND EARTH
THERE ARE MORE THINGS IN HEAVEN AND EARTH
THERE ARE MORE THINGS IN HEAVEN AND EARTH
THERE ARE MORE THINGS IN HEAVEN AND EARTH
THERE ARE MORE THINGS IN HEAVEN AND EARTH
THERE ARE MORE THINGS IN HEAVEN AND EARTH
THERE ARE MORE THINGS IN HEAVEN AND EARTH
THERE ARE MORE THINGS IN HEAVEN AND EARTH
THERE ARE MORE THINGS IN HEAVEN AND EARTH
THERE ARE MORE THINGS IN HEAVEN AND EARTH

THERE ARE MORE THINGS IN HEAVEN AND EARTH
THERE ARE MORE THINGS IN HEAVEN AND EARTH
THERE ARE MORE THINGS IN HEAVEN AND EARTH
THERE ARE MORE THINGS IN HEAVEN AND EARTH
THERE ARE MORE THINGS IN HEAVEN AND EARTH
THERE ARE MORE THINGS IN HEAVEN AND EARTH
THERE ARE MORE THINGS IN HEAVEN AND EARTH
THERE ARE MORE THINGS IN HEAVEN AND EARTH
THERE ARE MORE THINGS IN HEAVEN AND EARTH
THERE ARE MORE THINGS IN HEAVEN AND EARTH
THERE ARE MORE THINGS IN HEAVEN AND EARTH
THERE ARE MORE THINGS IN HEAVEN AND EARTH
THERE ARE MORE THINGS IN HEAVEN AND EARTH
THERE ARE MORE THINGS IN HEAVEN AND EARTH
THERE ARE MORE THINGS IN HEAVEN AND EARTH
THERE ARE MORE THINGS IN HEAVEN AND EARTH
THERE ARE MORE THINGS IN HEAVEN AND EARTH
THERE ARE MORE THINGS IN HEAVEN AND EARTH
THERE ARE MORE THINGS IN HEAVEN AND EARTH
THERE ARE MORE THINGS IN HEAVEN AND EARTH
THERE ARE MORE THINGS IN HEAVEN AND EARTH
THERE ARE MORE THINGS IN HEAVEN AND EARTH
THERE ARE MORE THINGS IN HEAVEN AND EARTH
THERE ARE MORE THINGS IN HEAVEN AND EARTH
THERE ARE MORE THINGS IN HEAVEN AND EARTH
THERE ARE MORE THINGS IN HEAVEN AND EARTH
THERE ARE MORE THINGS IN HEAVEN AND EARTH
THERE ARE MORE THINGS IN HEAVEN AND EARTH
THERE ARE MORE THINGS IN HEAVEN AND EARTH
THERE ARE MORE THINGS IN HEAVEN AND EARTH
THERE ARE MORE THINGS IN HEAVEN AND EARTH
THERE ARE MORE THINGS IN HEAVEN AND EARTH
THERE ARE MORE THINGS IN HEAVEN AND EARTH

III

She hadn't heard the song in – God knows how long. It came on first in the gym. She took out her earphones to listen. And then she played it again on the tube on her way home, and then in the shower. She listened to it through the sound of the shower water.

As she walked in a towel through the flat, Catarina asked through the kitchen door – Are you singing Britney Spears?

Yes

I don't know this one?

It's from her comeback album. Post breakdown.

If Britney made it through 2008 ...

You mean 2007?

Exactly.

That night Melissa went to sleep early. It was late autumn, outside had been dark for hours but she drew the curtains. As she lay in bed, Melissa played it quietly on her phone by her pillow.

She hum whispered –

DUM dah dada da DUM

I know it's been a while

and again –

I know
I know it's been a while
But

It's been a while

(I know I shouldn't have kept you waiting)

But I'm here now

The next day after work she didn't go to the gym. That evening they were on the street outside the little Soho pub, like always after work towards the end of the week. Femi bought the drinks but he wasn't really paying. It was a little cold a little dark to be outside but Melissa was smoking and it was too loud inside anyway. Melissa leant against the pub front wall smoking a roll up. Like always Femi emerged holding the drinks – Estrella Guinness.

And between speeches on the state of the party and the state of the left and the state of the sector – but the thing that most people don't realise is *and the thing that most people don't realise is* – Femi touched her wrist with the flat of his hand – Oh and by the way, Ruth is coming. I invited her.

Melissa felt burning under all her clothes.

Femi looked at her.

I'll get you another drink, he said.

Her hair was different; longer fluffier plainer unhighlighted mousy browner. Still nice though.

Her hips were wider, her arms a little bigger.

She was wearing a dusty yellow coat with a Paddington Bear hood.

Melissa was in her black jeans with her boots and glasses on.

Ruthie put a hand on her arm and kissed her cheek.

You look great.

And then, looking at Melissa, she said, her voice still exactly the same and so suddenly alive again –

I'm living in Kilburn now.

Of course Ruth lived far away in Kilburn. At the end of the quick clean silver line that ran through the night. Joo-bih-lee. They had been in school during the Queen's Jubilee. But the line had been built before that, obviously.

Melissa looked at Ruth.

I've never been to Kilburn.

Really?

It was a little dark a little cold a little loud to be outside. Ruth wasn't shivering or shaking. Ruth looked her in the face.

But it's where all your Zadie books are set.

Melissa's breath caught in her swollen heart.

Ruth

Ruth Lily

Lily pad

Ruth Lily-pad Curtis

Miss Ruth Curtis

Ms R L Curtis

Ruth

Ruthie

Ruthie stupid Lily Curtis

Roo

Ruth

There was only
once and
only
always only

But not only
just and let's be honest just forever never sometimes

Ruth

Like teenagers they exchanged numbers outside the tube station.

Ruth's had changed, it had loads of sevens in a row now, but Melissa's had stayed the same. Melissa read the digit patterns self-consciously. She remembered how Ruth had known them by heart, how her number had been top of Ruth's speed dial when speed dial and flip phones had been a thing. Don't call mobiles off the house phone, querida it's expensive.

Immediately, standing in her Paddington Bear coat, in the weekday nighttime under the lights in the foyer of the newly refurbished Tottenham Court Road station, Ruth said –

Can I text you?

Yeah –

Melissa looked at her. Brown fluffy hair.

Yeah of course.

Ruth had texted her that night, almost straight away. She had asked, Can I see you? What about Saturday? What about breakfast?

Yes —

They met in a café near King's Cross.

They had almost sat outside under the dry browning leaves but of course it was too cold.

They ate sweet pastries, round croissants, and Melissa got an espresso. Ruth had — a cup of tea, no actually a pot. Thank you.

They sat opposite each other.

Melissa looked at Ruth.

I heard you got a house with a mortgage.

Ruth looked embarrassed. Yeah. It's a little one bed small place.

With um?

No no. He's gone.

Oh

We broke up about two years ago. I wasn't sure if you had heard

Um

It was bad. I was all —

She shook her head.

Ruth looked at Melissa. But around then mum and dad were thinking of selling the house and moving anyway, so they gave me the deposit money.

Oh right. Congratulations

Yeah. Ruth bobbed her head.

Where did they go live?

Cornwall.

Oh

Mum won that argument in the end

Melissa smiled

They live next to these three women, they remind me of—

Jean, Janine and Jasmine

Ruthie smiled.

And you are – you look so successful and well

Yeah – thanks

Where are you living? What are you doing? I hear some things, and obviously the internet but –

I'm living in Mile End, it's in the East End, after Bethnal Green.

On the Central line

Yeah.

Ruth was nodding

I'm a software developer

Amazing

Melissa looked at her

Your mum died.

Melissa looked behind her through the glass to the street, and then back.

Ruth was silent. She looked at Melissa.

She spoke quietly, I'm so sorry.

Melissa looked at her.

I should have called you – I

Melissa looked at her

I didn't know what you wanted

They breathed. Inside the café was the colour of early winter.

Melissa began again. I live with my friend Catarina.

What's she like?

She's Brazilian, you know from Brazil Brazil. She's from the Northeast, a place called Olinda. She's very political

I would love to meet her.
Yes

Are you happy?
Yes. I think so.
Are you happy?

Yeah. Ruth looked at her.
What do you do
I'm a social worker, I work with women some children, for Barnet
Council
Yeah?
Yeah you know kids and families who experience abuse or
She looked at her moving hands and then she looked at Melissa.

Melissa –

She looked up.

Outside the brown leaves fell on the leaf brown streets and it became
dark. A waiter came to ask them to leave; the café was closing. Ruth's
tea had gone cold hours ago but she hadn't ordered another because she
hadn't wanted to draw attention to how long they had been sat there.
Outside it became dark.
    And Ruthie had said –
    Well if you do ever want to see Kilburn – exhale laughing nerv-
ously, the street light behind her, looking across the low coffee table at
Melissa.

    Well if you ever want to come to Kilburn –

Ruth unlocked the front door, they walked into the little flat. The rooms were dark with the light of the late sun. Victorian brick and walls, just a ground floor.

They were both grown women now, but neither of them said it

Melissa remembered what Catarina had told her – about how saying a person's name was the most erotic thing you could do

so, when she got on her knees, her hands not together, but as if in prayer

(and it had been seven whole years – yes it had been seven lucky unlucky, half dozen and one years – can you even imagine that length of time?)

And, after seven years, Melissa Ana Maria Moraes got on her knees, her hands not together but as if in prayer, through her breathing mouth she whispered said –

Ruth

Author's note

Some of the things mentioned in *there are more things* did really happen. Of those, some have been well documented in many languages and are easy to google, like Brexit or the death of Princess Diana. But others have been partially documented, documented in one language or place only, censored, or buried by trauma. For that reason, and because those parts should be remembered too, I've included this note.

Amen Corner

The £90/month that Melissa receives when she starts sixth form is her Educational Maintenance Allowance (usually known as 'EMA'). EMA was introduced in 2000 by the Labour Party, and cut in 2010 as part of the Tory-Liberal Democrat Coalition Government's austerity measures.

In 2010 the Labour Party proposed a bill to raise university tuition fees from £3000/year to £6000–9000/year. This sparked mass protests across the UK. However, the bill passed and came into effect in 2011.

Mark Duggan, a twenty-nine-year-old Black man of Irish and Caribbean descent, was shot and killed by the Metropolitan Police on Ferry Lane in Tottenham, north London on 4 August 2011.

Mile End II

'Pinakin, Rubel, Christine, Sheku' refers to Pinakin Patel, a thirty-four-year-old Indian man who died at Yarl's Wood detention centre in Bedfordshire on 20 April 2015; Rubel Ahmed, a twenty-six-year-old Bangladeshi man who died in Morton Hall detention centre in Lincolnshire on 5 September 2014; Christine Chase, a forty-year-old Jamaican woman who died in Yarl's Wood detention centre on Sunday

444

30 March 2014 and Sheku Bayoh, a thirty-one-year-old Sierra Leonean man who died after being restrained by police in Kirkcaldy, Scotland on 3 May 2015. These are only a few of the people who died while in the custody of, or after contact with, the British state between 2014–2015.

'Seeta, Amy, Jill, Sarah' refers to Seeta Kaur, a thirty-four-year-old woman who died while at her husband and in-laws house on 31 March 2015; Amy Gough who was killed on 29 March 2015 after being assaulted by her partner some days before; Jill Goldsmith, a forty-nine-year-old woman who died on 26 March 2015 after being assaulted by her husband (a police officer) and Sarah Pollock, a forty-one-year-old woman who was killed by her husband on 25 March 2015.

On 16 October 2015, 300 people protested at St Pancras station, six of whom glued themselves to the ticket barriers, blocking international travel to shouts of 'Your borders kill'. This action was organised by activist group The London Latinx.

The activist collective that Catarina and Melissa join is not a real group. I have borrowed its anti-deportations stance from Lesbians and Gays Support the Migrants (LGSM) and its meeting structure and policy of including women (trans and cis), non-binary and gender variant people from Sisters Uncut.

Mile End III

Maricumbia is a queer Latinx club night, held in various locations across London since 2016.

The song Pedro is half-humming on page 295 is 'London, London' by Caetano Veloso.

On page 296, 'I'm alive' is from the song 'Nine Out of Ten' by Caetano Veloso.

Rua do Bomfim

Miguel Arrães was the real Governor of Pernaumbuco between 1962 and 1964. Following the military coup he was imprisoned on the island of Fernando de Noronha for eleven months. He spent 1965–79 in exile in Algeria, returning after the amnesty of 1979. He was re-elected Governor of Pernambuco in 1986 and 1994, and died on 13 August 2005.

This list of Indigenous groups is taken from terraindigenas.org.br and is my attempt to list all indigenous groups living in Brazil now. I spent some time searching for a list of peoples who lived in (the territory now known as) Brazil before the Portuguese invasion in the year 1500, but could not find one.

Laura's account to Sônia of the discussion about whether the amnesty should extend to 'common' prisoners or not is based on an real account of such a meeting told to me by my mother, Laura Rodrigues. According to her memory, the meeting occurred in the city of São Paulo in 1977 or 1978.

Pedaço de mim

Carlos Marighella was the leader of Ação Nacional Liberadora (ANL) from 1964–1969. He was the son of Augusto Marighella, an Italian immigrant, and Maria Rita do Nascimento, whose parents were of Sudanese origin and had been enslaved. He was assassinated by the military police in November 1969. You can read his *Minimanual for the Urban Guerrilla* in both English and Portuguese on marxism.org. *Marighella*, a film based on his life has been made by Wagner Moura and at the time of writing had recently been released in Brazil.

'VOCÊ CONSTROI O BRASIL' was a real slogan of the military dictatorship.

The communists in the forest that Clitemnestra and Laura visit are based on the armed guerrillas who attempted to establish a liberated zone in Araguaia between 1968–72. I have taken nearly all details of this section (diet, celebrations and so on) from the diary of Maurício Gabrois, who was a commander in Araguaia. This diary was seized by the military police and only published in 2011 by journalist Lucas Figueira in *Carta Capital*.

The 'commander who studied in Prague and was descended from people who were enslaved' is based on 'Osvaldão' or Osvaldo Orlando da Costa, one of the commanders in Araguaia. Osvaldão was born in 1938, studied engineering in Rio and Prague, and according to several accounts was very popular with the local population in Araguaia.

Gabrois' diary includes a prayer for the guerrillas by 'a local Terecô priest', which I have reproduced on page 362. Terecô is an Afro-Brazilian religion.

The story about Commander Lamarca is taken from Elio Gaspari's *Ditadura Escancarada*. The story of the Japanese consul is taken from the documentary film *Repare Bem* (2012, Maria de Medeiros).

'ABAIXO A DITADURA. POVO NO PODER' means 'Down with the dictatorship. People in power' and was a popular slogan of anti-dictatorship movements at the time.

'FIM ÀS PRISÕES, TORTURAS E ASSASSINATOS' means 'End [to] prisons, torture and murders' and was another popular slogan at the time. I am grateful to Edmar Victor Rodrigues Santos for both suggestions.

The quotation on page 356 is taken from Ferreira Gullar's 'Poema Sujo' ('Dirty Poem').

The image on page 378 was taken by Apollo 8 on 24 December 1969. It can be viewed in colour on the NASA website.

The description of what happened to the Guerrillas in Araguaia is taken from the report released by Brazil's Truth Commission (Comissão Nacional da Verdade) in 2014, which investigated state violence under the Military Dictatorship.

The report also describes how many trade unionists, like Edivânia, were blacklisted by factories, forcing them away from their communities; arguably an equally painful form of torture as the kind which has been more formally recognised.

Mile End IV

On 11 April 2017, twenty-year-old Syed Jamanoor Islam was stabbed by a teenager on Wagner Street.

In the early hours of 14 June 2017, a fire broke out in Grenfell Tower in Notting Hill in West London, eventually killing 72 people. Residents had been campaigning for better fire safety for several years before the fire broke out.

Other

All recipes, translations and mistranslations from Portuguese are my own, except for the translation of Chico Buarque's 'Pedaço de mim', which I co-wrote with my mother, Laura Rodrigues.

Acknowledgements

Lots of people made this book with me.

I am indebted to the following living artists and writers, who greatly influenced my way of thinking, feeling and/or writing this novel—

Sara Ahmed, Margaret Atwood (for *The Blind Assassin*), Jay Bernard, Vincent Bevins, Anne Boyer, Chico Buarque, Anna Burns, A. S. Byatt (for *Possession*), Anne Carson, Aviah Sarah Day, Mike Duncan (for the *Revolutions* podcast), Tracey Emin, Barbara J and Karen E Fields, Nicole Froio, Gilberto Gil, Vivian Gornick, Juno Mac and Molly Smith, Bridget Minamore, Wendi Muse, Joana Nastari, Lola Olufemi, Alison Phipps, Arundhati Roy (from whom I borrowed '*die-able, viable*') Elza Soares, Britney Spears, Liv Wynter. RIP George Michael.

The following texts made the historical portions of the novel possible—

Na Trilha do Golpe edited by Túlio Velho Barreto and Laurindo Ferreira; *A resistência da mulher à ditadura militar no Brasil* by Ana Maria Colling; *Coleção Ditadura* by Elio Gaspari (especially Volume II, *A Ditadura Escancarada*); *Mulheres na luta armada* by Maria Claudia Badan Ribeiro; the film *Repare Bem* (Maria de Medeiros, 2012); the PhD thesis 'Olinda: Uma leitura histórica e psicanalítica da memória sobre a cidade' by Eliana Maria Vasconcelos do Nascimento; *Diário de Maurício Grabois* and the *Relatório da Comissão Nacional da Verdade* (especially Vol 1 parts III and IV and Vol II).

I am deeply grateful to everyone in Brazil who helped me—

Thália Velho Barreto de Araúju and Ricardo Ximenes, for being my leftwing family in Brazil; Thália, especially, for arranging for me to meet all kinds of people and for hanging out with me on the veranda. João Ximenes, for taking me out in Olinda and sharing your experiences. To Gabriel Rodrigues Santana for your literary insights, and Fred Caju for your poetry. Isadora Rocha Velho Barreto de Araújo for taking me out in Recife, telling me about motels and for reviewing the parts of the text about Catarina's life in Brazil. Túlio Augusto Velho Barreto de Araújo, for giving me *Na Trilha do Golpe,* and answering via email my questions about Recife and Olinda during the dictatorship. Hermes Xandó Rodrigues, my beloved cousin, for reviewing Pedro's sections with me. UFPE and the Instituto Capibaribe, for allowing me to visit. Edmar Victor Rodrigues Santos, for reviewing 'Pedaço de mim' with linguistic creativity and academic rigour (and Carly Rodgers for putting us in touch). Lucas Figueiredo, for your time emailing with me and for publishing Maurício Grabois' diary in the first place. All remaining errors are my own.

And I am deeply grateful to everyone in London who helped me—

Many people who grew up in South London in the early 2000s volunteered to speak to me about their experiences of drugs, sex, sexuality and class. I'm grateful for your trust and hope you recognise the spirit of our conversations in this book, especially in 'Amen Corner'. Paulo Drinot, Professor of Latin American History at UCL, for sharing the essay questions from your 'History and Politics of Latin America, c. 1930 to the Present' module, and allowing me to use them verbatim on p45. The London Latinx, to Maricumbia, to LGSM and most of all to Sisters Uncut, for creating new worlds – for an hour, a night, over the years.

Money-wise—

I am grateful to the Society of Authors for awarding me the John C Lawrence Award in 2018, worth £3,000, which funded my trip to Olinda and Recife in December that year, and to Hay Festival and British Library's Eccles Centre for shortlisting me for the Eccles and

Hay Festival Writers Award 2019, for which I received £2,500, covering two months of writing. Through 2020 and early 2021, I received quarterly furlough payments from the UK government, enabling me to write almost full time. I would therefore like to thank Rishi Sunak personally for providing me with the means to write this novel about queer communists.

For turning a patchy word doc into a book—

Rhiannon Smith, my editor, I owe this whole book to you, really. Thank you for giving me the artistic freedom and confidence to make this text, for treating its characters like real people and for caring for me as a friend when I have struggled.

Imogen Pelham, my agent; I owe you everything, too. Thank you for your patience with me and for all the time you gave this book before it was a book: setting me deadlines, reading chapters. Thank you for being open-minded and honest with me, for believing in me and getting me published.

Thank you to the whole publishing team: Marie Hrynczak, the production controller, and M Rules, for your forbearance typesetting and creating this book. Maya Berger for your brave, radical copyediting; Anne O'Brien for your careful proofreading; Sophia Schoepfer for your insights into the text, your extreme patience with my errors and your wrapping; Hayley Camis for your care, your warmth and your tenacity; Emily Moran for your pragmatism and humour and skill; Nico Taylor for your thoughtful brilliance commissioning Niki Usagi to design the cover; Niki, thank you for this beautiful piece of art, which is somehow Olinda, and London, and the neon spirit of the novel.

Lastly, to my family—

Mum, you are the person I owe the most. Thank you for sharing your memories with me, especially your memories of Paulinho. Thank you for translating with me, and always being up for chatting it through on whatsapp. Thank you to all my mother's friends – my many aunties – for showing me how big a family is. Thank you Cleide and Hannah for being in my life. Thank you Dad for your unruly, revolutionary spirit; George for your steadfastness, your kindness and your loyalty to your friends, which I have borrowed here for Melissa.

Thank you Babatunde Williams for naming Femi; Loukia Koumi for naming Eleni; Vi Tran for naming Ivy and being my oldest friend; Ben Cross for reading it and always telling me it was great, and for taking me to see Elza Soares at the Barbican in 2016; Vinay for always believing in me. Thank you Janet, Naomi, Georgia, Shana, Alice for our terrible, amazing adolescence. Thank you Irene, the baddest bitch. Thank you Charlotte Goodman, for talking me through the Oresteia in the cafe at the Gower Street Waterstones back in 2016 when I was looking for killer women, for our safe and love-filled home, for Moishy, for our Shabbat dinners (which appear here in all but name); for our own communism of two. And thank you Andrew McLean, for all the printing, of course, but most of all for your example, your patience and your love.